Did she dare bare her ugly past and risk turning him away forever?

"You know," John murmured, "the first time you got me talking about what happened to my folks, it was almost like living it over again. I was angry at you for making me remember."

She nudged her horse a little closer to his. "I'm sorry."

"Don't be. What I'm trying to say is, I've thought about it since. Talked a little about it. Each time it gets a little easier, and I never would have found that out if you hadn't made me speak of it the first time."

Jane's heart seemed to swell within her until she wondered how her small body could contain it. Here was something more she could give this man who offered her so much. She could give him balm for his wounded heart, because she, too, had known hurt and bereavement....

* * *

Whitefeather's Woman
Harlequin Historical #581—October 2001

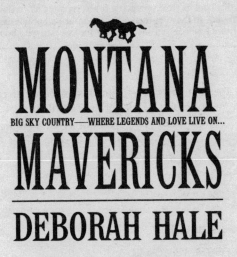

MONTANA

BIG SKY COUNTRY—WHERE LEGENDS AND LOVE LIVE ON...

MAVERICKS

DEBORAH HALE

WHITEFEATHER'S WOMAN

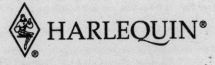

HARLEQUIN®

TORONTO • NEW YORK • LONDON
AMSTERDAM • PARIS • SYDNEY • HAMBURG
STOCKHOLM • ATHENS • TOKYO • MILAN • MADRID
PRAGUE • WARSAW • BUDAPEST • AUCKLAND

Special thanks and acknowledgment are given
to Deborah Hale for her contribution
to the MONTANA MAVERICKS series.

ISBN 0-373-29181-7

WHITEFEATHER'S WOMAN

Visit us at www.eHarlequin.com

Printed in U.S.A.

Please address questions and book requests to:
Harlequin Reader Service
U.S.: 3010 Walden Ave., P.O. Box 1325, Buffalo, NY 14269
Canadian: P.O. Box 609, Fort Erie, Ont. L2A 5X3

To my editor, the phenomenal Margaret Marbury, who trusted me with John, Jane and their wonderful story.

And to two of the most gifted writers of American historical romance, Cheryl St.John and Carolyn Davidson, from their adoring fan.

Chapter One

May 1897, Whitehorn, Montana

A frontier saloon was just about the last place on earth Jane Harris had ever expected, or wanted, to find herself. Why, Mrs. Endicott and her Ladies' Temperance Society back in Boston would have been properly horrified. They'd have been more horrified still by the knowledge that Jane had stolen and sold a brooch of Mrs. Endicott's to get here.

The jarring notes of a tinny piano pummeled Jane's throbbing head, and the reek of raw spirits and tobacco smoke made the flesh at the back of her throat constrict. If she'd had anything to eat in the past twenty-four hours, the stink, the noise and her own overwrought nerves might have conspired to make her violently ill.

Perhaps it had been a harsh blessing that she'd run out of money for food back in Omaha.

"Kin I pour ya a drink, little lady?" bellowed the man behind the bar, his voiced laced with genial mockery.

Jane gasped, her heart hammering against her corset like the pistons of a runaway steam engine.

"N-no thank you, sir." She raised her voice louder than

she'd ever spoken in her life, to make herself heard above the "music" and the babble of voices. "I'd be most obliged if you'd point out the foreman of the Kincaid ranch to me. The gentleman at the telegraph office told me I might find him here."

As she turned to speak to him, the bartender flinched. At the sight of her face, most likely. She'd hoped the bruises and cuts would have healed by the end of her long trip West. They must still have a ways to go if her appearance distressed a man who worked in such a rough establishment.

"Yep, ma'am. I seen him come in a while back and he ain't left that I know of." The bartender squinted through the haze of smoke around the cavernous room, with its sinister shadows and a huge, lowering buffalo head mounted behind the bar.

Raising a gnarled finger, he pointed to one particularly murky corner. "That's John Whitefeather, over there. He don't come in here much as a rule, but when he does it's always off by hisself."

Jane heard nothing after the bartender spoke the name. *Whitefeather?* An Indian! Her knees commenced to tremble beneath her skirts and petticoats.

Back in Boston, Jane's sole dissipation had been reading Western dime novels from Beadle's Library. Along with stories of legendary gunslingers like Jack Spade, they often featured lurid accounts of Apache atrocities. Were there any of that fierce tribe this far north? Perhaps she was about to find out.

"Thank you…sir. I—I appreciate your assistance." As much as a condemned prisoner appreciated a deputy's "assistance" to climb the scaffold.

Jane tried to smile at the man, but between her mounting

agitation and the still-healing gash on one side of her mouth, she didn't make a very good job of it.

Step by halting step, she crossed the saloon floor, painfully conscious of curious, predatory eyes following her movements. Had young Daniel felt this way walking through the lions' den? Probably not, for Daniel had been a man and he'd had the Lord on his side. With the sin of her desperate theft weighing on her conscience, Jane was certain she'd left any slight protection of the Almighty far behind her in New England.

John Whitefeather sat at a corner table, all alone, his back to the wall, as though he did not care to turn it upon the denizens of the Double Deuce. The bartender's pointing finger must have alerted the man that she wished to speak with him, yet he did not rise or otherwise acknowledge her approach.

Reason assured Jane that the Kincaids' foreman was hardly apt to pull out a tomahawk and scalp her in the middle of a crowded saloon. But her tautly stretched nerves refused to unwind for logic. She stopped before his table and stood like a convicted felon in front of a hanging judge. For a wooden nickel she'd have turned and fled, but she'd been told the Kincaids lived miles outside of town. John Whitefeather might be her only means of reaching them.

For perhaps the hundredth time since stealing out of Boston, Jane wished she'd been able to spare the money for a wire to advise her new employers that she was on her way. Mrs. Kincaid might have come to the depot to meet her, or at least have sent her a less alarming escort to the ranch.

"A-are you Mr. Whitefeather, the Kincaid foreman?"

The man gave a slow nod. Jane sensed his gaze sweep-

ing over her, but unlike the bartender, he betrayed no sign
that her battered face affected him.

"What can I do for you, ma'am?" His voice, a soft
rumble with a queer melodic inflection, was barely audible
over the raucous hubbub of the saloon.

"I'm Jane Harris, Mr. Whitefeather." She tried to sound
competent and businesslike to convince him of her iden-
tity. Instead, her words came out stiff and prissy. "I've
arrived from Boston to work for Mr. and Mrs. Kincaid,
taking care of their boys."

Her syllables began to trip over one another in their
haste, and she had to pause frequently to gasp for breath.
"I regret that I was unable to send a wire to announce my
arrival. I'd be most obliged if you could arrange my trans-
portation to the ranch."

He muttered something to himself, but what Jane could
hear made no sense to her. Was he speaking some Indian
dialect?

Draining the contents of a tall bottle, he rummaged in
his pocket and tossed several coins onto the table. Then
he scooped up his hat, pushed back his chair and stood.

Jane's last sound nerve shattered.

He was so big. John Whitefeather towered over her, his
shoulders alarmingly broad under an enormous duster coat
that fell almost to his ankles. And his hands... Jane nearly
swooned, imagining the horrible damage they could inflict
on a woman's vulnerable face and body. Emery Endicott
had been a runt compared to this giant. Before she'd run
away to Montana, though, her fiancé had managed to beat
her badly enough to put her in the infirmary.

"I expect you'd better come along with me, ma'am."

Any man who spoke so softly and with so respectful a
tone could never harm her. Jane didn't really believe it,
but the alternative was too terrible to contemplate. He

brushed past her, a man-of-war in full sail, while she bobbed along in his wake like a dinghy swamped by his bow wave.

To her surprise, John Whitefeather held the saloon door open for her like the most fastidious gentleman. Squinting against the bright setting sun, Jane stepped outside onto the boardwalk that ran in front of the businesses on Main Street. The air was dry and dusty, but otherwise clean. The rowdy noise of the Double Deuce immediately muted to a faint echo.

Behind her, John Whitefeather's voice rumbled, ominous, yet absurdly reassuring in its hushed tone. "Are your bags at the stage office here, or still back at the rail depot in Big Timber? Either way, we probably ought to leave them be until you've talked to Caleb and Ruth."

She spun around to face him. "I, er, don't have any bags."

Before she had time to lose her nerve, or recover her scruples, she rattled off the lie she'd carefully rehearsed all the way from the Atlantic.

"One of the trains got derailed just outside Chicago, you see. We passengers were thrown around the car, which is how I came by my...injuries. Then the baggage car took fire. I believe a lamp fell and burst when we went off the tracks. My trunk and both my valises were burned to a cinder, but of course I was relieved to have escaped with my life."

Quite against her will, the inflection of Jane's voice rose at the end of her account, as though questioning whether her listener was prepared to swallow this barely probable tale.

"That's too bad about your train, ma'am. Do you have any money to tide you over?" He took a few long strides down the boardwalk that abutted the false-fronted buildings of Main Street—a hardware store, a butcher shop and an alarming number of saloons.

Jane scurried to keep up with him. "M-money? What makes you ask?"

Why she clasped her reticule to her bosom, Jane wasn't sure. It contained nothing more valuable than a pair of damp, crumpled handkerchiefs, the pawn ticket for Mrs. Endicott's brooch and a newspaper cutting of the Kincaids' original employment notice.

"I'll be getting room and board working for the Kincaids, and they'll be paying me wages. I can get by until then."

John Whitefeather stopped in his tracks and glared at her with a sullen severity that almost brought tears to her eyes.

Oh dear. Had she offended him by implying she feared he might steal from her?

He didn't raise his voice. If anything, it grew quieter. The temperature of it dropped, too, until Jane fancied his breath frosted the air. "Forget it."

Her eyes were becoming accustomed to the sun's glare. At last she was able to take in more about the Kincaids' foreman than his general shape and size.

Beneath a battered brown hat with a broad brim, John Whitefeather's coal-black hair was tied back with a leather cord and cascaded down past his shoulder blades. He had skin the color of oiled teakwood, with the dark shadow of whiskers on his firmly hewn jawline. Above high, jutting cheekbones blazed deep-set eyes the startling blue of an infinite Montana sky.

His fierce, intensely masculine beauty unsettled Jane almost as much as his height had. What a mousy, battered eyeful he must be getting by comparison.

Heaving a sigh from deep within his vast frame, John

Whitefeather made a subtle movement as though adjusting an awkward load upon his powerful shoulders. He untied the reins of a tall, white-spotted horse from the hitching post, then started across the hard-packed dust of Whitehorn's main street with his mount in tow. Not knowing what else to do, Jane followed.

Over his shoulder the Kincaids' foreman called, "I reckon we'd better get you back to the ranch so we can sort all this out."

Sort what out? What was there to sort? Even if she'd had breath left to speak, Jane would not have dared ask. But she disliked the sound of it. She'd come West in answer to the Kincaids' letter, to work for them. Far from Boston. Far from Emery. Far from danger.

Except that Whitehorn, Montana, didn't seem very far from danger at the moment. Was there a safe haven for her anywhere in the world? Jane wondered. If there was, she'd barter her very soul to find it.

John Whitefeather would have bartered a month's pay to wriggle out of the situation in which he now found himself.

Why had he gotten saddled with Miss Jane Harris from Boston and all her problems? He seldom came into town. When he wasn't back at the ranch or out on the range, he spent most of his time at Sweetgrass. With the help of his brother-in-law, Caleb Kincaid, he'd purchased that parcel of land over a year ago. He'd settled a group of his Cheyenne kinsmen there, to keep them out of a government reservation.

With bitter amusement, John wondered how Miss Jane Harris would react if he took her back to Sweetgrass instead of to Caleb's ranch. Scream her lungs out or faint dead away? With one foot in the world of *ve'ho'e*, the white man, and the other in the realm of the *Tsitsistas,* John knew Miss Harris had far less to fear from his people than they had to fear from the likes of her.

Outside Briggs Livery, he spun around and thrust Hawkwing's reins into the stranger's tiny gloved hand. "Hang on to him while I go see about hiring a wagon."

By the look on her face, he might as well have given her a writhing rattler to hold. What in blue blazes was a woman like this doing in Montana?

"He won't hurt you," John barked. "And I'll only be a minute."

Ignoring her doubtful looks on both counts, he turned away, blowing out an impatient breath as he entered the livery stable. Ordinarily, he avoided the place, and he resented the woman for making it necessary to come here.

"Afternoon, Mr. Briggs." He nodded to the liveryman, who also doubled as the town undertaker. "I'd like to hire a wagon. Doesn't have to be big or pretty. I can get it back to you by this time tomorrow."

Lionel Briggs had a long, mournful face that somehow befitted his second occupation. He looked his customer up and down. "What'cha need it for? I'll have to have a deposit."

A ripple of heat crept up John's neck, speeding toward his face. He knew Lionel's father had been killed in a skirmish with some Pawnee decades ago, yet John never got used to the liveryman's hostile suspicion of anything and everything to do with the native people of the Plains. John's own parents and younger brothers had been massacred at the hands of white men, yet he didn't treat all *ve'ho'e* with embittered distrust.

At least not once he got to know them.

He jerked his head toward the street outside. "Lady just

got into town from back East. She needs to see Ruth and Caleb, and I'm the only one around to fetch her out there.''

He felt in his pockets. Damn! He'd left his last penny on the table at the Double Deuce to pay for his sarsaparilla. ''Can't you just bill it to Caleb?''

Lionel Briggs made a noncommittal gurgle deep in his throat and scratched the stubble on his chin.

''S'pose I *could*.'' His tone left no doubt that he didn't much like the idea. ''Don't reckon as I'd have anything to suit, though.''

John had swallowed as much as he was prepared to. He had never done violence to a white man in his life, unless you counted the time at residential school when he'd kicked one of his teachers in the shin. But he'd accepted the fact that some *ve'ho'e* would never alter their opinion of his people.

He shrugged and turned to leave. ''It's your business if you want to turn away customers, Mr. Briggs.''

''It *is* my business, and don't you ferget it, White-feather!'' the liveryman huffed. ''Just 'cause you married your sister off to a rich rancher don't make you the boss of me.''

John did not look back.

Out on the street again, he looked around for Hawk-wing. The skewbald gelding had made his way over to a nearby water trough, and Miss Jane Harris had been powerless to stop him.

Marching over to the horse, John climbed into the saddle and held out his hand to the troublesome visitor from Boston.

Her nervous glance darted from his hand, to his face, to the horse and back again until it threatened to make John dizzy.

''Grab hold and I'll pull you up,'' he snapped.

She continued to hesitate. "I thought you were going to hire a wagon for us."

So did I. "Briggs claims he doesn't have anything to suit." John could hear the disdain in his own voice.

Her lower lip, still swollen from the train accident, commenced to quiver. John wanted to throw his head back and howl, like a he-wolf at the full moon.

He could read the thoughts running through her head as clear as the sign above the No Bull Meat Market across the street. She saw him as some heathen savage, just waiting for a ripe moment to ravish and slaughter her while they rode across open country with daylight waning.

"It's up to you." John straightened in his saddle. "It'd be just as easy for me if you stay in town tonight and I send somebody from the ranch to fetch you in the morning."

When she darted an anxious glance farther up the street to the Carlton Hotel, John almost laughed aloud. The woman wasn't only afraid of him, she was scared of everyone and everything about Whitehorn. Talk about your fish out of water!

"I—I don't have any money to pay for a room."

John softened his tone as he leaned down and offered her his hand again. In spite of some harsh lessons from life, he believed in second chances.

"Well, that makes two of us, ma'am. Come on, now. I'm pretty near as harmless as Hawkwing, and only a bit more stubborn. We'll make better time getting to the ranch if we ride across the range, anyway. You do want to get to the Kincaids, don't you?"

That did it. Her baby mouth set in an attempt at a determined line, which John found strangely comical. And even more strangely appealing. No question, she was prepared to wade through hell itself to reach his brother-in-law's ranch.

She extended her absurdly tiny hand up to meet his.

Drawing her up off the ground, John set her on top of Hawkwing's generous hindquarters. "Hang on."

For the first minute or two, she settled for clutching a handful of his coat. But as the horse's pace picked up, she clenched her arms around his waist. John Whitefeather had never felt so uncomfortable on the back of a horse as he did on that endless ride out to the ranch with Miss Jane Harris perched behind him, clinging like grim death.

Everything about the woman irritated him. Her small size. Her New England fussiness. Her barely controlled panic, so intense it was almost contagious.

For the last twenty of his thirty years, John had struggled to tread the thin, brittle line between two races vastly at odds and often at war. Among his late father's people, he had found a measure of acceptance, though always clouded by the necessity to prove himself and a personal sense of guilt for the crimes of the whites. Among his late mother's race, he doubted he would ever find tolerance, let alone favor.

Over and over, he had told himself he didn't care. Until he'd almost come to believe it. His meeting with Miss Harris had ripped away those comforting illusions, and he wanted to hate her for it.

"Is the ranch much farther?" she squeaked when they had been riding for a quarter of an hour.

So, she'd finally worked up the nerve to make conversation. John heard her suck a breath in through clenched teeth.

"Why? Did you hurt your..." he searched for a polite word, but found he could only think in terms of horses "...your *rump* in that train crash?"

Her whole body stiffened behind him. "How dare you ask a lady such an improper question!"

So, the quivering little rabbit had teeth, after all. For no sane reason he could think of, John found himself grinning. Luckily, she couldn't see his face.

He shrugged. "We can stop and stretch your legs if you like, but I'd just as soon not be caught out in open country when the sun disappears behind those mountains. Easy to get lost unless there's a good moon. Lot of animals come out to hunt at night—wolves, wildcats."

He sensed her looking around, taking in the waving green grassland in one direction and the wooded foothills of the Crazy Mountains in the other.

A shiver ran through her and she tightened her arms around his middle. "By all means, let's keep riding."

John could tell he'd spooked her. A bucketful of ice-cold shame doused the spark of gleeful satisfaction within him. Some men found fun in baiting wild creatures, but he had never been one of them. On the contrary, he had a gift for gentling such animals—deer, pronghorns and especially wild mustangs.

For all her show of Boston prudery, Jane Harris reminded him of a wounded doe. Beneath a tiny scrap of a hat that would be useless against the beating sun, she had hair of a sorrel shade, like a yearling just losing its protective spots. Her features were as delicate as a fawn's, too, and she had the same enormous, liquid brown eyes. Those eyes held a restless wariness like a deer's, as if ever alert for predators, yet powerless against them. He had never met a woman so vulnerable and so completely unfit for Big Sky Country.

She provoked his pity as well as his resentment, and they were like twin burrs beneath his saddle. Truth be told, pity was the more nettlesome of the two.

Little Miss Harris had landed in Whitehorn alone, injured and without a single belonging she didn't wear or carry on her. What would she do, John wondered, when she found out Ruth and Caleb *didn't* want her to work for them?

Chapter Two

Something was wrong. Jane sensed it from the moment John Whitefeather ushered her into the big, two-story house with a wide porch that wrapped around it like a protective embrace. Standing in the generously proportioned kitchen, dominated by a big cast-iron stove, she wondered why her new employers didn't appear happy to see her.

"Ruth, Caleb, this is Miss Jane Harris, from Boston." John Whitefeather hung his long coat and leather hat on a peg by the kitchen door. "She just got into Whitehorn this afternoon. She's come about the job looking after Barton and Zeke."

A slender woman with warm bronzed skin dropped her washing cloth into the dish tub in the far corner of the kitchen. Wiping her hands on her apron, she approached Jane. Her dark hair was plaited in a thick braid that coiled far down her back. She wore a long skirt that looked to be made of very fine leather, and a bright red shirtwaist embroidered with tiny colored beads in an intricate design.

Beside the area where his wife had been working, Caleb Kincaid sat in a big wooden armchair upholstered with leather. A rugged-faced man with shaggy blond hair, he slowly lit a pipe without speaking a word.

Mrs. Kincaid shot her husband an odd, searching look, then she caught sight of Jane's face. "What happened to you, *kâse'ee'he?* Did you fall off the horse on your ride out here? No, these bruises have begun to heal."

Jane took a deep breath, ready to launch into the contrived explanation for her injuries. At the last moment, she faltered. What if she got confused and told Mrs. Kincaid a slightly different story than she'd told the foreman? Might he trip her up in the lie?

To her surprise, John Whitefeather came to her rescue. "Some cars on her train got derailed back in Chicago. She lost all her bags in the accident, too."

Ruth Kincaid shook her head and made a crooning noise of sympathy. "You must be hungry and tired, dear. Sit down and eat, then we'll talk. Before you go to bed, I'll put a poultice on your cheek. It might draw that bruise. And you need some salve for the scrape on your chin."

Gratefully Jane sank down onto one of the plain, solid chairs ranged around the big kitchen table, and took off her hat and gloves. Eking out her last few crackers on the train, she thought she'd grown accustomed to the vague biliousness of constant hunger. It had gnawed at her stomach like a toothless old dog worrying a bone. Now, as she inhaled a savory blend of meat and onions, her appetite suddenly grew the fangs of a wolf.

Mrs. Kincaid set a plate of stew in front of Jane and another in front of John Whitefeather, who had taken a seat opposite her. Years of strictly minding her manners, and the consciousness of her new employers' eyes upon her, kept Jane from falling on her supper like a starving beast.

Nothing could stifle her groan of pleasure upon sinking her teeth into a tender morsel of richly flavored meat.

Mrs. Kincaid smiled as she set a plate of biscuits and a crock of butter on the table between Jane and the foreman. "Is this the first time you've tasted venison, Miss Harris?"

Jane abruptly stopped chewing. She swallowed hard to work that mouthful down. "Deer meat?"

She reached for a biscuit at the same moment as John Whitefeather. His large, brown knuckles swiped across hers, making them look smaller, softer and paler. She suddenly had a vivid flash of memory—Emery's sallow, bony fist flying toward her eye. With a gasp and a start, she jerked her hand back, as though she'd touched a red-hot stove.

"Don't worry, Miss Harris." The foreman glanced at Mrs. Kincaid, his dark brows raised. "There's plenty of biscuits here for both of us."

Jane caught the rancher's wife returning John Whitefeather's dubious look. A sense of impending trouble ambushed her again.

Caleb Kincaid smoked in watchful silence as Jane and John Whitefeather finished their meal. Only when his wife had removed the plates from the table did he speak.

"I'm afraid we have a problem, Miss Harris." The rancher stared hard at the kitchen floor, as if suddenly finding its wood grain of absorbing interest.

Here it came. Jane's insides constricted into a tiny little lump, heavy as lead.

"Problem?" She almost gagged on the word.

Three thousand miles from home, with *nothing*. There couldn't be a problem with her only means to earn a living. There just couldn't.

The rancher was a big man. Not quite as big as his foreman, but still tall and powerfully made. Having broached the subject, he now cast a helpless glance at his wife, who looked every bit as ill at ease.

"Did you not read the letter we sent you, *kâse'ee'he?*" Ruth Kincaid set the dishes in the washtub, then stood beside her husband's chair.

"Of course I read it," blurted Jane, then she hesitated. What if the Kincaids asked her to quote particulars? "I mean...not with my own eyes. It...arrived on a rainy day...and the ink ran."

Oh dear, why could she not invent a more plausible explanation for coming all the way to Montana without actually having seen the Kincaids' offer of employment? After all, she'd had years of practice lying about the injuries Emery had done her.

She toyed with the notion of telling them the humiliating truth, but firmly rejected it. Better to let the Kincaids turn her out on the empty grasslands, with wolves howling in the distance, than have to admit her fiancé had burned their letter before her eyes, then beaten her insensible for trying to escape him.

"I just assumed you must be writing to offer me the job." Though she struggled against it, her voice rose, shrill and plaintive. "No one writes all the way from Montana to Boston to say they *don't* want you."

Neither Caleb Kincaid nor his wife would meet her eyes, so she addressed her hopeless question across the table, to the only person in the room who did not flinch from her imploring gaze.

"Do they?"

For the first time since she'd come face-to-face with him that afternoon, John Whitefeather's sternly handsome features softened in a look of sympathy. He cleared his throat.

"We can't do anything about this tonight." He addressed his words to the Kincaids. "Miss Harris is here and she can't go back to Whitehorn until morning. Maybe after a good night's sleep we'll all see our way clearer."

Jane wasn't certain what to make of a hired man advising his employers with such authority. She couldn't picture herself bidding Mrs. Endicott to do anything.

After spending so many nights dozing fitfully on the upright seat of a jolting railway carriage, she yearned to lie flat on her back to sleep. As John Whitefeather had said, the situation couldn't help but look a little brighter in the morning. At the moment, her problem seemed insurmountable.

Unfortunately, nothing was going to make it disappear overnight.

"Why...?" Her lower lip began to quiver. She drew a breath to steady herself, only to exhale a humiliating sob. "Why don't you want me? You need someone to look after your baby, and I've looked after Mrs. Endicott since I was twelve years old. She's not a baby, I know, but sometimes when she won't take her pills like the doctor orders, and when she rings the bell for me half a dozen times in the night, she's every bit as much trouble. And she doesn't smell sweet like a baby or hold out her arms and smile like babies do to let you know they..."

The forlorn little words *love you* were lost as Jane shielded her face with her hands and fought to compose herself.

Suddenly she felt a pair of strong arms warm around her shoulders. Her breath caught in her throat and she jerked back from the comforting embrace. She relaxed slightly when she found it was Mrs. Kincaid, not John Whitefeather, holding her.

Ruth Kincaid crooned some words Jane could not understand before easing into English. "It was not *you* we turned down, Jane Harris. I asked Caleb to make that plain in his letter. There must have been a mix-up. We didn't even run our notice in any newspapers so far East.''

Jane remembered. She'd read the Kincaids' advertisement in one of the newspapers Mrs. Endicott's cousin had sent her from Saint Louis. Wanting to get as far away from Emery as possible, Jane had scoured the western papers for employment opportunities. Of several inquiries she'd sent, only the Kincaids in distant Montana had answered.

To say they didn't want her.

Ruth Kincaid patted Jane's shoulder, then took a seat beside her at the table. "I'm a healer, and when my people call on me in an emergency, I have to go. Someone needs to be here to care for the baby and for Caleb's boy, Zeke, while I am away. Women who come to Montana from back East often don't stay. Our land is too big and too hard for them. When the letters came applying for the job, we chose a widow from Bismarck. She knows this country. She'll stay for as long as we need her.''

"I w-w-would have stayed." Jane fought the urge to give way to tears harder than she'd ever fought anything. Childish blubbering would only convince the Kincaids they'd been right to hire someone else.

Smoothing the tumbled strands of hair back from Jane's face, Ruth nodded gravely. "I think you would have. I'm sorry you came so far and through so many troubles for nothing.''

"It's my fault. I'm sorry." By rote, the words fell from Jane's lips. This time, she meant them. "I should have taken the time to confirm what was written in your letter and not come dashing out to Montana based on a hopeful assumption.''

After her ride from Whitehorn on the back of John Whitefeather's spotted horse, she understood what Mrs. Kincaid meant about women from the East Coast not staying long in Montana. Everything about the place was on such a vast scale. It dwarfed all her efforts and her dreams. Such country demanded strength from its daughters, and Jane sensed it would not take kindly to a foundling like her.

The dispiriting fact remained: she had nowhere to go and no means to get there if she did.

Jane took a deep breath, trying to make herself look fearless, capable and steady. She doubted either the Kincaids or John Whitefeather would be fooled. "I'll be obliged to you for letting me stay the night. I don't suppose you know anyone else hereabouts who needs help looking after their children?"

"Well now, let me think on it." Caleb Kincaid scratched his chin in a pensive fashion.

"Think tonight and we'll talk more in the morning." The rancher's wife beckoned to Jane. "Come along, dear. Let's find you a bed and a nightgown, then I'll bring my medicines."

Despite her worries, or perhaps because of them, Jane longed to stretch out on any excuse for a bed and to flee from her troubles into the land of dreams.

As she rose from the table to follow her hostess out of the kitchen, John Whitefeather spoke. "I have a thought, if you want to hear it."

Ruth Kincaid chuckled. "Was there ever a time we didn't pay you mind, *hestatanemo?*" To Jane, she added, "It was my brother who advised me to leave our people and make a life with Caleb Kincaid."

Brother? Jane tried to mask her surprise as she berated herself for not guessing sooner. Her stomach churned as she recalled all the subtle ways she must have offended John Whitefeather since the first moment she'd approached him in the saloon. What wise counsel was he going to give his sister and brother-in-law concerning their unwanted houseguest?

Jane braced herself.

"When's this other lady supposed to come?" John asked, drumming his fingers on the table.

Caleb Kincaid shrugged. "Mrs. Muldoon didn't rightly give a date. Said she had to settle her affairs in Bismarck first. Another few weeks, a month, who knows?"

Nodding, as if gravely pleased with the answer, John Whitefeather cast a look at his sister. "Didn't you get called out just the other night, when Ghost Moon had trouble birthing her twins?"

"You know I did, since you rode with me."

"Well, then, since Mrs. Muldoon won't be coming for a spell and Miss Harris is already here and could use a job, why don't you let her look after the boys? That way she could at least earn the price of a train ticket back to Boston."

Before Jane could help herself, the words burst out. "I'm not going back to Boston—not ever!" Not as long as Emery Endicott was there, at least.

They all ignored her outburst. Ruth and Caleb Kincaid exchanged a long gaze, as though sharing each other's thoughts without words.

Jane held still, scarcely breathing as she silently willed them to give her a chance. Her eyes met John Whitefeather's, and she offered him a timid half smile for intervening on her behalf. She couldn't remember the last time anyone had spoken up for her.

At last Ruth Kincaid nodded. "My brother's plan is a good one for all of us. Would you be willing to stay, Miss Harris, until Mrs. Muldoon can come?"

"Yes." Jane blurted out her acceptance before the Kincaids had time to think better of the idea. "Thank you."

The matter settled, Mrs. Kincaid hustled her upstairs to a rustic but snug little room under the eaves. A narrow bed stood in one corner, while a small bureau and a washstand of matching, pale-hued wood bracketed the window. Green curtains, a round braided rug and a patchwork quilt added touches of color and warmth.

Her new employer fetched Jane a pitcher of hot water, a nightgown and an extra quilt.

"The nights can still get cold this time of year, and you don't have much meat on your bones, dear. We must try to fatten you up while you're with us."

When Mrs. Kincaid returned later with her medicines, Jane was standing at the window, staring out at a small, sturdy cabin not far from the main house.

"I can't think why my brother insists on sleeping out in the foreman's cabin when he takes all his meals with us." As Ruth Kincaid spoke she set several clay pots of salve on top of the bureau.

Jane remembered what the bartender in town had said about John Whitefeather always keeping to himself. That would suit her just fine. The fewer men she had to deal with in her new position, the better.

Casting dubious looks at Ruth's medicines, Jane wrinkled her nose at some of the smells. Patiently Ruth Kincaid told her the ingredients of each compound and what good it would do. Then she applied generous daubs on Jane's injuries with a whisper-light touch.

"Do you hurt anywhere else that needs tending, dear?"

Jane's stomach churned at Ruth Kincaid's matter-of-fact question.

"No." Her hand flew to the modestly buttoned throat of her borrowed nightgown before she could stop it. "I guess my clothes must have protected the rest of me when I got thrown around the train carriage."

In truth, she wished Mrs. Kincaid could employ her healing touch on the ribs a doctor at the Boston infirmary had pronounced cracked. That injury and the ugly purple bruising on her bosom could easily be explained by the train-crash story. For Mrs. Kincaid to examine her ribs, though, Jane would have to expose her shoulders and upper arms. Those wounds, where Emery had dug in his nails and gouged her flesh, would betray her shameful secret.

When she'd changed for bed, Jane had noticed the injured skin was still red and swollen. She feared the wounds would leave telltale scars.

Mrs. Kincaid gathered up her medicines. "If that's all I can do for you now, I'll say good-night. Sleep well—it's the best healer. In the morning we'll find clothes for you."

She turned down the wick on Jane's lamp, easing the tiny gable room into a warm cocoon of darkness.

With a sigh of contentment Jane gave herself up to the modest luxury of a clean, warm bed. She could scarcely remember a time when she'd been cared for with the tenderness Mrs. Kincaid had shown her tonight. The sturdy construction of the ranch house made her feel safer than she had felt in a long time. Already she shrank from the prospect of leaving it.

She would repay the Kincaids for their kindness, Jane vowed as exhaustion overcame her. She would work hard to care for the children and do everything possible to help Mrs. Kincaid around the house.

If she really, really tried, perhaps she could even make herself indispensable.

As she lapsed into dreams, Jane found herself reliving her ride from town in the untalkative company of John Whitefeather. Even when she'd doubted whether she could trust him, her arms had instinctively latched on to his warm, solid frame. She had breathed his scent, a faint mas-

culine compound of sweet dry hay mingled with the musk
of horses and leather. The contrast to Emery's overpowering pomade comforted her somehow.

Why had John Whitefeather not mentioned he was re-
lated to the Kincaids? And what had prompted him to in-
tercede on her behalf? Jane had lived too long and been
hurt too often not to question his motives. She knew from
bitter experience the danger of fraternizing with a member
of her employer's family.

Not that such a thing was apt to happen in her case. For
all she knew, John Whitefeather might be happily married,
though his sister's comment about the foreman's cabin
made Jane doubt it. Even if he was a bachelor, such a
handsome man must have plenty of ladies waiting at his
beck and call. What interest would he have in some
mousey, penniless hired girl from the East? None at all,
Jane insisted to herself as her cracked ribs began to ache.

Or was it, perhaps, her heart?

"I swear I could see her heart thumping." John shook
his head, recalling the spectacle of Miss Jane Harris venturing into the Double Deuce Saloon. "Like a rabbit come
calling in a coyotes' den."

Caleb Kincaid threw back his tawny head and let out a
whoop of laughter. "I'll bet a few of those hungry coyotes
were licking their chops, all right! She could be a fetching
little filly if she didn't look like she just lost a barroom
brawl."

Somehow the thought of those cowboys at the Double
Deuce casting hungry eyes over Miss Harris sobered
John's mood of levity. He didn't reckon he had any call
to make fun of the lady. She'd shown some backbone
traipsing into a tough spot like the Double Deuce to find
him. The fact that she'd done what she had to in spite of

her obvious fear kindled a grudging glimmer of respect in him.

As far as John Whitefeather was concerned, *that* was the true mark of courage.

"What do you reckon brought her all the way out here, from Boston?" he asked, as much to himself as to Caleb. The woman was a bundle of mysteries and contradictions, all of which intrigued John too much for his liking.

Caleb Kincaid took a long draw on his pipe, as if the tobacco smoke fueled his thoughts. "Could be most anything. Maybe she got itchy feet and figured Montana would be a big adventure. Or she might have read about the gold fields and figured this was prime hunting ground for a rich husband."

John shook his head slowly. Neither of these guesses tallied with what he'd so far experienced of Miss Jane Harris. Not that he had much practice with women, but he knew enough of men and horses to recognize a look of desperation when he saw it.

"I got the feeling she wouldn't be in Montana if she had a choice."

Caleb mulled that over for a long, silent moment. "Think she might be on the run from the law? Maybe I ought to send a wire to the police in Boston. Don't want some criminal taking care of my boys, no matter how good-looking she is."

For no good reason that John could figure, his brother-in-law's words provoked him. He responded in a sharper tone than he intended. "How come you're so set on thinking the worst of this poor gal, Caleb? I can't picture her getting up the gumption to do anything against the law."

Caleb replied with a smug, mocking smile that John wanted to wipe off his face—by force if necessary. "How come you're so set on defending her? That's a far more entertaining question, if you ask me.''

"I *didn't* ask.'' John rose abruptly from the table. "Can't sit around jawing with you all night. Got to work some more on that little maverick filly tomorrow. Maybe she got to missing me while I was gone today, and she'll be ready to make friends.''

As he fetched his hat and coat from the hook by the door, his brother-in-law rose and stretched. "Always plenty to do, is right. A man needs to grab his sleep when he's got a soft, warm bed.''

He ambled over to the stove, lifted the lid off the firebox and knocked the ashes from his pipe into it.

"Be careful around *this* little maverick filly, John.'' Caleb nodded upward to signal that he meant Jane Harris. "I've got a bad feeling about her. Reminds me of Zeke's mama, God rest her soul. She just wasn't fit for this kind of life, and she made the boy and me miserable for a long spell before and after she died. I don't know what would have become of us if Ruth hadn't come back into my life again when she did.''

The rancher's rugged features softened and his wary tone warmed as he spoke of his wife.

John knew how many years his sister had quietly suffered, her heart held captive by a married man who couldn't claim her. One of his greatest joys in life was to see her so happy and fulfilled in her union with Caleb Kincaid. Part of him envied what Ruth and Caleb had together, while another part shied from going after it himself. Every moment of happiness they enjoyed now had cost them a matching moment of pain.

Besides, a wife was a responsibility, and he already had more than enough responsibility for the folks at Sweetgrass. One day, perhaps, if he found a woman capable of easing his burdens, rather than adding to them, he might be willing to gamble his heart and his hard-won peace of spirit.

"Save your warning, Caleb." John jammed on his hat and pulled open the kitchen door. "Once I delivered Jane Harris to the ranch, my obligation and my interest both ended. Even if I was fool enough to hanker after her, you never saw the way she looked at me in town today. I reckon the lady would sooner be courted by a grizzly."

Caleb's husky laughter followed him out into the night.

Though the clean, still air was chilly for late May, John didn't bother to put on his coat for his short saunter from the Kincaids' kitchen door to the foreman's cabin, where he spent his nights.

In the distance, lights flickered from the windows of the cowboys' bunkhouse. The sounds of talk, laughter and the plaintive croon of a harmonica spilled out into the night. John knew if he set foot inside, the music and gossip would stop and the cowboys would hit their bunks, where they belonged. Tonight he didn't have the heart to interrupt their fun.

He hesitated at the door of his cabin, a refuge of solitude between the homey bustle of Ruth and Caleb's place and the bachelor commotion of the bunkhouse.

Overhead, the wide, black Montana sky glittered with a mother lode of tiny silver nuggets—calm and beautiful, but also distant and cold. For the first time since coming to the Kincaid ranch, over a year ago, John Whitefeather went to bed in a foreman's cabin that felt lonesome and empty.

Chapter Three

"Indispensable. In-dispensable." Over and over, Jane muttered the word to herself as she confronted her first day of provisional employment.

To her surprise, she'd slept deeply and peacefully, untroubled by nightmares of Emery hunting her down. Between Mrs. Kincaid's pungent salves and the healing night's rest, Jane did not wince too painfully at the sight of her face in the oval looking glass above the bureau.

A soft knock on the door made her jump. Her newfound sense of security must not run very deep, after all.

"W-who is it?"

"It's Ruth, Miss Harris. I heard you stirring and thought I should bring you some clean clothes."

Jane pulled open the door. "That's very kind of you."

Expecting only Ruth, she started at the sight of a boy, nine or ten years old. If he was home from school, this must be Saturday. Jane realized she'd lost track of the days during her exhausting journey west from Boston.

If she noticed Jane's jumpiness, the rancher's wife gave no sign. "Jane Harris, this is Zeke, Caleb's son. He helped me bring down this trunk of clothes from the attic. They belonged to his mother and they're too small for me. They might fit you until we can make some new ones.''

"Thank you." Jane looked from the trunk to Zeke Kincaid. "If it'll upset you to see me wearing clothes that belonged to your mother, I can get by with the blouse and skirt I wore from Boston."

The boy shoved his hands in his pockets and stared at the floor. "I don't mind, ma'am, honest. My ma's been gone quite a spell now and Ruth told me all your bags got burned up in a train wreck." He glanced up at her, then looked away again, blushing. "That must've been exciting."

"I suppose so." Jane hoped Zeke wouldn't pester her for details that might unravel her tangled falsehood. "Not exciting in a good way, I'm afraid."

Was there a good kind of excitement?

Before the boy could inquire further, a loud and sustained wail rang out downstairs.

Ruth Kincaid turned to her stepson. "Go see what your brother's done to himself this time, Zeke. I'll be right down."

The boy grimaced. "Aw, do I have to?"

"Please, Zeke."

Muttering to himself about the bother of baby brothers, the boy headed downstairs.

Ruth pushed the trunk over Jane's threshold. "You're kind to think of Zeke's feelings. Don't worry, though, he won't have many memories of his mother wearing these things. Use whatever will fit."

"What about Mr. Kincaid?" The impossibly tactless question slipped out before Jane could help herself.

To her surprise and relief, Caleb Kincaid's second wife shook her head. "I asked him, and he doesn't mind. Come down to breakfast when you're dressed. You can meet Barton and we'll talk about this job you have with us.''

When her new employer had gone, Jane found it took longer than she planned to rummage through the trunk for something to wear. The clothes fit her well enough, but few looked suitable for a Montana rancher's wife, let alone a hired girl.

To Jane, who had never owned pretty clothes because Mrs. Endicott disdained such frivolity, the trunk was a treasure trove. She couldn't resist trying on one or two of the fanciest dresses before settling on a comparatively simple style in apple green. If she borrowed an apron of Ruth's to cover the front, it might not be too fancy for doing chores.

Employing a dainty hairbrush she found in the trunk, Jane dressed her plain brown hair in a style that veiled as much as possible of her healing face. After making her bed, she followed the tantalizing smell of coffee down to the kitchen.

There she found Ruth adding chopped vegetables to a big cast-iron pot on the back of the stove. Young Zeke was shoving oatmeal into the mouth of a baby, whose plump cheeks were caked with drying porridge.

Jane tried to guess how old he might be. Not a young infant, for he held himself erect in the chair. A year old, perhaps? Two? Should a woman be caring for young children if she couldn't place the age of a baby better than that?

Stifling that nauseating qualm of doubt, Jane stooped in front of the high chair. She offered her forefinger for the baby to grasp in his chubby fist. ''This must be Master Barton. He looks like a hearty eater.''

''Watch out if you're trying to feed him something he

doesn't like." Zeke pulled a face. "Pa says Barton can spit farther than a rattlesnake."

Jane could scarcely imagine this chuckling cherub being any trouble. As much as Zeke looked like his father, little Barton was the image of his mother, with golden-brown skin, fine black hair and dark laughing eyes. When he cracked a wide gummy smile and crowed his delight at seeing her, Jane surrendered her heart to him.

After what Emery had done to her, the idea of marriage now frightened Jane too much to contemplate. Which meant she would never have babies of her own.

To distract herself from that wrenching regret, she asked Zeke, "What sorts of food does your little brother dislike?"

"Mashed peas." The boy rolled his eyes.

"Oh dear." Jane laughed, and Barton's big brother laughed with her.

"I'll be glad when he's older." Zeke passed Barton's bowl and spoon to Jane. "Then I can take him riding with me and fishing down at the creek. Right now, he's not much use."

Jane nodded. She couldn't find it in her heart to tell Zeke that by the time his baby brother was able to ride and fish, he probably wouldn't want the little fellow tagging along. She could hardly remember her older brother, who had sickened and died of the typhoid along with their mother. She did recall how Ches had discouraged her from following him and his friends.

Ruth Kincaid gave one last stir to the contents of the pot, then she opened the warming tray above the stove and lifted down a bowl and a plate. "Come eat breakfast, Miss Harris. I kept it hot for you."

Planting a kiss on the baby's fat fist, Jane pried her finger from his sturdy grasp. She took her place at the table and tucked into her breakfast gratefully. When Ruth brought her a cup of strong black coffee, she savored each sip.

"Today I'll show you around the house." Mrs. Kincaid brought her own steaming cup of coffee to the table and took a seat opposite Jane. "I'll explain what chores I want you to do while you're with us. After that we can—"

Before the rancher's wife could finish, a stampede of footsteps thundered out on the porch. Jane cringed at the sound, then exhaled a breath of relief when Caleb Kincaid burst through the kitchen door.

"Can you come, Ruth?" he called to his wife. "Bring your medicines. Lizzie's brother's been thrown by his horse out on the range. Broke some bones and may have cracked his skull. I don't want to move the young fellow until you look him over first."

With a nod to her husband, Ruth rose from her chair and strode out of the kitchen. She returned a moment later wearing her bonnet and shawl, and carrying a brown leather satchel.

She glanced at Jane. "Good fortune brought you to us last night, Miss Harris. Take care of the boys while I am gone."

Before Jane could ask how long that might be, the Kincaids had hurried out of the ranch house. Caleb shot her a glance as they were leaving—wary and vaguely hostile. Perhaps he didn't like her wearing his late wife's clothes, after all.

Young Barton stared at the door for a moment, as if expecting his parents to come rushing back in again. When a little time passed and they did not materialize, he screwed up his face and began to cry loudly.

Zeke scowled at his little brother. "He don't like it when

Ruth goes off like that. If I was you, I'd stuff rags in my ears, miss.''

"He'll settle down." Jane hollered to make herself heard over Barton's shrill lament. Hunting up a damp cloth, she wiped the baby's face, which made him cry harder still. Then she scooped him up out of his high chair and bounced him gently, trying to comfort him.

The child's sobs gradually subsided into wet hiccups. A warm surge of success buoyed Jane—*indispensable.* "There now, that wasn't so bad."

Time to wipe off the tray of his high chair and wash the breakfast dishes. Giving his warm little body a final squeeze, Jane set Barton down on the floor so she could tend to the other chores.

"Waaaa!" The crying returned in full force and increased volume.

Jane picked the baby up again. My, he was a heavy little armful! The gentle ache of her ribs sharpened. It took her longer to quiet him this time, but at last his tears subsided and he poked a plump thumb into his mouth. Shifting him to her hip, Jane managed to carry her breakfast dishes and his porridge bowl to the corner washtub. She dampened a rag and swiped it over the tray of his chair. It wasn't as thorough a job as she would like to have done, but the best she could manage one-handed while balancing a heavy baby on her hip.

Zeke ambled to the kitchen door, grabbing his hat and coat from their pegs.

"Where are you going?" Jane asked.

The boy shrugged. "Poke around the corrals. Maybe saddle up Windsinger and go for a ride."

Jane thought of the cowboy thrown from his horse. The one Mrs. Kincaid might be tending at this very minute. And what animals might be out in the ranch's corrals?

Bulls with sharp horns and heavy hooves, perhaps. Wild mustangs whose powerful bucking legs could shatter a man's skull with one kick.

Ruth and Caleb Kincaid had left her in charge of their boys. Ruth trustingly. Caleb warily. More than anything, Jane wanted to justify Ruth's faith in her and to win Caleb's trust. How else could she make herself indispensable around the Kincaid ranch? If Zeke came to harm while in her care, she might find herself on the next train back to Boston, or perhaps hired to ply some unspeakable trade at the Double Deuce Saloon.

"I'm sorry, Zeke. I'm responsible for your safety. I'll have to ask you to stay in the house with me until your folks get back."

"Aw!" The boy thrust his hat back on its peg, but kept his buckskin jacket on. "I ain't a baby like Barton. I've been going where I please around this ranch as long as I can recollect. Two years ago I ran off and joined the Cheyenne."

If Zeke expected such a boast would impress Jane into setting him at liberty, he miscalculated.

"I'm sorry, Zeke." He seemed like a good boy. If she denied him and he came to resent her presence, what chance was there that his father and stepmother would keep her around? "I could use your help while Ruth is gone. Barton doesn't know who I am, and I haven't got any idea where to find things. I'd be much obliged if you'd stay close by to advise me."

He heaved a great sigh that reminded Jane of Mrs. Endicott when she finally submitted to the tiresome necessity of taking her pills. "I suppose I can hang around till Pa gets back. Best advice I can give you—if Barton starts to cry again, try sitting with him in the rocking chair."

"Thank you, Zeke. I'll remember that."

Just to impress upon her that he was obeying under protest, the boy stalked off to another part of the house. Later Jane heard loud banging noises from upstairs, but she didn't have the courage to go investigate what he might be up to.

Not that she had the opportunity, for Barton kept her well occupied. As long as she sat in the rocking chair, talking or singing to him, he was perfectly contented. And he would tolerate being held in Jane's arms while she walked through the house, wistfully taking note of all the chores she *could* be doing to impress the Kincaids with her industry.

If she set him down, though, the baby would suck in more air than his small body seemed capable of holding. Then he would release it at high volume with a distressing infusion of tears. The sound of his crying made Jane's insides contract and the muscles between her shoulders bunch up tight.

What was that smell? Something burning?

Ignoring Barton's shrieks, Jane popped him into his high chair and checked the stove. The savory concoction of beef and beans had begun to scorch on the bottom of the pot. Jane stirred it several times.

Was it her imagination, or did she smell the tang of sourdough working?

A quick glance in the warming tray revealed a number of loaf pans covered with damp dish towels. Had they risen sufficiently? Was the oven hot enough to bake them? Back in Boston, Mrs. Endicott's cook had prepared all the meals. Jane wished she'd shown more curiosity about culinary matters.

She could always leave the dough and later claim not to have known it was there. But by then it might have overflowed the pans and made a sticky mess all over the bottom of the warming tray. She owed Ruth better service than that.

Desperately hoping she was doing the right thing, Jane lifted the pans down and set them in the oven. Then she dug in the wood box for a couple of good-size sticks to stoke the fire.

"Hush, Barton, hush. I'm coming." She hoisted the squalling baby back out of his chair and bounced him on her hip until she feared her cracked ribs would break for sure. Did something else ail the little fellow besides missing his mother? Was he hungry? Thirsty? Tired?

The Kincaids had been right not to hire her in the first place. What had made her think she could look after a baby when she had almost no experience, only a pack of romantic daydreams about motherhood?

Jane collapsed into the rocking chair and snuffled back tears of sympathy for young Barton. And despair for herself.

The new filly shied away from John Whitefeather's approach. The last shreds of patience slipped from his grasp like a greased rope. He'd tried a number of his most reliable techniques on the tetchy beast and she still wouldn't let him near—not even to feed from a bucket of oats he held.

Finally he let her out into the paddock with Hawkwing and Zeke's pony, Windsinger. Maybe they would let the filly know he was a man a horse could trust.

When his stomach gave a loud growl, John realized the time had gotten away from him. That often happened when he threw himself into gentling a particularly reluctant horse. Still, he could always count on his sister to drag him into the ranch house for meals.

But Ruth had gone with Caleb to tend young Cicero

Price, and there was no sign of them back yet. Just then, John remembered Caleb's parting words to him.

"Keep an eye on that Harris gal, will you? Can't put my finger on it, but there's something about that gal I don't trust."

"Better late than never," John muttered to himself as he headed for the ranch house. How much mischief could she have gotten into since breakfast? Even if she was the mischievous type—which John doubted. "I could use a cup of coffee and something to eat, anyway."

The minute he walked through the kitchen door, the smell of burned food overpowered John's nose, while the piercing howls of his infant nephew all but deafened him. The room looked like an orange Kansas twister had just blown through it.

A strange, frantic sensation tightened the flesh of John's throat as his eyes swept the kitchen, looking for Jane Harris. Had she run off or locked herself in her room, leaving the boys to fend for themselves?

In front of the oven, a disheveled figure straightened up and set a loaf pan on the counter. The aroma of fresh bread almost battled the stench of burned beans. Three more times Jane Harris bent and straightened, like some kind of wading bird bobbing for food. Then she closed the oven door and rescued Barton from his chair.

As she stood there clutching the bawling baby, John thought he'd never seen such a pathetic looking creature in his life. The injuries to her face still had some healing to do, and her warm brown hair straggled from a once-neat roll at the nape of her neck. Her dainty green dress, better suited to a garden party than a Montana ranch, was spattered with gobs of bright orange, as was her face. She shrank from his gaze as though she expected John to draw a six-shooter and gun her down.

As Barton's cries quieted, she spoke. "I don't think the bread is ruined."

She made it sound like a single hard-won victory in a day of disastrous defeats. For reasons he could not explain or justify to himself, John Whitefeather began to chuckle and then to laugh.

"This isn't funny!" The terrified look left her eyes, replaced by a rather becoming flicker of fury. "I've tried my best, but everything's just gone from bad to worse, and I can't get a blessed thing done when I have to hold the baby every blessed minute."

When a frightened filly had her back to the wall, often she would rear or buck, rather than cower. The Boston gal put John in mind of such a horse. And she wasn't done yet.

"He spit out every spoonful of mashed carrots I tried to feed him. His brother's off tearing the house apart nail by nail for all I know. Any minute, Mr. and Mrs. Kincaid are going to arrive home and put me on the next train back to Boston. If they don't decide it's cheaper just to throw me to the wolves!"

For an instant John feared the woman was going to burst into hysterical tears. Instead, she glanced around the kitchen and down at her carrot-dappled dress, then began to laugh with an edge of frenzy.

Two swift strides brought John close to her. When he held out his arms for his nephew, she surrendered the child without any pretense of reluctance.

John lifted little Barton high in the air and spoke to him in Cheyenne. "What kind of warrior are you to pour tears like a rain cloud and howl like thunder? Why do you torment the woman so she cannot work?"

Two deep dimples blossomed on either side of Barton's mouth as he crowed with laughter.

John lowered the child to his shoulder. "I'll keep him quiet for you and I'll go talk to Zeke while you clean up the kitchen."

"Why?" Suspicion brooded in the woman's eyes.

He'd expected some timid sign of gratitude, like the smile she'd offered last night when he'd convinced Ruth and Caleb to let her stay on at the ranch. Her question, posed with a guarded posture and wary tone, puzzled him.

"Why should you clean the kitchen? If you can't see that for yourself, ma'am, I don't think you're going to be much help to my sister."

"I know why the kitchen needs to be cleaned." She stiffened and pushed a fallen lock of hair out of her eyes. "What I want to know is why you're willing to help me. When I first arrived in town yesterday, you looked at me like I was a dead whale rotting on your shore. Later you spoke up for me with the Kincaids and now you propose to take charge of the children so I can set this mess to rights. What is it you want from me, Mr. Whitefeather?"

The maverick filly out in the corral had exhausted his patience. He didn't have a scrap left for this Boston filly who provoked a dust devil of contrary feelings within him.

"What do I want?" he snapped. "How about a crumb of thanks? Or is that too much for a Montana half-breed to expect from a prissy New England lady?"

Her fair complexion paled even further, until Barton's spewed carrots stood out like a faceful of bright freckles. In John's arms, the baby began to fuss. Rubbing the child's back and rocking him, John softened his reproach of Jane Harris so as not to upset Barton further.

"Last night, when you found out you didn't have a job, you looked like somebody pretty near the end of her rope. When I walked through that door a few minutes ago, you appeared to have gone downhill in the meantime. Call me a gullible jackass, Miss Harris, but I've always had a soft spot for folks who are in trouble. If you can't accept a little help with good grace, I reckon that's *your* problem.''

She thought his words over for an instant, then whispered, ''I suppose it is.''

Miss Harris looked too doggone appealing, and he wanted to stay mad. So John spun away from her and headed off to find Zeke.

Over his shoulder he called, ''Get busy and clean up around here. I'm doing this for my sister, not for you. She'll be tuckered out when she gets back from doctoring Cicero. I don't want her coming home to a kitchen that looks and smells like this one does.''

Behind him he heard absolute silence, which pricked his curiosity so much he almost looked back. Instead he forced his feet down the hall and up the stairs to Zeke's room.

He tapped on the door. ''Zeke, it's me and Barton. Can we come in?''

The door swung open. John almost flinched at the sight. He'd seen hog wallows cleaner than Zeke's bedroom.

The boy must have been cracking walnuts open with a hammer, for shells were spread across the wood floor like a crunchy carpet. Either the bed hadn't been made that morning, or Zeke had climbed back under the covers recently. Discarded clothes lay everywhere. A company of painted toy soldiers littered one corner of the room where they had fallen in some pretend battle. Others sprawled behind a fortress of building blocks whose walls had been breached by imaginary artillery.

Picking his way through the walnut shells, John cleared a spot on the rumpled bed, then sat down and began to bounce Barton on his knee.

Zeke glanced around his room, as if noticing the mess

for the first time. He knelt down and began sweeping the walnut shells into a pile.

"Did *she* say you had to hang around indoors all day, too?" The boy's lower lip thrust out in a stubborn pout.

Sometimes John wondered if his young friend didn't have the worst qualities of both his parents—Caleb's stubborn streak and Marie's spitefulness.

"Nope." John shook his head. "I came in to get some coffee and a bite to eat." Jane Harris had driven any thought of food or drink from his mind. "You housebound for the day?"

"Uh-huh. She thinks I'm some kind of danged baby, like Barton. I told her I've been going where I want and doing what I please on this ranch since I been out of dresses. Told her how I ran off and joined the Cheyenne."

John swallowed a smile and nodded, remembering how the boy had appeared at their camp, wanting to become a Cheyenne warrior to avoid going to school. "Was that likely to convince her it's safe to let you out of the house?"

"Reckon not."

"I don't think she was trying to be mean to you, or treat you like a baby, Zeke. Your folks went off in a big hurry this morning and left Miss Harris to look after you boys without any time to prepare. It's not easy being put in charge when you aren't ready. Lot of responsibility. Lot of things can go wrong and it'll be your fault if they do."

That's how he'd felt when Bearspeaker and the other elders had made him their chief. Always, he worried if he was doing the right thing. Like now—working in the white man's world to provide a place that belonged to them. Would he have done better to settle them on the reservation with other Cheyenne bands? If any of his people suf-

fered because of his decision, John wondered how he
would bear the burden on his conscience.

"If you say so." Zeke gathered up his dirty clothes and
set them on the end of the bed. "She's kind of pretty, ain't
she?"

"You reckon?" John shrugged and wrinkled his mouth
into a dubious frown.

"Yep." Zeke dug out a wooden box from under his bed
and put all his soldiers away. "Not pretty like Ruth or
Aunt Lizzie, of course. And for sure not like Jon Watson's
ma, that Uncle Brock married."

John had to agree. His sister and Caleb's sisters-in-law
were all very striking women, each in her unique way.
Ruth with her long raven hair, Lizzie with her riot of
golden curls and Abby with her bright coppery mane.
Alongside them, Jane Harris looked like a drab little mead-
owlark in the company of a raven, a goldfinch and a robin.
Still, the little lady from back East had a waifish charm
that drew his eye far more than it ought to.

Zeke stacked his blocks into a neat pile in the far corner.
"She ain't a Montana kind of gal, that's for sure."

A yelp of laughter burst out of John, which set Barton
gurgling along with him. "We're agreed on that, son. You
appear to know a whole heap about women."

"I oughta." Zeke winked. "Plenty of courting going on
around here lately." He continued to tidy his room in silence, then he added in a more serious tone, "I reckon
Miss Harris needs somebody to take care of *her*."

For some reason the boy's words dug into John's conscience like cold steel. "If she's going to last in Montana,
Miss Harris needs to learn how to take care of herself,
son."

A tentative tap sounded on Zeke's door, followed by a
bolder one. With a guilty start, John wondered how much

of his conversation with the boy Jane Harris might have overheard.

Perhaps Zeke was pondering the same thing, for he looked a little shamefaced as he pulled the door open.

Before Jane Harris could get a word out, he launched into his apology. ''I'm sorry I didn't stick around and give you a hand with Barton, ma'am. And I'm sorry I didn't tell you he hates carrots even worse than he hates peas. Night Horse explained to me about you being respons'ble in case I get hurt while my folks are gone.''

Jane Harris looked from Zeke to John and back, a shadow of uncertainty in her eyes. ''Night Horse?''

''My Cheyenne name.'' The gruffness of his voice took John aback.

''So you're not Apache?'' One slender hand flew up to cover her mouth—too late to prevent her words escaping.

Zeke scowled with boyish scorn. ''Don't you know nothing, ma'am? Apaches live way in the south. This here's Cheyenne, Crow and Sioux country. Night Horse is a real live Cheyenne warrior chief, and he made me an ornery Cheyenne brave.''

''*Honorary* brave, Zeke.'' John bit back a grin. So had Jane Harris, unless he missed his guess.

''Why is a Cheyenne warrior chief working as a ranch foreman?'' The lady's wide eyes betrayed a shade of fear. And possibly a glow of respect?

''Long story, ma'am. Long, dull story.''

''No it ain't,'' piped up Zeke.

John gave the boy a warning look, but addressed his words to Jane Harris. ''Was there something you wanted, ma'am?''

''Ah—yes, there was, as a matter of fact. I've got the kitchen scrubbed down as best I can and I managed to save some of those beans. The scorched ones I fed to the pigs. It won't be enough for supper, I'm afraid. Especially if Mr. and Mrs. Kincaid get home in time to join us. After I change my dress, I wondered if you gentlemen might give me a hand fixing something more.''

John rose from his seat on Zeke's bed, little Barton gathered close to his chest. The baby blinked heavy eyelids and sucked on his thumb.

''I reckon we could do that, ma'am.'' Somehow, during his conversation with Zeke, the flash of anger he'd felt toward Jane Harris had eased. ''Later, I can show you how Cheyenne women keep their hands free to work when they've got little ones to mind.''

''Thank you, Mr. Whitefeather. Or should I call you Night Horse?''

He liked the sound of his Cheyenne name on her tongue. A little too much, perhaps.

''Plain *John* will be fine, ma'am.''

Chapter Four

"That cradleboard was a fine idea. Thank you…John."

How would she have managed this past busy week without it? Jane wondered as she took a hasty bite of her own dinner, then offered Barton a spoonful of applesauce. Fortunately, the child liked fruit a great deal better than he liked vegetables.

"Glad I could help." John glanced at his nephew and winked. "You seemed to have your hands full that first day."

Except for Barton's company, she and John were eating their midday meal alone. Zeke was in school and Caleb had ridden out to a place called Sweetgrass after breakfast to check on Ruth. An outbreak of scarlet fever among the Cheyenne children had kept her there for several days.

"You were kind to help me out after I was so ungracious." Jane kept her eyes fixed on the baby. As she brought another spoonful of applesauce to his mouth, her hand trembled slightly. "I've wanted to apologize to you before this, but I never had the chance." Or the nerve.

Over the past week, John Whitefeather had proven himself a very different kind of man than Emery Endicott. He did have a temper, though. Jane hadn't wanted to risk rousing it by reminding him of the rocky start to their acquaintance.

"No harm done." John reached for a biscuit.

His sudden movement made her flinch, but if he noticed, he pretended not to. He spread butter on his biscuit without missing a beat. "You seem to be getting along better, lately."

Jane smiled to herself. If only he knew how many mistakes she'd made in the past few days. How many chores she'd had to do over two or three times until the result satisfied her. But she'd persevered. On the Kincaid ranch, she felt needed in a way she never had in all her years with Mrs. Endicott.

"If Mrs. Muldoon would tarry in Bismarck another few weeks, I might develop a knack for this domestic routine."

As she glanced around the tidy kitchen and at the contented baby, a strange feeling swelled in Jane's heart. Though she couldn't be certain, she wondered if it might be…pride?

John reached over and tickled his nephew under the chin. "You and Barton got any big plans for this afternoon?"

"Nothing special." Noticing John's dinner plate was empty, she fetched him a slice of plum cake and a cup of coffee. "We washed the laundry and hung it out this morning. If I can work up the courage, I might fry a batch of doughnuts while Barton takes his nap."

John bit into the cake. "This tastes good." He sounded more than a little surprised. "I saw you hanging out the wash. That was a clever idea, tethering Barton to the clothesline so he wouldn't wander off."

She'd come up with it all on her own, too. The peculiar feeling in Jane's heart burned warmer. "He's steadier on his feet every day, and he does like to walk. Besides, it was too hard on my back, stooping to get wet clothes out of the basket with him in the cradleboard.''

Jane didn't mention the fat green grasshopper she'd had to fish out of Barton's mouth. Why he spit out peas and carrots, but not live insects, was more than she could figure.

''Maybe later you could bring this little buckeroo over to the corral and we could take him for a ride.'' John leaned back in his chair and took a long drink of his coffee. ''He always gets a kick out of that.''

''Are you certain it would be safe?''

Jane wiped Barton's face and lifted him out of his high chair. For a moment, she cradled his warm, sturdy little body against hers. The swiftness and intensity of her fondness for the child frightened her. It would be hard enough to leave the Kincaid ranch when the time came, even without strong emotional ties.

She looked up and caught John watching her with intense, perplexing concentration. The blue of his eyes sparkled as clear and brilliant as sapphires. And twice as hard.

His stare stoked a sudden fevered blush right to the roots of Jane's hair. She tried to break eye contact with him, only to discover she couldn't. His piercing gaze held her, probing her secrets. Then he let her go and she found herself capable of breathing again.

''The boy's not made of glass, Miss Harris.'' He spoke quietly, as always, but in a tone that brooked no argument. ''Even if he was, we'd have to toughen him up.''

''At the risk of shattering him?'' Jane heard herself ask.

Where had this unaccustomed defiance come from? Had John Whitefeather's relentless blue gaze planted it within her?

''I'm not going to set him on the back of a bucking bronco, ma'am. Just a gentle old mare who can't do much better than walk. I'll hold on to him good and tight in front of me.''

John held out a large brown hand to the baby. ''What do you say, Thundercloud?''

Barton immediately grasped one of his uncle's fingers and pulled it close to Jane's face.

She thrust the baby into John's arms, trying not to sound as alarmed as the sudden movement made her feel. ''Is that his Cheyenne name?''

''That's what it means. Ruth gave it to him because he makes a lot of noise for a critter so small. You'll come riding with us to keep an eye on him, won't you, ma'am?''

Jane shook her head with some vigor. ''Except for that trip in from Whitehorn, I've never sat a horse in my life.''

''Why didn't you say so? I would have made Lionel give us a wagon to drive out here even if I had to steal one. No two ways about it—you'll have to learn to ride if you're going to survive in Big Sky Country. Tell you what. I've got an old gelding who couldn't work up a gallop if you dropped a jar of nitroglycerin behind him.''

A bubble of laughter swelled inside Jane, all the more buoyant for being so unexpected. It rose and burst from her lips. ''I suppose I could try.''

''Sure you can. Unless I miss my guess, you've done plenty of things this past week that you've never tackled before.''

Did a hint of admiration warm his words?

''That's true.'' She'd made a fair job of them, too. But riding high off the ground on the back of such a large, powerful animal? ''Then again, I've never heard of a person getting bucked off a washboard.''

* * *

John saddled both horses, though he had more than a few doubts that Jane Harris would show up for their ride. To his surprise, she did.

To his greater surprise, she looked almost beautiful.

In the week since her arrival, the scrapes and bruises on her face had healed. Suddenly, John noticed.

Somewhere in that trunk of Marie Kincaid's, Jane had found a riding habit. The cloth was a little rumpled in places, but the fitted black jacket showed off the curve of her bosom in a way that made the collar of John's shirt tighten. A ruffle of white lace at the throat emphasized the daintiness of her features. She might not be as striking a beauty as Ruth or Lizzie or Abby, but she was every inch a lady.

A lady far more suited to the refined city life back East than to the vital, rough-edged existence in Big Sky Country. She was a woman who needed a wealthy, cultured gentleman to pamper her the way she deserved. With a sudden pang of regret, John realized he wasn't doing her any favors by helping her fit in around the ranch. Sooner or later, she'd figure out this wasn't the place for her.

Then she'd go away.

"I hope we won't be keeping you from your work." Her voice held a note of uncertainty, as though she was fishing for any excuse not to do this.

John thought about the maverick filly he'd privately dubbed Cactus Heart. "I haven't got a single thing in the world I'd rather do than take my nephew for a ride."

Barton clearly felt the same way. He held his stout little arms out to the horses and babbled with delight. John mounted the mare and reached down to lift the baby from Jane's arms.

She let him go reluctantly. "You will keep a tight hold on him, won't you? He squirms like the dickens when he gets excited."

"I know that, ma'am. Been around this young fellow since the day he was born." Somehow, John felt he should resent her protectiveness of *his* nephew. But he couldn't work up a pinch of the feeling that usually overwhelmed him when he was dealing with white folks.

Her arms looked strangely empty without the baby in them.

"I'm sorry," said Jane.

John had never met a person so quick to say those words. They usually stuck tight in his own craw.

"You're right, of course," she continued. "It's just that he's my responsibility and I've become very attached to him in the short time we've been together."

John knew that, too. It showed in the way she held the boy. It glowed in her smile and warmed her words when she spoke to him. That soft, maternal quality flattered her appearance far more than all Marie Kincaid's fancy clothes. Maybe that was why he found it impossible to resent her.

John Whitefeather had never been much given to smiling, and he didn't smile now. But he cast Jane a look he hoped would reassure her.

"Don't you fret about young Barton. I'm partial to the little rascal myself. I'll see he doesn't come to any harm."

Too late, John realized Barton's pretty nanny would need his help to mount the gelding.

So did she, by the look of it.

"You and Barton go ahead and ride. I'll just watch from here." Sounding more relieved than anything, she waved them on their way.

Out of the corner of his eye, John noticed one of the ranch hands approaching the corral.

"Can I be of service, ma'am?" Floyd Cobbs removed his hat. John didn't think the fellow was much to look at, but by all accounts Floyd fancied himself a ladies' man. "Help you onto that horse, maybe?"

John's brows tightened into a scowl. "Aren't you supposed to be keeping an eye on the Price boy, Floyd?"

"I've been watching him real close, boss." The words were respectful enough. To John's ears at least, the tone was anything but. "He's having hisself a little siesta right now, so I thought I'd stretch my legs."

The cowboy turned his attention back to Jane. "Pardon my manners, ma'am. I reckon we haven't been properly introduced. Name's Floyd Cobbs. I've been working the Kincaid spread for over three years now."

"Pleased to meet you, Mr. Cobbs." She didn't sound pleased. In fact, John could have sworn she took a couple of small steps back, until the corral fence prevented her from retreating any farther. "M-my name's Jane Harris. I'm just here for a short while to give Mrs. Kincaid a hand with the children and the house."

She reminded John for all the world of a rabbit doe cornered by a weasel—skin paler than usual, movements twitchy.

A blaze of rage kindled deep in his belly, but John did his best to ignore it. The lady wasn't in any real danger. And besides, he couldn't look after every stray who crossed his path.

"Well, that's real fine." The cowboy eyed Jane slowly from the crest of her saucily veiled hat to the tips of her high button boots peeping out from beneath the skirt of her riding habit. "Maybe you'll take a fancy to Whitehorn and decide to stay. If there's one thing wrong with the state of Montana, it's that we need more women."

John fought the urge to scramble down from his horse and pummel the insolent cowboy. What right did he have, though? Miss Jane Harris was nothing to him.

"Perhaps." She didn't sound very certain. Was her little Western adventure beginning to pale already?

"What do you say, ma'am? Want me to help you into the saddle?" Floyd spoke the words in an innocent tone, but John thought he detected a mocking double meaning.

"T-thank you for the offer." She eyed Floyd Cobbs as if he was a giant-size bedbug. "But I don't believe I'll ride today, after all."

"Good enough, ma'am." Floyd grinned and took another step toward her. "Then you and me can keep each other company here while Mr. Whitefeather trots young Kincaid around."

Absorbed in watching Jane and the cowboy, and trying to sort out his unduly strong reaction, John didn't notice Barton dig his fists into the mare's mane and yank. The horse tossed her head and whinnied. If she'd been a couple of years younger, she might have reared.

"On second thought," gasped Jane, "perhaps I'd better stay as close as possible to Barton, in case he gets himself in trouble." She ducked past Floyd Cobbs and fled into the corral.

Jane stuck one foot in the gelding's stirrup—the wrong foot—then grabbed hold of the saddle horn and tried to hoist herself up. She fell back into Floyd's waiting arms.

"Careful there, little lady, you could hurt yourself."

The way Floyd spoke the words *little lady,* as though they were some kind of endearment, set rage buzzing in John's head like a swarm of bees.

"Set Miss Harris on her feet, Cobbs," he rumbled, with all the menace of a death threat. "Then hustle yourself back to the bunkhouse to watch Price."

"If she'd have let me help her mount in the first place, she wouldn't have fell." The cowboy hoisted Jane upright, his hands lingering on her far too long and far too intimately to suit John.

"Pleasure to meet you, ma'am." With an exaggerated bow and a parting scowl at John, Floyd Cobbs meandered back to the bunkhouse.

Jane stood pale and tremulous as an aspen leaf.

"Are you hurt?" John edged his horse toward her.

She forced a tight little smile that didn't fool him for a second. "Only my dignity."

"Can we try again, then? You take Barton back and I'll lift you both into the saddle. Then you can pass him to me once I've mounted."

"Well…"

Before she could object, he lowered the baby into her arms and sprang from his saddle. Then he lifted them onto the gelding's back, letting go the instant he could tell she was seated securely. The sensation of her soft, slender frame in his arms unsettled him too much to risk prolonging it.

Words of protest died on Jane's lips before she could get them out. She gave a little laugh that sounded both nervous and a bit excited. Barton chortled.

"That's all very well for you, Thundercloud." She nuzzled the baby's fat cheek. "You're more accustomed to being on horseback than I am."

Back astride his own mare, John reached over and took the baby from her. "Hold your reins loose, now, and hang on to the saddle horn if you have to."

"How do I make him go?" Jane clutched the saddle horn so tightly her whole hand whitened.

"Don't worry about that, today. He'll follow along wherever the mare goes. They're kind of like an old married couple—easy with each other and always sticking close together."

He urged the mare to a slow walk and, true to his word, the gelding followed.

"Is that what your parents are like?"

Jane's casual question almost knocked John out of his saddle. He'd been thinking of old Bearspeaker and Walks on Ice.

A hundred possible responses raced through his mind, some bitter, all pained. "My folks didn't get the chance to be that way."

For a few moments the horses continued their sedate walk, while Barton wriggled in John's arms and made loud noises of delight.

So loud, they almost drowned out Jane's next words. "I'm sorry. Did they pass on long ago? My father was lost at sea." She balked for an instant. "Then my mother and my brother died of the typhoid when I was twelve."

John didn't intend to answer. He had never talked about the deaths of his parents and his brothers with anyone. Not Bearspeaker. Not even Ruth.

But Jane's experience paralleled his own too closely not to acknowledge. "Mine were killed by white buffalo hunters when I was ten."

He didn't look at her as he spoke, and he hardly noticed her horse pulling alongside his. Then her hand settled on his arm, with no more force than a hovering butterfly. Through the sturdy cotton of this shirt, her gentle touch communicated so many things words couldn't express.

Understanding. Sympathy. Comfort.

Sometimes he could bring himself to offer such gifts to others. Receiving them, especially from so foreign a creature as Miss Jane Harris, gave him a chilling sense of vulnerability. A warrior of the Big Sky could not afford that dangerous indulgence.

Abruptly he pulled away from her and wheeled his mare back toward the ranch house.

If John Whitefeather had lashed out and struck her, as Emery had so many times, Jane could not have been more shocked. Or dismayed.

His guarded confession of their painful common bond had rocked her. It had also called to her on a level deeper than her fears, and she had battled her fears to respond. She had little to offer a man like John Whitefeather. But she did have a heart that remembered and understood the loss of a family to cruel, capricious forces beyond a child's control.

She'd reached out to him, and he had slammed the door in her face. It might have hurt less if she had not sensed that door momentarily held ajar for her, a warm hearth light flickering from within. Or had she only imagined that because she wanted it to be true?

The way she had imagined strength and protectiveness in Emery's character where there had been only a domineering will and an easily provoked temper.

Men had other ways of hurting a woman that left no visible bruises or scars. From what she'd come to know of John Whitefeather over the past week, Jane doubted she had reason to fear for her physical safety with him. Just now, he had served her warning that she needed to be cautious around him, all the same.

The more she found herself drawn to him, the more cautious she must be.

Perhaps her poor gelding was as startled by the abrupt turn of John's mare as Jane herself. With more energy than he'd shown since she mounted him, the horse swung about to follow his companion, speeding his pace to catch up. Jane bit back a scream and hung on for dear life.

As she bounced and swayed in the saddle, the hard-packed earth beneath the gelding's hooves looked a long way down. She imagined it lunging up to meet her, like an enormous brown fist.

She was almost faint with relief when her horse caught up with John's at the corral fence. Then a fresh worry rocked her back in the saddle. Would John Whitefeather pass Barton back to her, then lift the two of them down off the gelding's back?

After the way he'd rebuffed her, she wasn't sure she could stand the sensation of his hands on her body. Nor the fleeting moment, as her feet touched the ground, when she stood in the circle of his arms with the baby cradled between them. Why, she'd sooner throw herself to the ground and be done with it. Experience had taught her that bones healed easier than hearts.

Fortunately, Ruth and Caleb Kincaid were waiting for them. As Ruth held up her arms to receive little Barton, Jane extracted her feet from the stirrups. Clinging to the saddle horn, she melted off the gelding's back until her feet gratefully touched the earth.

She shrank from a sharp look Caleb Kincaid shot her. Despite his gruffly respectful manner, Jane knew he didn't have much use for her. But his wife liked her and so did his sons. That made three more friends than she had back in Boston.

Jane couldn't bear the thought of being exiled from them so soon. If only some kindly matchmaker in Bismarck would set up the widowed Mrs. Muldoon with a new husband. Then she might stay put in North Dakota and leave Jane to the relative peace and security she'd found in Whitehorn.

Chapter Five

"That girl needs a husband." Ruth Kincaid looked up from her beadwork at her husband and brother.

John spared a glance from his late evening checker game at the kitchen table with Caleb. His sister had a determined look in her eye. It made him uneasy.

"What girl?" Caleb asked absently as John jumped two of his checkers.

"Why, Jane Harris, of course. What other girl is there?"

John plucked Caleb's black checkers from the board and said, "King me," as though he hadn't heard his sister.

But his conscience squirmed like a heifer under the branding iron. In fact, he wondered if the memory of Jane's white face and stricken eyes had been seared into his brain along with the recollection of her hand squeezing his arm. Like a brand, they stung. They would never go away.

And in some baffling fashion, they had put her claiming mark upon him.

"She's a willing little thing." Ruth bowed her dark head over her beadwork again, but kept on talking as the men jumped their red and black disks across the checkerboard. "She works hard and she's eager to learn, but she needs looking after. I can't help feeling bad that she came all this way and lost everything in that train wreck on our account.''

Caleb's head snapped up. ''It's not our fault the fool gal didn't even stop to read the letter we sent.''

Hard as John tried to clamp his mouth shut, the words spilled out. ''I reckon there's more to that than she's letting on, Caleb.''

His sister nodded. ''There's much more to Jane Harris than she's willing to tell.''

Turning his attention back to the checkerboard, Caleb muttered, ''Don't expect an argument from me on that score. I sent off a wire to the Boston police yesterday, just to make sure she isn't on the wrong side of the law.''

''Oh, Caleb, of all the foolishness! That girl hasn't got it in her to hurt a fly. Can you imagine her holding up a bank or a train?''

The iron-willed rancher looked shamefaced by his wife's gentle rebuke. ''I don't suppose I can, at that. I'll admit, she's been real handy around here while you were gone, and the boys have taken a shine to her. Just something about that gal doesn't sit right with me. She always looks as though she expects I'm going to bite her head off.''

''I'm sure she'd rather you did that than telegraph the Boston police about her behind her back. If you'd just give her half a chance you'd soon see what a nice little thing she is.'' Ruth concentrated on rethreading her needle. ''I think you don't like her because she reminds you too much of Marie.''

''Fiddlesticks.'' Caleb scowled at the checkerboard as John handily won the game.

Had Caleb forgotten that he'd openly compared Jane to his late wife on the night she arrived? John wondered.

The men set up the board for a rematch, and for a while the kitchen was quiet except for the soft crackle of the fire in the stove and the click of checkers.

''She's bound and determined not to go back East,'' Ruth murmured at last, almost as though she was talking to herself.

John swallowed a grin. His sister had learned this trick from their aunt, Walks on Ice. Raising a subject again and again with a question here, a chance remark there, until she wore Bearspeaker down, like a hunting party trailing a wounded buffalo.

''I don't reckon she has much to go back to, poor child.'' Ruth shook her head.

His sister's words hit John like a gunshot.

He knew perfectly well Jane Harris had nothing and no one waiting for her back in Boston. If he hadn't been ambushed by painful memories from his past or terrified by his own involuntary confession, he might have paid closer attention when she'd told him about the deaths of her family.

Most folks might say it was a greater tragedy to have your parents murdered than to have them die of sickness or be lost at sea. Either way, they were still dead.

At least he'd had Ruth and their Cheyenne band. As far as he could tell, Jane Harris had been left completely alone in a pitiless city. All at once, John felt a sense of responsibility for this winsome little stray who'd landed here by mistake. Setting her adrift again in a few weeks' time with the price of a train ticket out of their lives suddenly felt like a callous act of cruelty.

''We need to find her a husband,'' said Ruth. ''No reason a smart, pretty little woman like her couldn't have her pick of the men around here.''

Part of John had to agree that it was a sensible plan. A

less sensible part of him resisted the idea of marrying Jane Harris off.

"It'll have to be a fellow who can look after her decently." John pushed one of his checkers forward, and Caleb promptly hopscotched all over the board at his expense. "She's not strong and she's not used to this country."

Exactly the opposite of what he'd need in a wife, if he could ever make up his mind to take one.

"Lionel Briggs has a good business," volunteered Caleb. "An undertaker never lacks for work." Jumping John's last piece, he packed away the checkerboard and retired to his favorite chair by the stove.

"I wouldn't wish a master like Lionel Briggs on a stray dog." John shuddered at the thought of the liveryman's cold hands on Jane. "Let alone husband for a lady like Miss Harris."

Ruth nodded. "They say his first wife died just to get away from him. Besides, I want to invite any likely suitors out to the ranch for dinner to meet Jane. I doubt Mr. Briggs would want to darken our doorstep any more than I'd want him in my house."

"On account of his pa being killed by the Pawnee?" Caleb lit his pipe and took a deep puff. "Good enough, then. Scratch Lionel off the list of husband candidates."

"There's the butcher, Mr. Lundburg," suggested Ruth. John shook his head. "He drinks."

"Lou Lambert." Caleb threw down the name like a challenge. "Hard worker. Churchgoer. Got a good spread."

"And seven kids." John stalked over to the stove and poured himself more tea. "Jane wouldn't last a month."

Several more possible suitors were proposed. John found some damning objection to every one.

Caleb shook his head. "We're never going to get this gal married off if you're going to be so particular." He poked the stem of his pipe at John for emphasis. "It isn't like she's got a big dowry or comes from a fine family or is any raving beauty."

John didn't care for the knowing, slightly mocking glint in Caleb's eyes that reminded him of the warning, "Be careful of this little maverick filly."

Did Caleb think John was objecting to these other men because he wanted Jane Harris for himself? Why, if Ruth *had* put his name forward, he'd be the first to name a dozen reasons why he'd be wrong for Jane and she for him.

"Winslow Gray." Ruth spoke the young doctor's name in the same tone John had heard poker players announce a royal flush. She pinned her brother with a stare that dared him to find fault with her latest choice.

"He seems like a good enough fellow." John wondered why he begrudged Dr. Gray this meager praise. "He hasn't been in Whitehorn long, though, and nobody knows much about him."

Caleb chuckled. "I'd say that makes him a perfect match for our Miss Harris. And if it turns out she isn't anxious to stay in Montana, he's got no ties to keep him here."

"That's settled then." Ruth folded up her beadwork and laid it in her work basket of woven reeds. "When you go into town tomorrow, Caleb, drop by Dr. Gray's dispensary and invite him out to dinner on Saturday night."

"Yes, ma'am." Caleb lavished a fond smile on his wife, and suddenly John felt like an outsider.

Would he ever experience that kind of bond with a woman? Where words were no longer necessary and a shared look could set them apart from the rest of humanity—in their own tiny kingdom with a population of two?

John realized his sister was speaking to him. What was she saying?

"I'll expect you to praise Jane up to Dr. Gray when he comes to dinner."

"You praise her. I'll be out at Sweetgrass."

"Go ahead, just be back in time for supper."

He headed off to bed, muttering about bossy little sisters and trying to convince himself that Winslow Gray would make the perfect husband for Jane.

"We're having company for supper tonight." Ruth handed Jane a dinner plate to dry. "Why don't you fish a pretty dress from Marie's trunk and I'll warm a couple of irons on the fire to press the wrinkles out of it?"

"Company?" said Jane in the same tone she might have said "Snakes?"

It had taken a while, but she'd finally grown accustomed to Ruth Kincaid's family. Even her sometimes gruff husband and her often pensive brother. Jane no longer jumped or gasped when either of the men made a sudden move toward her. Her heart hardly sped up at all when one of them raised his voice. Now, the thought of a strange man at the supper table set her stomach aflutter.

Ruth nodded. "Caleb often takes pity on the bachelors and widowers in town and invites one of them out for a square meal. I think he remembers what it was like when he and Zeke had to shift for themselves to get a bite to eat in the evenings."

"Of course," murmured Jane. "That's kind of him."

How selfish to think only of how the presence of unfamiliar company would affect her, she chided herself. When this poor man was probably looking forward to a good, home-cooked meal after weeks of boardinghouse or saloon fare.

"We'll eat in the dining room tonight," said Ruth. "Put out the good china and silver. I'll roast a nice rib of beef."

"I could wait on the table for you." Jane offered a hopeful suggestion.

That would be the perfect solution. From her years in Beacon Hill, she knew well-trained servants were practically invisible. She wouldn't be expected to make conversation with this strange man, only fill his plate or fetch him a drink. Afterward, she could eat her own meal in the quiet sanctuary of the kitchen.

Ruth glanced up from her vigorous scrubbing of a tin pot. "Don't be silly. You'll eat with the rest of us, like always. We'll set all the food on the table beforehand so everybody can help themselves."

"What about sweets?" Jane tried to disguise the pleading tone in her voice. "Tea and coffee?"

"We can both fetch those from the kitchen when the time comes. Now I don't want to hear another word about you not eating with the rest of the family. You and Dr. Gray will have plenty to talk about. He's from back East, too."

The tumbler Jane was drying slipped out of her hands and crashed to the floor.

"I'm sorry! What a butterfingers. I should have been paying more attention to what I was doing. I'll get the broom."

"Don't fret about it." Ruth grabbed the dustpan and held it while Jane swept up the broken glass. "As I was saying, Dr. Gray is from back East. Saint Louis, I think Caleb said."

Jane let out a quivering breath. Saint Louis was a long way from Boston. In fact, Mrs. Endicott would have called it "out West." Even if this doctor had been from the Atlantic coast, that didn't mean he'd necessarily be acquainted with her former employer. There must have been a few physicians between Portland, Maine, and Charleston, South Carolina, who Mrs. Endicott *hadn't* consulted about her various aches and pains.

"I have a notion to heat some water for a bath," said Ruth when the last of the dishes were put away without further breakage. "Might as well wash our hair while we're about it. I brew a rinse of vinegar and herbs that'll make your hair shine like a mink's pelt."

Jane replied with a halfhearted smile. It was good of Ruth to fuss over her like this, especially since she wouldn't be staying around much longer. She couldn't enjoy it, though. The thought of entertaining company tonight left her vaguely bilious. The men would probably take a glass of whiskey before dinner. Perhaps more than one. She remembered all too vividly the effect of strong drink upon men's manners and tempers.

Undaunted by Jane's lack of enthusiasm, Ruth Kincaid nudged her through preparations for the evening, while Zeke kept the baby amused. The two women oiled and buffed the dining table. Ruth seared the roast and put it in the oven, while Jane peeled potatoes and set them to soak. Together they baked plum puffs for dessert. All the while, Ruth sang the praises of Dr. Winslow Gray.

When all the work had been done to Ruth's satisfaction, she contrived that Jane should bathe first.

"What do you think of this?" Ruth asked when Jane emerged from her bath with hair cleaner and more fragrant than she could ever remember.

Staring at the swath of taffeta in Ruth's arms, Jane gnawed on her lower lip. How had Ruth guessed that this dress, the color of daffodils in warm spring sunshine, was her favorite of all the beautiful gowns in Marie Kincaid's trunk?

Not to mention the most impossible to wear outside the privacy of her bedroom.

"Don't you think it's a bit too fancy just for dinner?"

"Where else are you going to wear it?" Ruth held the gown up in front of Jane and nodded her approval. "No matter what the sign outside Big Mike's saloon says, Whitehorn doesn't have a proper opera house like they've got in Denver. Caleb tells me Marie used to dress up like this all the time. I say it's too pretty *not* to wear."

"Do you think it'll be warm enough? The nights are still rather chilly and I'm prone to the cold."

"It will leave your shoulders bare," Ruth agreed.

Though Jane didn't dare admit it, that was what made this dress so unsuitable. The wounds Emery's nails had gouged were finally healing, but they had left scars on her flesh that might never disappear. A physician would be sure to recognize what they represented. That she was a woman who'd merited a beating at the hands of a man she'd cared for.

Just framing the notion in her mind left Jane nauseous with shame.

"I've got it!" Ruth thrust the dress into Jane's arms and charged up the stairs.

She returned a moment later bearing a cream-colored shawl of the finest brushed wool. "This will keep you from catching cold. Just pull it around your shoulders if you feel a draft. Besides, catching cold will be in a good cause if you can catch a—"

"Catch what?"

"Catch…a chance…" sputtered Ruth, "to enjoy some fresh company. You must be getting so tired of seeing nobody but Caleb and me and the children. And John, of course.''

Jane shook her head. ''I could never get tired of any of you. You've all been so kind to me after I showed up here, out of the blue and by my own silly mistake. I love this place. It's so solid and safe.''

''You wouldn't have said that a few years back when the winters were so bad. Plenty of folks from the East think this country is full of danger. I'm not sure there's anyplace a body's safe from all harm. Even if there was, you might be bored to death.''

''I'd take my chances.'' Jane hoped her reply sounded lighthearted.

Matchmaking must be in the air, John decided ruefully, as he rode back to the ranch from Sweetgrass.

He'd first suspected something was afoot when Walks on Ice had introduced him to a distant cousin who'd come to visit from her reservation farther north.

''This is Moon Raven. Her grannie is my cousin. She's a good worker, like all the women in our family. Smart and respectful. Pretty, too, isn't she, Night Horse?''

John couldn't deny it. The girl was attractive, with hair the color of her namesake bird and eyes the hue of ripe wild plums.

''Welcome to Sweetgrass, Moon Raven. I hope you'll have a good visit.''

To Walks on Ice he asked, ''How are the children? Have any more come down with the fever?''

The old woman shook her head. ''Not since Ruth put all the sick ones together, away from the rest. Two are still weak, but the others are better. Moon Raven was a great help to Ruth.''

''I'm sure she was. Thank you, Moon Raven.''

"Your sister is a skillful healer. I was honored to work with her and learn from her."

Walks on Ice beamed. "I like a girl with a mannerly tongue in her mouth. You can tell she's been well brought up—no *black robe* schools to fill her head with foolishness. How old are you, Night Horse?"

"Have you forgotten how to count, Auntie? Your hands brought me into this world. You should know it was thirty years ago."

"As many as that?" The old woman shook her head dolefully. "And still no children. My Lame Elk is younger than you, yet he has four fine sons and a new little daughter who is the joy of his eyes."

John didn't need to be told. He had noted the arrival of each new addition to Lame Elk's family with joy. And envy.

"Lame Elk is a lucky man. Well, I must go talk to Bearspeaker. Goodbye." Before Walks on Ice could get another word out, John strode away.

If he thought he'd left Moon Raven behind, he was wrong.

"So you met our pretty visitor, Night Horse?" Bearspeaker eyed John slyly. "What did you think of her?"

"A fine girl. How's the hunting been? Do you need any supplies from town?"

"Small herd of buffalo grazing to the north. Can't you smell the meat smoking? Not enough snow last winter, though. The ground is dry and no sign of rain."

Bearspeaker pointed to the waving sea of grass, which looked green and plentiful to John. "The herd may leave in search of better forage as the summer goes on. Did Walks on Ice tell you the girl is a granddaughter of Blind Wolf? And on her mother's side, she has the blood of Tall Snow. He was a fierce warrior of great honor."

Before John could stop him, Bearspeaker began reciting a litany of Moon Raven's ancestors back several generations. Was this how buffalo felt when they were being harried over the edge of a cliff? John wondered.

When they ate, his aunt instructed Moon Raven to bring John his food and sit beside him. He might have warmed to this paragon of Cheyenne womanhood a little more if she'd shown just a flicker of embarrassment.

"Say again how old you are, Night Horse—twenty-five?" This was the third time Walks on Ice had asked his age.

"Your ears must be failing, Auntie, or else your memory. I'm an old man of thirty."

"That much? And still alone in the world. The wife of your friend Red Stone gave birth to twins not long ago."

"I'll buy him a cigar," John muttered in English.

Walks on Ice could not have cast him a darker look if she'd understood what he was saying.

She made one last try as he was saddling up for his ride back to the ranch. "One year working on that ranch has pulled you away from our people more than all your time at the white man's school, Night Horse."

His irritation vanished and he tried to reassure her. "I have to work there to repay Caleb for helping us buy this land. You know my heart will always be Cheyenne, old one."

Taking a Cheyenne wife would prove it to her and to the rest of their band. John mulled the notion over as he rode away from Sweetgrass.

Moon Raven was exactly the kind of wife he needed—calm, strong, bred for Big Sky life. As his aunt had pointed out so often that day, he wasn't getting any younger.

But there was a difference between knowing something with your head and feeling it in your heart. As John approached the Kincaid ranch, that chasm stretched before him, wider than a badlands canyon.

With the setting sun at his back, he saw Jane Harris before she saw him.

She stood on the verandah at the rear of the house, her sorrel-colored hair unbound and rippling behind her in the breeze. Beside the stout timbers of the ranch house, she looked so fragile. Vulnerable to every powerful, pitiless force of nature on the frontier.

If there was a woman more wrong for him on so many counts, John had never met her. Yet almost from the first moment he'd encountered Jane Harris, she had stirred something inside him.

Now, for instance. Spying her in an unguarded moment, with her hair flying wild in the wind, John caught himself picturing her splendidly bare. Like the Bible story he'd learned at residential school—Eve in the Garden of Eden.

She had no business provoking such thoughts in him.

"Getting prettied up for tonight?" he called to her. He almost asked if she was primping on account of Dr. Gray, but at the last minute the words soured in his mouth.

Jane let out a squeak that might have been a pathetic excuse for a scream. If she'd been a prairie dog, she would have disappeared down her hole. A bird and she would have taken to the air.

"Don't you know it's impolite to sneak up on folks?" She gathered her drying hair and pulled it over one shoulder.

John edged his horse right up to the verandah. "For a gal who scares so easy, you aren't much good at staying alert."

"I wish I could find a place where I didn't *have* to be on guard all the time." The wistful tone of her voice and the longing in her eyes whispered past John's defenses.

They raised a lump in his throat and made his arms ache to hold her.

He understood her craving for sanctuary. But life's harsh lessons had taught him that no such place existed. In truth, the illusion of security represented the greatest threat of all.

"Maybe what you need isn't a place, but a person."

He couldn't be that person, for a hundred solid, practical reasons. Once again John struggled to reconcile the contrary bidding of his sensible, prudent head with that of his baffled, bewildered heart.

Chapter Six

"Jane, this is Winslow Gray." Ruth gave her a gentle push toward the doctor. "He's come all the way from Saint Louis to be our new doctor in Whitehorn."

Jane tried to summon up a smile.

With Barton fast asleep and Zeke spending the night at his uncle Brock's place, the adult members of the Kincaid household welcomed their guest in the parlor—Jane's least favorite room in the house. Elegantly appointed by Montana standards, with furniture Marie Kincaid had ordered from Chicago, it made Jane feel like she was back at Mrs. Endicott's Beacon Hill mansion.

"Dr. Gray, this is Miss Jane Harris. She's here for a while helping me with the children. She's from Boston."

"Miss Harris, a pleasure to meet you." Dr. Gray held out his hand.

Jane reached up to grasp it tentatively. Did all the men in Montana have to be so tall—even the ones who came from elsewhere? Aside from his height, he wasn't so very alarming in appearance. But then, Emery hadn't been, either.

"G-good evening, Dr. Gray." She couldn't bring herself

to mouth a polite falsehood about being delighted to meet him.

A pleasant-featured man, the doctor had a full head of dark hair and a lean muscular figure that looked very distinguished in a suit. Behind his spectacles, a pair of perceptive green eyes appraised the world. Including her.

Jane wished he'd go jump on his horse and ride back to Whitehorn at top speed.

A wave of panic engulfed her as she felt the cashmere shawl begin to slip off her shoulder. She wrenched her hand from the doctor's firm grip to rescue it before her scars blazed out for all to see.

Dr. Gray drew back when she pulled away from his handshake so abruptly. "Is something the matter, Miss Harris?"

"Of course not." Jane tugged her shawl securely over her right shoulder and tucked one end under her arm to anchor it in place. "What makes you think there's anything the matter?"

The Kincaids, God bless them, had politely ignored her intermittent signs of alarm. Clearly a physician was used to taking note of such things and probing until he discovered their cause.

"I thought perhaps I'd gripped your hand too hard." The doctor sounded apologetic.

"Nonsense," chimed in Ruth, leading their guest toward the horsehair sofa. "Jane may look as delicate as a flower, but she's really very capable. I don't know how I'd have managed the past little while without her."

"I heard you had an outbreak of scarlet fever among the Cheyenne children, Mrs. Kincaid. Is there anything I can do to help?"

"That's kind of you to ask. Isn't Dr. Gray a kind man,

Jane? There haven't been any new cases in a while and the ones who were sick seem to be getting stronger.''

As Ruth and the doctor talked, Jane began to relax. If the two of them would spend the rest of evening discussing medical matters, this dinner might not be so bad, after all.

She glanced across the room to where John stood behind a stiffly upholstered brocade armchair. He seemed every bit as stiff and formal in a starched collar, string tie and dress suit. His long hair, which looked so natural hanging down the back of a coarse cotton work shirt, suddenly appeared exotic and out of place to Jane. Though not un-attractive for all that.

His singular blue eyes surveyed her, too, but without the doctor's searching scrutiny. Jane sensed a hint of warmth in his gaze, and for the first time in her life she felt pretty.

From his place beside a low, glass-fronted cabinet, Caleb called out, "Can I offer you a little something to moisten your throat, Doc?''

"I wouldn't say no to bourbon and branch.'' The doctor winked at his host as Jane tried not to cringe.

"Anything for you, John?''

"Sarsaparilla.''

"Sarsaparilla it is. Jane, could I trouble you to take the doc his drink?'' Caleb held out a glass containing a liberal measure of the whiskey-and-water mixture.

Mooring her shawl securely, Jane crossed the carpeted parlor to fetch Dr. Gray his drink. She willed her hand not to tremble as she passed it to him, and for a wonder she succeeded.

Ruth shifted from her place on the sofa beside the doctor. "I must go see how dinner's coming. Jane, you sit right down here and keep Dr. Gray company. Tell him about what happened to your train in Chicago.''

"I'm sure he wouldn't be interested in that, Ruth.'' Jane

headed for the door. "I'll be glad to check on the dinner for you."

In her haste, she tripped on a wrinkle in the rug and took a couple of staggering steps before she regained her balance. Ruth grabbed the trailing end of Jane's shawl and pulled her back.

"Of course you're interested, aren't you, Doctor? The train was derailed. Jane barely escaped with her life—lost all her clothes and personal things when the baggage car caught fire."

With a firm hand, Ruth hauled Jane down onto the sofa between herself and Dr. Gray. "Go ahead, dear. Tell him about it."

The doctor took a long drink from his glass. "A train wreck, you say? Funny, I don't recall reading anything about it in the papers. How long ago did it happen?"

When he spoke to her, Jane smelled the spirits on his breath. Her own breathing picked up tempo, yet she felt as if she could not draw in enough air. She wasn't sure what unsettled her more—the whiskey fumes that reminded her so potently of Emery at his worst, or the doctor's relentless inquisition about her invented train wreck.

"Not the whole train, just a couple of cars. I don't expect the papers made much of it."

As Ruth bustled off to the kitchen, Jane wiggled over onto the part of the sofa she'd vacated, putting as much space as possible between herself and the doctor.

"Ruth makes it sound much worse than it was." Jane tried to laugh, but she couldn't catch her breath. Her lungs felt like a pair of bellows being pumped by an overeager youth.

"Are you sure you're feeling all right, Miss Harris?" The doctor made a sudden lunge toward her, his hand upraised.

The last thing Jane remembered was the sound of her own scream.

"What the devil...?" Winslow Gray put a practiced hand to Jane's throat, a couple of inches below her ear. "Good lord, her pulse is galloping like a runaway horse. I think the lady's swooned!"

John dashed across the parlor. His own pulse had been pounding in his ears as he watched Jane being squeezed onto the sofa almost thigh-to-thigh with Dr. Gray.

She had been acting very nervous this evening, even for her. Somehow her dismay had communicated itself to him. It upset him to see her upset, even though he didn't understand the reason. He didn't like seeing her gussied up in that lacy yellow dress, either. It looked so much more appropriate for Boston or Saint Louis than Montana. John resented the notion that another man might recognize her fragile beauty. He had a crazy desire to keep it a secret between himself and Zeke.

"Jane?" He knelt by the sofa, clutching her impossibly delicate hand in his. It was as cold as a Montana winter.

The doctor scrambled up from his seat. "My bag's just in the kitchen. I'll dig out my smelling salts."

"Marie used to faint at the drop of a hat." Caleb sounded bored. "Give the lady a belt of neat whiskey when she comes around."

John shot his brother-in-law a venomous glare. "Get it through your thick head—Jane Harris is *not* like Marie!"

"If you say so." Caleb shrugged, clearly not convinced.

"Jane, can you hear me?" For the first time, John felt the softness of her skin beneath his fingertips.

It intoxicated him as surely as Caleb's whiskey would have done, filling his mind with tantalizing urges, preposterous desires.

"Come on, now. Wake up." He smoothed a wisp of golden-brown hair back from her brow, barely holding back the urge to pull all the pins out and let her hair tumble down as he had seen it on the verandah. A river of honeyed silk that a man would gladly drown in.

Her eyelids fluttered, as did her golden lashes, fine as cobwebs.

Swift, purposeful footsteps sounded behind John, and he felt himself shunted aside by the doctor, who thrust a vial of smelling salts under Jane's nose.

John wanted to push back, hard. He resented being elbowed out of the way by this well-groomed Easterner, with his polished manners and superior education. The fact that Winslow Gray would make an ideal husband for Jane did nothing to improve John's opinion of him.

As Jane inhaled the pungent whiff of ammonia, she jerked awake. Clutching the shawl tight around her shoulders, she shrank from the handsome doctor.

"Please don't touch me. I'm fine now. I can't think what made me faint." Her eyes sought and found John's. In them he read a desperate plea for rescue.

It was all the invitation he needed.

John pulled the doctor away, none too gently. "You heard the lady. Leave her be while she catches her breath."

"Perhaps her memories of the train accident overwhelmed Miss Harris." Dr. Gray straightened his tie and replaced the smelling salts in his satchel. "I've seen it before. Patients keep their heads while they're in peril only to suffer delayed shock afterward."

That certainly explained Jane's queer behavior since she'd arrived in Whitehorn. Capable and composed one minute, jumpy as a scalded cat the next. John had put it down to a highstrung nature, not taking into account what she must have been through.

''She needs rest and quiet.'' His words came out like a harsh reproach of their guest.

When Jane gazed up at him, her soft hazel eyes glowing with gratitude, his heart seemed to swell in his chest. John fought the urge to grin like a simpleton.

He scooped her off the sofa, lurching slightly as he straightened up with Jane cradled in his arms. Not because she was heavy to carry, but because the smell of her hair wafted into his face, momentarily turning his knees to water.

As John took a step toward the parlor door, his sister suddenly appeared in his path.

''What's going on here? Where do you think you're taking Jane?''

''She fainted.'' John nodded toward the doctor. ''He upset her, asking all kinds of questions about the train accident. I'm putting her to bed.''

''I'm sure she'll be fine. Just give her a minute to collect her wits.'' Ruth shot John a look that reminded him of Walks on Ice.

''Give her whiskey,'' suggested Caleb again.

''I'm putting her to bed.'' John stepped around his sister and headed for the stairs.

Behind him, John heard Dr. Gray apologizing to Caleb and Ruth. ''I'm sorry if I upset the lady. I had no idea her memories of the incident were still so vivid and painful.''

John's conscience smarted. He had no business blaming the new doctor, when he hadn't guessed Jane's problem after having known her a good deal longer.

She nestled in his arms, as weak and trusting as a newborn foal. John found his steps slowing as he approached her bedroom door, overpowered by a reluctance to let her go.

Slowly he turned the knob and nudged the door open.

Setting behind the Crazy Mountains, the evening sun cast just enough light into Jane's bedroom for John to find her bed. As he eased her down onto the mattress, his arms ached with a chill emptiness.

"Can I get you anything?" he murmured. "Glass of water? A drop of whiskey?"

"Not just now." Her voice sounded weak and weary.

He picked up the extra quilt Ruth always kept folded at the foot of the bed and pulled it over Jane.

"Thank you for rescuing me. Tell Ruth I'm sorry I made such a fool of myself. I'm not much used to entertaining."

"Don't fret about Ruth. Or about Dr. Gray." John's hands itched to stroke her hair. He almost had to sit on them to keep them still. "Rest, now. That train crash must have been a lot worse than you let on."

She shook her head. "I don't want to talk about it."

John understood. But that didn't make it any easier for him to hear. "That day on the horses, when you told me about your folks and I told you about mine. I'm sorry I turned away when I did."

Anxious as she was to keep a safe distance from folks, what had it cost her to reach out to him?

The quilt lifted as she shrugged. "I guess there are some things we can't trust an outsider to understand, no matter how well they mean."

An *outsider*. The word clouted John like a sack of horseshoes. He knew about being an outsider, all right. To be a half-breed meant living permanently on the outside. A woman like Jane Harris was the ultimate outsider on the Montana range. Perhaps that was the mysterious force drawing him to her, in spite of his reason and his will.

"It was right after Little Big Horn," John heard himself say. "Bunch of buffalo hunters ambushed our camp. They got my parents and two little brothers."

In the quiet, shadowy little room, the sound of distant voices and footsteps drifted up from the bottom floor. Ruth, Caleb and the doctor must be going to eat before the food got cold.

"How did you and Ruth escape?" He heard the hesitation in Jane's voice. A fear that her question might hurt or anger him.

"Ruth wasn't much older than Barton is now. Some relatives were looking after her."

He expected Jane to ask again about him, but she didn't. At least not with words. John felt her silent sympathy wrap around him, though, coaxing him to lighten the burden on his mind.

"I was a little ways off from the rest. My mother screamed a warning to me and I…ran. I don't think they'd have killed her if she'd kept quiet."

The blanket stirred in a barely noticeable rise and fall.

"Jane, what is it?" His hand brushed her cheek and came away wet.

"Oh, Jane." He gathered her in his arms, nuzzling his cheek against her fragrant hair as she wept all the silent tears he had kept locked in his heart for twenty bone-dry years.

During the past weeks, he'd watched her come close to crying many times, but never completely surrender. Now she wept for him, and John struggled to breathe as impossible feelings for her ransacked his heart.

"Shh. Are you sure there isn't anything you want to tell *me?*"

"I can't. I'm sorry. I…just can't."

She stopped crying, and John knew there was no reason for him to keep holding her. Unless he gave in to his stubborn yen to kiss her.

And he mustn't do that on any account. It would be a

dangerous indulgence on his part. Not to mention taking mean advantage of her in a moment of weakness.

John Whitefeather had performed many difficult deeds in his life, but few as difficult as easing Jane Harris back down onto her pillow and slipping out of her room without a backward glance.

Was this how a beach felt after the wind and waves of a hurricane had finally died away? Jane lay in the darkened room, spent after a storm of emotion.

Thinking back on her disastrous meeting with Dr. Gray, she cringed at her own foolishness. Their guest wouldn't have hurt her, whiskey or no whiskey. If he'd tried, Ruth and John wouldn't have let him. Even Caleb Kincaid, for all his unspoken aversion to her, wouldn't have let her come to harm under his roof.

As for Dr. Gray's inquiries about the fictitious train accident, he'd soon have lost interest if only she'd made light of it and changed the subject. Instead, she'd worked herself into hysterics over nothing and probably made everyone more suspicious.

When all was said and done, that irrational terror had left her less shaken than those quiet, sheltered moments in the sanctuary of John Whitefeather's arms. Perhaps there had been a time, long ago, when someone had held her and whispered to her. Offered her comfort and made her feel safe, however fleetingly.

Perhaps. But Jane had no conscious recollection of it. Why, she scarcely knew how to comfort herself. Her behavior in the parlor tonight proved that.

She had never imagined welcoming a man's touch instead of flinching from it. But she had welcomed John's. Was this what he meant when he'd spoken about finding safety in a person rather than a place?

It made a kind of sense. If she could find a person with the strength to protect her. A person she could trust never to turn his strength against her. A few hours ago Jane would not have believed such a person existed. Now she wondered if he might.

Lying there, inhaling the faint scent of a man that lingered in the air, Jane thought back to the moment she'd wakened from her faint, roused by the murmur of John Whitefeather's mellow, melodic voice and the soothing gentleness of his touch. Once she had feared the damage those large, powerful hands might do to a woman's face. Tonight she'd discovered their capacity for tender healing.

When he had swept her into his arms and whisked her up the stairs, she'd felt lighter than air. In body and in spirit. Each moment from then until John had left her, Jane remembered and relived. Gloating over them like a miser over hoarded coins.

He had given her two gifts a hundred times more precious to Jane than gold. The gift of a few moments of complete peace and safety. Now she knew what it felt like, and understood why she craved it so. The second gift Jane treasured even more, if possible, for it had obviously cost John dearly.

A piece of his past. A piece of himself. Jagged and bloody. Exhumed from the dark depths of his heart.

She'd wept for the boy who had seen his parents and brothers killed, and for the girl who'd watched her mother and brother perish of fever, and had waited in vain for the father who would never come home.

She understood the ache of his grief, the void of his loneliness and the crippling burden of his guilt. For all their superficial differences, they were very much alike at heart.

* * *

"That was a delicious supper, Mrs. Kincaid." The doctor pushed back his chair. "I appreciate the invitation. I get so busy with my new practice I sometimes don't remember to eat regularly."

"You'll need to put a little more meat on your bones to keep you warm through a Montana winter," replied Ruth.

John didn't need a road sign to see where she was headed.

"A doctor spends all his time looking after other folks. He needs a good wife to look after him."

But not the woman lying upstairs in her darkened room. John's cheek still tingled from the sensation of pressing against Jane's hair.

Dr. Gray exchanged glances with Caleb and John as he chuckled. "I'm not sure my profession leaves me enough time to do justice to a marriage, Mrs. Kincaid."

For the first time that evening, John looked on the doctor with approval.

Ruth waved away Dr. Gray's protest. "Oh, you'll change your tune once you meet the right woman, isn't that so, Caleb?"

"Can't argue with that, my dear." Caleb Kincaid reached over the table and laid a hand on his wife's. "Running a ranch keeps a fellow on the hop, too, Doc. But having a family is what makes everything else in a man's life worth doing."

Ruth's dark eyes glowed as she smiled at her husband. It wasn't only a sense of obligation to Jane that made his sister take up matchmaking, John realized. She also wanted to help others find the special happiness she and Caleb had discovered.

"I wish you'd got the chance to know Miss Harris a little better." Ruth shot John a sharp glance, as if Jane's fainting spell had been all his fault. "She's the one who cooked this dinner you enjoyed so much."

John knew perfectly well that Ruth had done at least half the work, but he kept his mouth shut for fear he'd never eat in this house again.

"Give her my compliments." The doctor rose. "Now, if you'll excuse me, I should be getting back to town."

Winslow Gray reminded John of a stag sniffing the wind for predators, bunching the muscles of his hindquarters to flee at the first shot.

"Why don't you give them to her yourself the next time you see her?" Ruth followed their guest to the front entrance, beckoning for Caleb and John to come along. "I'm planning a housewarming for Caleb's brother and his family as soon as their new place is finished. Jane would be glad to have a handsome gentleman like you to squire her to the party, I'm sure."

John caught a glimpse of himself in the looking glass by the coat tree. He hardly recognized the man scowling back at him.

The doctor didn't say a word as he put on his coat, then picked up his hat and satchel. He shook hands with Caleb and with John.

And finally with Ruth. "Can I tell Jane to expect your invitation?" she pressed.

John winced at his sister's lack of subtlety. Why didn't she just lead Jane down the main street of Whitehorn in a bridal gown with a sign on her back saying Groom Wanted?

Dr. Gray shook his head. "I don't think so, Mrs. Kincaid."

A whole evening's tension ebbed out of John's body.

"Give the girl a chance, Doctor," Ruth pleaded. "It's

plain as can be you need a wife and Jane needs a husband.''

"That girl doesn't need a husband, ma'am." The doctor jammed on his hat. "She needs a good stiff bromide. Good night, folks."

"Well, how do you like that?" grumbled Ruth as the sound of the doctors footsteps faded. "He doesn't have much manners for a city boy, does he?"

"Don't you reckon you might have a come on a little strong, honey?" Caleb made a manly effort to suppress a grin.

"We don't have time to beat around the bush. Mrs. Muldoon will be here before we know it, and what's poor Jane to do then?"

Ruth headed back to the dining room, where she began clearing dishes off the table. John and Caleb each carried a load out to the kitchen.

"I reckon that doctor is a confirmed bachelor," announced Ruth as she poured steaming water from a kettle over the dirty dishes. "Well, that's his loss. Now who's next on our list?"

Chapter Seven

"Who's next on our list?" asked Ruth, a note of desperation creeping into her voice.

Henry Hill, proprietor of the Four Kings Saloon, had just ridden back to Whitehorn after an awkward evening that had ended with Jane spilling a bowlful of creamed peas into his lap.

John chuckled again, remembering it. Jane had fled upstairs in an agony of embarrassment, and for that he was sorry. But Henry Hill had those creamed peas coming to him, the way he'd been looking at her. As though she was one of his saloon girls. Why, if John had been the one passing those peas, they'd likely have landed on top of Henry's Macassar-slicked head.

"What are you laughing at?" Ruth glared her brother. "This isn't comical. First the doctor, then the minister, now Mr. Hill. We're soon going to run out of prospects. Who'd have thought it would be so hard to find a decent husband for a smart, pretty girl in Montana?"

"Jane Harris is too good to be a saloonkeeper's wife, anyhow." John had said so from the start, but his sister had overruled him.

Ruth shook her finger at him. "If we don't soon find a

husband for Jane Harris, she could end up serving drinks in a saloon.''

''Why can't you just keep her on here if she's willing to stay?''

Caleb frowned. ''My ranch isn't a settlement house for runaway gals from the East Coast. Besides, three women in one kitchen is nothing but a recipe for trouble.''

''The Mormon folks down in Utah seem to make out fine.''

''Then maybe we ought to ship Miss Harris off to Salt Lake City.''

''Now who's being comical?''

Ruth hurled a dish towel at John and another one at Caleb. ''Stop it this minute, both of you. Caleb's right, there won't be enough work for three of us when Mrs. Muldoon gets here. Besides, Jane deserves a home and family of her own. She'd make a wonderful mother—have you seen the way she is with Barton?''

John growled something like a *yes* as he dried the bowl that had earlier held the creamed peas. Of course he'd seen how tenderly Jane cared for his nephew. He'd also seen how some folks in town looked askance at the little fellow on account of his Cheyenne blood. Jane had never once looked at Barton like that, or shown any favor toward Zeke, the child of two white-skinned parents.

Ruth was right, though; Jane deserved a better future than tending other people's houses and children. He'd taken selfish glee in watching Ruth's matchmaking go sour. Just because he wanted to keep Jane around where he could enjoy the pleasure of her company without taking any responsibility for her.

Well, enough of that. He was not the man for her, no matter how she had begun to plague his dreams.

The way she'd behaved around Dr. Gray, Reverend

McWhirter and Henry Hill proved beyond doubt that she had too sensitive a nature to withstand the life of a ranch foreman's wife. Besides, he already had a family—the folks at Sweetgrass. He owed his first duty to them.

Time for him to stop playing dog in the manger and do whatever he could to help Jane. Even if that meant helping her become the wife of another man.

"As far as prospective husbands go, Amos Carlton's our ace in the hole," said Caleb. "Recent widower. Bags of money. A fine house. Upstanding citizen. Not as young as he used to be, but still a fine figure of a man. I don't know but Jane might be all the better for an older husband."

John kept his eyes on the glass he was drying. Amos Carlton? The hotel proprietor was easily old enough to be Jane's father. Not to mention fastidious to the point of being prissy. John had often wondered what drew a man like Amos to the Montana frontier.

But Amos did have a nice house and plenty of hired help. Jane wouldn't have to work as hard as she did around Ruth and Caleb's place. Amos was a soft-spoken man, too. If he took a fancy to Jane, John didn't doubt he'd treat her like a queen and defer to her the way he had to his late wife. Perhaps not demand too much from her in the bedroom.

John privately wondered if fears about the marriage bed might account for Jane's reaction to the suitors Ruth had been throwing at her head.

"Amos Carlton wouldn't have been my first pick." Ruth stared off into space, nodding her head slowly. "But the better I get to know Jane, the more I think he might be just the man for her. Let's not waste any time, then. We can take Jane into town for dinner at the Carlton Hotel. Caleb, you have a word with Amos beforehand, coax him to be Jane's escort to Brock and Abby's housewarming party.''

Caleb held up his hand. ''Hold your horses, now. If we fix Jane up with Amos and she carries on like she has with the last three, it'll be time to throw in our hand. That gal is just a bundle of nerves around strangers. Do you suppose we could slip her a nip of spirits before the party to calm her down?''

''Is whiskey your answer to everything?'' Ruth flashed her husband a wry grin as she handed him another wet plate.

''No.'' He leaned over and whispered something in her ear that made Ruth laugh and pretend to swat him.

As John watched the two of them carrying on, he felt like a starving dog peering in a butcher's window. Picking up a stack of plates and saucers, he carried them into the dining room to put away in the sideboard.

He returned to the kitchen just in time to hear Ruth say, ''You're right about one thing. We have to find some way to calm Jane down around strangers, or Amos'll never be able to court her, let alone propose. I declare that girl's as skittish as a mustang filly.''

The kitchen went quiet.

John glanced at his sister, only to find her watching him the way a hawk would watch a prairie dog hole.

''What did I do?''

A slow smile spread across Ruth's face. It made the hairs on the back of John's neck rise.

''It's not what you've done, *hestatanemo*. It's what you're going to do.''

''Ooh, and what's that, exactly?''

''You're going to gentle our nervous little filly so Amos Carlton will stand a chance with her.''

* * *

If Jane hadn't known better, she would have sworn John Whitefeather was nervous.

The big ranch kitchen was empty but for the two of them. Zeke had gone off to do his chores, and Ruth was upstairs giving the baby a bath while Jane fixed supper. John had ambled in a few minutes earlier, looking mysteriously shamefaced, then proceeded to pour himself a cup of coffee.

Ever since that night John had carried her up to bed, Jane had found herself more awkward than ever around him. He'd never mentioned those moments of chaste intimacy they'd shared, nor had he made any move to touch her since. Jane was beginning to wonder if she'd dreamed it all. Certainly she'd relived it in her dreams often enough in the past two weeks.

The silence in the kitchen grew oppressive. Jane cleared her throat. "Looks like rain. I'm glad Ruth and I retrieved the laundry from the clothesline."

"A few drops maybe." John avoided her eyes, staring instead into his coffee cup as if he could divine the weather by reading the dregs. "Not as much as the ground needs."

He looked as if he wanted to say something more to her, then he changed his mind.

Jane tried again. "Busted many broncos lately?"

"I don't break horses, ma'am. I gentle 'em. Some cowboys think my way takes too long, but Caleb's wise enough to see that it's better in the long run. Maybe you could bring Barton out sometime to watch me at work."

"Thank you. I'd like that." She also liked the sound of his work—*gentling* horses. No question, John had the strength and the will to master an animal by brute force, but he chose to go about it another way.

"Say, Jane..."

"Yes?"

"The Kincaids are having a housewarming party for Brock and Abby this Friday night. Get a jump on celebrating the Fourth of July, too."

Jane nodded. "I know. Ruth and I are going to be busy the next few days cooking for it."

She had heard all about Caleb's pretty redheaded sister-in-law from Zeke, who was best friends with Abby's son, Jonathon. It flabbergasted Jane to think of Abby running her own hardware business and raising a child single-handedly before she'd married Brock Kincaid. No question, Abby was the kind of strong, determined woman a Montana man needed for a wife.

"I was wondering..." John looked out the window, then back at the tabletop, anywhere but at her. "Zeke and me are riding over early to take some of the food. We wondered if you'd like to come along with us?"

"Oh, I can't go to the party." She didn't want to, either. A whole evening in the midst of a bunch of strangers was her notion of hell. "Ruth'll need me to stay home and look after Barton."

"No I won't." Ruth strode into the kitchen with Barton in her arms, all glowing and downy-headed from his bath. "Folks back East may leave their young'uns at home when they get together with their neighbors, but hereabouts we just bring them along. There'll be plenty of young girls at Brock and Abby's place anxious to mind the babies. We can't all drive over in the one buggy, though, so it'd be a big favor to me if you'd tag along with John and Zeke to watch that they don't eat all the food I'm sending with them."

"I suppose...if you really need me to." She could always just sneak off to a quiet corner somewhere until it was time to come home.

"Good. That's all settled then. Tomorrow, we bake."

* * *

Bake they did, starting not long after sunrise and well into the afternoon of the next day.

Trays of buttermilk biscuits and cinnamon rolls. Crocks of rusty-brown baked beans. Pans of red flannel hash. Apple pies, rhubarb pies, red bean pies and vinegar pies. Plum cake, lemon cake and Ruth's specialty, cinnamon cake.

By midafternoon, when Ruth sent her to take Barton for a walk, Jane wondered if her cheeks hadn't been baked to a permanent rosy glow from bending over a hot oven. She had a fat cinnamon roll, still warm from the oven, wrapped in a napkin and tucked in the pocket of her apron as a treat for John. Barton was gnawing on a hard rusk Ruth had baked specially for him to cut teeth on.

Though she still shrank from the prospect of an evening spent in the company of so many strangers, Jane found herself looking forward to the buggy ride with John…and Zeke. The night before, she'd sifted through Marie Kincaid's trunk, looking for a pretty dress to wear to the party. One that wouldn't expose her shoulders.

"Would you like to go visit your uncle John and watch him gentle a horsey?" she asked Barton.

"Unka-unk!" The baby squealed, rocking up and down in her arms doing a good imitation of a rider's motion on horseback. "Or-*sey!*"

Jane laughed and rubbed noses with him. "That's right—horsey! You'll soon be chattering up a storm, won't you, my little cowboy?"

Instantly, her smile melted. By the time Barton was talking well, she wouldn't be here to enjoy his conversation. Mrs. Muldoon would be capably in charge, no doubt. A sensible woman who could be counted upon not to faint on the sofa or spill creamed peas all over the Kincaids' guests.

Jane's skin crawled as she remembered the way Mr. Hill had reached under the tablecloth and laid a hand on her knee. Why couldn't she have passed him the dish, then casually slid her chair out of reach?

With a sigh, she set Barton on his feet and held tightly to his hand so he could toddle the last few steps to the corral, where John spent most of his time. As they walked, Jane fell into her melancholy musings again.

She'd worked her heart out to win herself a permanent place at the Kincaid ranch, and she was proud of all the new skills she'd mastered in the past several weeks. Though she sensed that Ruth liked her, the Kincaids hadn't offered to keep her on. Only the other night, Caleb had let slip a reference to Mrs. Muldoon's expected arrival in another couple of weeks.

So much for making herself indispensable.

The sturdy, cosy ranch house had come to feel like home to Jane in a way Mrs. Endicott's grand, cold mansion never had. But would anyone here remember her name when she'd been gone a week?

"What's wrong, Jane? You look like you've just lost your last friend."

She glanced up to see John leaning over the corral fence, wearing a look of earnest concern.

I'm about to lose my only friends. The words crowded on the tip of her tongue, begging to be spoken, but Jane refused to utter them. How was she ever going to survive here in the West if she didn't toughen up a little?

"Why does everyone always think there's something wrong with me?" John Whitefeather was perhaps the only person with whom she felt safe to express annoyance. "First Dr. Gray taking my pulse and prescribing bromides. Then the minister wondering if I had some sort of burden on my conscience."

"I'm sorry if I misread your look just now, but I don't reckon I did." John held out his arms for Barton, and Jane lifted the little fellow up to him. "Folks tell you a lot about how they're feeling by the way they move and how they hold themselves. Horses are like that, too."

He nodded toward a horse in the corral behind him, an equine patchwork of white, black and brown. "See how that little paint has her tail down tight between her legs? That means she's nervous. If she tilts her chin way up, it'll be a sign she's bothered about something, like maybe I'm walking toward her too fast."

"What if she keeps her head down?" For a moment, Jane forgot her own troubles, fascinated by John's profound understanding of the animals he worked with.

One corner of John's straight, solemn mouth arched upward. "If she does that, it tells me she's not paying attention. What I watch for is the minute a horse will lick her lips. It usually means she's willing to try what I'm asking of her."

"And what might that be?" The words tickled in Jane's throat.

"Just to get close to her and touch her for a start. Then to let me slide a light rope of rawhide around her neck. After a spell, to tolerate a hackamore bridle and the weight of a saddle on her back. Finally to let me ride her, and to follow my signals. Once she trusts me enough to let me handle her, the rest usually comes pretty easy."

"And if she shies away when you try to touch her?" Jane got the feeling they were talking about something other than horses.

The corner of his mouth curved higher. "Oh, I've got my ways of winning a balky horse over. Can't give away all my secrets, though, can I, Barton?"

Jane remembered the warm cinnamon roll in her pocket.

"Could we bribe them out of you?" She pulled out the napkin and peeled its corners back to reveal the contents.

"Well now!" A full, true smile flashed across John's face, coming and going as swiftly as a bolt of lightning. Just as bright, just as electrifying. "I reckon you know a thing or two about getting a man to do whatever you ask him, Jane Harris."

Jane's gaze dropped. "I wish that was true."

She hadn't been able to *gentle* Emery Endicott. If anything, he'd gotten more fractious and violent as time went on. All the cinnamon rolls in the world wouldn't have sweetened him when he was in a temper.

"It's true for me—that's what matters."

He spoke the words so softly they might have been sighed on the Big Sky breeze, and when Jane looked up his lips were no longer moving. If they ever had been.

A long, quivering sigh escaped John's lips as he watched Jane return to the ranch house, a child of his blood toddling along beside her. Slowly he licked the last traces of cinnamon and sugar from his lips. He had a suspicion Jane's rosebud mouth would taste even sweeter.

Would he get a chance to find out before he was finished the task Ruth had set for him?

John found himself looking forward to Brock and Abby's housewarming in a way he'd never anticipated any social gathering. Though he'd reluctantly donned the mantle of a Cheyenne leader, John had never felt a true sense of belonging to any group. He could join one pack or another for a time, observe their rituals, run with their hunt. But at the end of the day, his spirit was that of the lone wolf.

Solitary and self-sufficient, he came as close to finding balance and peace as he ever expected to in this life. When he was in the company of whites, his Cheyenne blood sang most potently in his veins. His English took on a different rhythm, like drops of water falling on pebbles. In the faces around him, he saw the men who had killed his parents and the Indian agents who had taken him from his band and thrust him into the alien world of residential school.

Yet at Sweetgrass he was always conscious of his lighter-colored skin and his peculiar blue eyes. His voice sometimes stuttered over the words of his father tongue, and he sensed a subtle distrust from the other young warriors. Only in the Kincaid household, with mixed blood of its own, did he truly feel a part of the circle.

Even there, he was not fully one of them. The rogue stag intruding on a comfortable family group.

Somehow, Jane's coming had eased that.

John felt a warm, moist nudge on his shoulder. Glancing back, he discovered the pinto filly standing behind him.

He reached up and scratched her behind the ears. "What do you think, Cactus Heart? Am I going to be able to gentle that skittish little filly like Ruth wants, or is she going to buck my old heart bloody?"

Chapter Eight

The team's hindquarters swayed and their hooves kicked up dust on the road into town.

Jane's stomach lurched in time to the rhythmic jingle of the harness. If only the party didn't loom before her with its prospect of loud noise and strange faces, she might have enjoyed this ride.

"What do you say, Zeke?" John glanced down at the boy who sat between them on the front seat of the buggy. "You ready to ride shotgun on all this good cooking in case we run into vittle rustlers?"

Zeke grinned. "I reckon so. It sure smells good, don't it?"

"Don't you go taking any notion to hijack this shipment, now. Ruth sent Miss Harris along to keep us honest." John winked at his young friend.

Jane had never imagined those piercing blue eyes could sparkle with fun. They did now, coaxing a smile out of her when she didn't think she had one to give.

As the team jogged along, and John and Zeke discussed the merits of various varieties of pie, Jane found herself gazing at the Montana countryside that surrounded her. During that ride out from Whitehorn on the day she'd arrived in Montana, she had been so worried about falling off the horse's back that she'd squeezed her eyes shut tight for most of the trip.

Today, she drank in the majestic landscape. Off to the east, miles of green, open range rolled on as far as the eye could see. Though the vast scale of it intimidated her, Jane drew some comfort from the wide buffer between White-horn and Boston. Surely Emery wouldn't venture so far to come after her.

Westward, the Crazy Mountains lunged toward heaven, with dark forest sprawled at their feet. Soaring above it all, a sun-gilded canopy of blue was strewn with gossamer clouds. No wonder they called this place Big Sky Country.

It would take a far stronger woman than her not to be awed by its power. On the Montana frontier, nature reigned unchallenged. And if he chose to flex his muscles... Jane shuddered at the thought.

"Don't tell me you're cold," said John.

Jane wished he wasn't quite so alert to her movements and expressions, even if he had misinterpreted the cause.

"I have a fleece robe you can put around your shoulders, but I didn't figure you'd need it until the drive home. It still gets a mite nippy on a clear night."

"I'm fine," Jane lied. "But speaking of coming home, do you plan on staying very late? I know Ruth said it's the custom out here to bring the little ones along. Surely she won't want Zeke and Barton to stay up very late past their bedtimes. Perhaps we could bring the boys home in a few hours so Ruth and Caleb can stay and enjoy themselves."

"Uncle Brock promised I could sleep over with Jona-thon tonight." Zeke's tone suggested that he didn't like being classed as a "little one." "We're going to stay up as late as we want on account of I'm leaving next week to spend the summer with my grandpa in Texas.''

John's hands tightened on the reins. Both his posture and his expression stiffened. Though she didn't have his talent for reading people, Jane knew he was worried what effect a summer with his maternal relatives might have on the boy.

Young Zeke didn't appear to notice his friend's lack of enthusiasm. ''Say, do you reckon Cousin James will be at the party tonight?''

''All the Kincaids should be there, son,'' John replied. ''Your uncle Will and aunt Lizzie, your cousin Jesse and his family. Makes sense James and Kate will be there, too.''

Zeke scratched his head. ''Since school just got out for the summer, do you reckon it'd be all right for me to call my teacher Cousin Kate?''

''I doubt she'd mind, if you say it real respectful. What do you think, Jane?''

''Well…'' She was not used to having her opinion solicited. Strange how it heartened her. ''It probably wouldn't hurt to address your teacher more informally at a family gathering. You could always leave it up to her. Say 'Mrs. Kincaid' the first time you speak to her. She may invite you to call her 'Cousin Kate' after that.''

Zeke thought it over, then nodded vigorously. ''That sounds real sensible.''

''Any questions you have about good manners, you just ask Miss Harris, here,'' John advised Zeke. ''Back where she comes from, folks set a lot more store by proper etiquette.''

Jane wasn't sure if he meant that as a compliment or not. Certainly the people she'd known back East worked hard to maintain appearances. That was why Emery had insisted they keep their engagement secret until after his aunt's death. Because Mrs. Endicott had her heart set on her only nephew "marrying well." If the Kincaids were any indication, folks in the West lived more on their own terms, with less regard for putting on airs or impressing their neighbors.

"We just finished studying all about Boston in school on account of the Fourth of July's coming. Mrs. Kincaid read us stories about the Boston Tea Party and Paul Revere. It sounds like a swell place. Are you hankering to go back there, Miss Harris?"

"No, I'm not." Jane's voice rang in her ears with positive conviction. "I like Montana far better than Boston, and I mean to stay here."

Over the top of Zeke's head, John's eyes met hers. Jane wasn't sure whether they held a flicker of respect or a specter of doubt.

If she meant to stay, she'd need to find another job. "Do you suppose anyone at the party tonight might be looking for a housekeeper or someone to look after children?"

John turned the team off the main road and up a wooded lane. "When Brock got married, Caleb gave him a parcel of the Kincaid spread closest to town, so Abby could still keep an eye on her store. She might need another clerk to spell off Sam Roland."

He seemed to sense Jane's renewed apprehension about the party. "Like I told Zeke, this will be mostly a family gathering. The Kincaids are nice folks. Just relax and have a good time."

How easy he made it sound.

"If you still want to go back to the ranch in a few hours time, I'll take you."

Jane's conscience smarted. She couldn't drag John away

from an evening with his friends, just because she felt uncomfortable.

She gulped a deep breath and raised her chin. "If Ruth doesn't need me to take the boys home, I'll stay as long as you want to."

Their eyes met again and John flashed her a smile so fleeting, Jane wondered if she'd only imagined it. Still, she felt rewarded for her tiny display of mettle. What greater challenges would she dare for more of John's smiles?

They pulled up in front of a house that looked much like Ruth and Caleb's, only smaller in scale. The pungent aroma of sawdust hung in the air. Out in the yard, a man who looked like a younger version of Caleb was improvising tables for the party by nailing big slabs of deal lumber atop pairs of sawhorses.

When he saw their wagon, he doffed his wide-brimmed hat and waved it at them. "John Whitefeather—just the man I wanted to see. Can I get you to give me a hand here, so we'll have someplace to sit and eat tonight?"

John reined the team to a halt in front of the house. "Be glad to, Brock. I'll be with you directly."

As he climbed down from the driver's seat, Zeke scrambled after him. In an instant John appeared on Jane's side of the wagon, his arms held up to her. He smiled—really smiled, and this time it did not vanish from his face as rapidly as it had come.

If he meant to encourage her, it worked. For one golden moment her fears fled, her shoulders straightened and she felt an answering smile warm her own features. John clasped her firmly, and Jane launched herself off the wagon, savoring the sweet moment before her feet touched the ground. And the even sweeter moment John Whitefeather searched the depths of her eyes, his hands lingering around her waist.

A boy ran out onto the porch. Though younger than Zeke, the youngster looked startlingly like his friend. "Ma, we got company!"

Abby Kincaid followed close on the boy's heels. Wisps of rich auburn hair straggled around her pink, freckled face. "Already? I must run and change my clothes so I'll be fit to receive guests."

She caught sight of the covered baskets and hampers loaded in the back of John's wagon. "Is all this for us? Why, Brock and Jonathon and I will be eating well for a week after this party's over. I hope you folks brought your appetites."

Brock Kincaid wandered over, fanning his face with his hat. "If they haven't, we'll just work them hard to make them hungry. Good to see you, John."

He began to fan his wife's face, and the two of them exchanged a special fond look that made Jane ache with envy.

"Brock, Abby, have you met Jane Harris?" John asked. "She's helping Ruth out for a spell."

Abby clasped Jane's hand warmly. "I'm glad you could come tonight. Ruth's told me what a godsend you've been to her. I wonder if I could impose on you to help me out? While the men are knocking a couple more tables together, perhaps I could get you and the boys to bring the food into the house. I have to throw on a clean dress and pin my hair up before the rest of our company arrives. Right now I look like something that was sent for and couldn't come."

The tightly knotted flesh of Jane's neck began to relax. Having a job to do made her feel much less awkward about being there. With the help of Zeke and Abby's son, Jonathon, she managed to tote all the food from their wagon into the kitchen of the new house. Then John and Brock needed her to hunt up the gingham yard goods Abby had basted into tablecloths.

Whenever she started to worry about the evening ahead, Jane would glance at John and catch his eye for a look of encouragement. Once or twice she caught him watching her.

By the time the lady of the house descended the stairs in a fresh dress and apron, Ruth and Caleb had arrived with Barton. Recognizing a good way to keep out of sight, Jane whisked the baby and the two older boys off to the back porch to keep them entertained. Now if the adults would just leave her be, she might have a tolerably good time at Brock and Abby Kincaid's housewarming, after all.

John lit and hung one final lantern, then scanned the throng of guests who had arrived while he'd been busy helping Brock.

Where had Jane got to?

The Kincaid men lounged at one end of the verandah, along with a few other ranchers and a couple of men from town. John recognized Harry Talbert, the barber, among them, and the Dillards, who owned Whitehorn Mercantile. The women had begun setting the deal tables with various crocks, pans and platters, which gave off tempting aromas. John watched their procession from the house for several minutes before concluding beyond doubt that Jane was not among them.

Neither were the children, and that was unusual.

Ruth had dragged him along to a couple of these family festivities since she'd married into the Kincaids. They were usually knee-deep in youngsters. Jesse and Haley's crowd. The Baxter brood. Zeke and Jonathon, now little Barton. Unless John missed his guess, the schoolmarm and the banker's pretty little doll of a wife would soon be adding to the flock of young Kincaids.

Welcoming an excuse to stay out of the thick of the party, John sauntered through the high grass to the rear of Brock and Abby's new house. Sure enough, he found Jane and the missing children.

He wasn't certain what to make of the silence at first, until he realized they were playing hide and seek. Zeke roamed around the yard peering up into the branches of a big cottonwood, then checking behind a cluster of empty barrels.

"One, two, three on Daisy!" he shouted as Jesse's little daughter emerged from her hiding place.

While Zeke continued his hunt, Daisy skipped over to the back porch, where Jane and the older Baxter girl sat with babies in their arms.

As John watched the children at their game, a queer pang went through him. He thought of his cousin Lame Elk and his friend Red Stone, with their sturdy sons and winsome little daughters. Perhaps it was a grave misfortune that John had reached his present age without siring any children of his own. Maybe he shouldn't fight his auntie's aggressive matchmaking.

While Zeke was busy flushing Jonathon Watson from behind a patch of alder bushes, his cousin Chris Kincaid stole out from his hiding place under the porch steps. Chris would be a handsome fellow once he grew into his height, John thought to himself. The boy had Jesse's strong features and thick head of dark hair, combined with Haley's striking green eyes.

Some whispering of the Great Spirit told John this mingling of a man's and a woman's flesh in their young was a mystical thing. Not to be undertaken for the wrong reasons or without the powerful medicine of great love.

Silently, Chris sped toward a tin can sitting in the middle of the yard and gave it a good hard kick. The can flew up in the air, then sailed back down into the boy's hands.

"Gotcha, Zeke! I'm *it* now."

Other boys and girls suddenly appeared around the yard. Matthew Kincaid shimmied down from the tree Zeke had inspected.

"Say, Miss Harris, this is a good game. Got any others you can teach us?"

Chris elbowed his brother. "Not till after I get my turn."

Pulling his lips taut with two fingers, John blew a piercing whistle. The children all turned to look at him.

"You might want to fill your bellies to give you strength for more games," he called. "Chow's on out front."

"Yippee!"

"Let's go!"

"Wait till you see the cake my ma brought."

The children thundered past him like a miniature buffalo stampede, until only Barton remained. The little fellow held out his arms after his departing cousins and began to rock himself up and down. "Uh-uh-uh!"

John sauntered over and lifted him out of Jane's arms. "I reckon this young dogie is anxious to join the rest of the herd at the feeding trough. It smells like a fine spread out there."

She made no move to rise from the porch steps.

"Barton and I would be honored if you'd sit with us at supper, ma'am." He cocked his elbow toward her.

A tiny sigh escaped Jane, and she worked up an uncertain smile. "Thank you for the invitation. It'll be nice to sit with somebody I know."

Straightening her shoulders and lifting her chin, she rose from her perch on the steps and placed her hand in the crook of his arm, with only a minor hesitation.

John could barely sense her featherlight touch through the sturdy cotton weave of his shirt, yet suddenly a peculiar warmth began to flow through his arm. As if the rest of his body had become a block of senseless wood, and every particle of feeling centered on the spot of contact between Jane and him.

When he tried to speak, the words caught in his throat. He had to push them out by force. "The truth is, you'll be doing me a favor, too. It's only since Ruth married Caleb and I went to work at the ranch that I've been coming to these get-togethers. It's kind of the Kincaids to invite me along, but most all the other grown-ups are married and…"

He couldn't bring himself to mention that, with the exception of his sister and nephew, everyone else was white.

Was his imagination working overtime, or did Jane's tiny hand press more tightly against his arm?

"That's exactly how I feel. Everyone I've met so far has seemed very nice, but they've all known each other for a long time and I'm a…stranger."

They reached the front yard, where the children were jostling to help themselves from the food table, while their mothers tried to keep order, with mixed success.

John nodded toward the women. "Plenty of these ladies were in the same boat when they first arrived in Montana. See Mrs. Jesse Kincaid over there? She came from back East to marry a land agent named Stoner. Real cuss of a fellow he was. Jesse held up the stagecoach she was riding to Whitehorn and kidnapped her. That's got to be every bit as vexing as your train crash."

Jane's face went white as sun-bleached bone, and John wished he hadn't reminded her of the accident.

"Mrs. James, there," he hastened to add, pointing out a tall woman with wire-rimmed spectacles who wore a rich plum-colored dress, "she came West to teach school. Her stage no sooner pulled into town than a couple of bank robbers tried to make their getaway in it. Caleb's cousin shot both the robbers. That's when the town council took a notion to make him sheriff."

"I think I'd have died of fright if those things had happened to me," Jane murmured, staring at Kate and Haley Kincaid with unmistakable awe.

John shook his head. "Don't go selling yourself short. I reckon those ladies were plenty scared at the time. Likely thought about bolting back East to where life was safer, but they stuck it out, just like you're doing. And by the looks of it, they're thriving, just like you will."

The festive hubbub almost swallowed Jane's whispered reply. Perhaps she didn't mean for him to hear it.

"I haven't any choice but to stay."

As the evening wore on, Jane found she had no choice but to enjoy herself. Whether because the Kincaids were such an infectiously friendly clan or because she wanted to help John feel more a part of the festivities, she wasn't certain. Perhaps the reason didn't matter.

The two of them loaded their plates from an improvised buffet table that fairly groaned under blue enamel pans of chicken and dumplings, platters of cold sliced ham and tongue, a mess of fried trout, braised short ribs and stewed venison, scalloped potatoes swimming in milk and butter. Though not the sort of dainty fare Jane was used to from Beacon Hill, it was wholesome and tasty. Just having her stomach pleasantly full of such food made her feel more hardy and confident.

"Jane made those baked beans," Ruth announced after several compliments on their flavor. "And wait till you taste her lemon cake. She's going to make some lucky man a fine wife.''

From one of the other tables, Jane heard the sheriff mutter, ''Just as long he gets her good grub into his stomach and not all over his trousers.''

The other men at the table began to chuckle, but were cut short by elbow jabs or reproachful looks from their womenfolk. A stinging blush rose in Jane's cheeks and the party food seethed in her stomach. Then she felt John's hand fumble for hers under the gingham tablecloth.

On his way to give her hand a quick squeeze of encouragement, his knuckles brushed her knee. Unlike the saloonkeeper's touch, it did not provoke a spasm of disgust. Instead it sent a ticklish sensation coursing up her inner thigh that culminated in an alarming, though curiously pleasant shimmer of heat between her legs. The blush in her cheeks intensified.

''I agree with you, Ruth,'' said a woman with chestnut curls, whom John had pointed out as Mrs. Jesse Kincaid. ''Miss Harris has a real way with children, too. It was good of you to keep them out from underfoot while we were getting everything ready, my dear.''

The boy sitting next to her piped up, ''The lady taught us a new game, Ma. It's like hide and seek, but more fun, 'cause if you're hiding you don't just sit around and wait till you're found. You have to try to sneak out and kick a can without getting caught. I did, so I'm gonna be *it* once we finish eating.''

''Say, that does sound like fun.'' The boy's father tousled his son's dark curls. ''Maybe I'll join you kids for a game to run off some of this good supper.''

Though his handsome features had a rugged cast, Jesse Kincaid didn't look like the kind of desperate outlaw who would kidnap another man's bride-to-be at gunpoint. No

more than Brock looked like a fearsome gunslinger—
something Jane had overheard Matt whisper to the Baxters' oldest daughter. Perhaps Haley and Abby had mastered the art of gentling their turbulent stallions.

Jane doubted she had either the courage to try or the
charm to carry it off.

Sneaking a sidelong glance at John Whitefeather bouncing little Barton on his knee, she wondered what kind of
husband he might make…for some woman.

He worked hard, and to her knowledge he never drank
anything stronger than sarsaparilla. He had a kind of steady
strength that reminded Jane of the mountains ranged along
the western horizon. Yet he had a gentle side, too, like the
tall prairie grass waving in the wind, or the warm caress
of a fleece wrap on a chilly night.

She admired the tender but powerful bond between him
and his family, almost as much as she envied it. The relationship between Emery and his aunt had been distant at
best, downright acrimonious at worst.

Once upon a time, she'd had a loving family, too. For
months after Mrs. Endicott took her in, she'd pined for her
folks, treasuring their memory. Gradually she'd put them
out of her mind because it hurt too much to recall the
happy times.

It had taken her a while to realize and trust that John
Whitefeather was nothing like Emery Endicott. All the
same, Jane sensed a difference between John and the other
men gathered around these tables. Was it just his mysterious Cheyenne heritage, or was it the wrenching tragedy
that marked his past?

Whether by circumstance or inclination, there could be
no doubt John Whitefeather walked alone. The kindness
he'd shown her of late had surely been prompted by pity.
She'd be a fool to think otherwise. And yet…

Some long dormant yearning made her wish he could just once slip his arm around her shoulders the way Caleb did to Ruth, or fan her flushed face with his hat, the way Brock had Abby's.

When the time came to dig into the sweet course, John followed Jane to the table spread with pies and cakes, cobblers, sweet rolls, bread pudding and turnovers. While she held Barton, he asked her what she wanted to eat, and heaped their plates accordingly.

The guests were all digging into dessert when Caleb rose and cleared his throat. "Brock and Abby, we're all glad to see you and Jonathon settled in your new place. Folks have a few tokens of remembrance they want to give you to warm your new home."

At a nod from their mothers, Matt Kincaid and the Baxters' eldest daughter stepped forward carrying a magnificent apple-leaf-pattern quilt in soft shades of green. The other women exclaimed, and Abby ran her hand over the intricate patchwork as if it was the most precious treasure in the world.

"Christine and I have been working away at that whenever we could get together," said Haley. "We hope you'll spend many happy nights snuggled under it."

Brock extended one long arm around his wife's shoulders and hugged her close to him. "I'd say that's a pretty safe bet."

All the married couples joined in an indulgent, knowing chuckle. Jane stared at her lap and blushed again. Growing up in Mrs. Endicott's household, she'd been strictly discouraged from learning the particulars of what went on between a husband and wife in the privacy of their bedroom. She'd almost come to believe there must be something vaguely shameful about it. These nice folks didn't make it sound that way, though.

"Thank you, ladies." Brock flashed a roguish smile at Haley and Christine. "I'll bet old Grover and Mrs. Cleveland don't sleep under as fine a quilt as this in the White House!"

More presents followed. A savings bond from the banker, William Kincaid, and his wife, Lizzie. Two finely bound volumes of Shakespeare from James and Kate. A handsome set of fire irons and screen from Caleb and Ruth. China from Mr. and Mrs. Dillard, who ran the mercantile. Everyone seemed to have a gift for Brock and Abby's new house.

Everyone except her.

Jane wanted to slide down in her chair and hide beneath the table. She wished Ruth had told her the other guests would be bringing presents. Not that she'd had money to buy a gift. The Kincaids were so much nicer than Mrs. Endicott, but it didn't change the fact that she was living on their charity.

Nobody else at the party would know that, though. They'd see her fancy dress, not realizing it was an old one of Marie Kincaid's, and think she was just too mean to buy a gift.

She didn't notice that John had left the table until she heard his voice behind her. "Here's a little something from me and Miss Harris and my folks back at Sweetgrass."

He set the brown paper parcel in Abby's lap and made his way back to Jane's side. The expression on his face was the most endearing mixture of embarrassment and fierce pride.

"Why, thank you, John," said Brock, as Abby unwrapped the gift.

"Oh, my stars!" Abby gasped.

Jane craned her neck to see, hoping none of the others would guess she hadn't a clue what *her* gift might be.

Abby held up three pairs of beaded moccasins—small, medium and large. "They're as soft as kid leather and lined with rabbit's fur. And look at that beautiful beadwork. Thank you, John and Jane. The three of us can wear these around the house to spare my new floors. You really didn't need to bring anything, but we'll think of you both whenever we put these on."

She passed the moccasins around for all their guests to admire as Caleb got to his feet again.

"I guess that's all the presents—I'd say you made a darn good haul. Between the quilt and the fire irons and your fine new moccasins, if your house isn't warm now, it's never going to be."

Under cover of the laughter that greeted Caleb's quip, Jane leaned close to John and whispered, "What made you say those moccasins were from me, too? You know I didn't have a thing in the world to do with them."

John shrugged. "I saw the look on your face while folks were giving their gifts. It was easier to read than a mustang rolling his eyes. It didn't take anything away from me to say the moccasins were from both of us."

"Let's clear away these tables," suggested Caleb. "Then if we can coax Harry to haul out his fiddle, we can get down to some dancing."

In a buzz of activity, the guests rose and began to prepare for the dancing. While John helped the men knock down the tables, Jane let the Dillards' youngest daughter take Barton so she could help the women clear away and clean up after the supper.

An hour later, John found her in Abby's kitchen drying the last of the dishes.

"So *this* is where you've been hiding." He leaned against the door frame. Though it looked to have been built tall, to accommodate Brock and the other Kincaid men, John filled the space.

"I'm *not* hiding," Jane protested, though the beginnings of a shamefaced grin might have betrayed the truth. "The other ladies had husbands wanting them to dance, so I told them to go."

"Well, now you have somebody wanting to dance, so hang up your dish towel."

"I couldn't. I don't know the first thing about dancing."

She'd longed to, though. Every time she'd accompanied Mrs. Endicott out to a society wedding or to the annual Temperance Society Benefit Ball, she'd stood behind the old lady's chair, watching with envious eyes when the dancers swirled past.

What had hurt most was having to watch Emery take the floor with another partner. He hadn't dared ask Jane to dance, of course, in case his aunt discovered their secret engagement. Sometimes, though, Jane felt certain he'd relished the opportunity to flaunt his attentions to some other girl in her face. Once she'd made the mistake of complaining to him afterward....

"Your spirit is wandering, Jane Harris," she heard John say. "Come on back to the Big Sky and try to work up the gumption to take a turn around the yard with me. I know a heap more about ceremonial dancing than I do about waltzes and such, but I'm willing to give it a whirl if you are."

He nodded toward the source of the music outside—the seductive croon of Harry Talbert's fiddle. "If we stay beyond the circle of lanterns, nobody will be able to see if we step all over each other's toes. Besides, all those married folks only have eyes for each other. They'll never even know we're around."

He must have sensed her hesitation waning, for he introduced his most potent argument. "I'd say one dance would just about square your half of those doeskin moccasins we gave Brock and Abby. You wouldn't want to welsh on your debt, would you?"

How could she refuse when he'd provided her with a perfect excuse to do what she wanted to? Jane laughed as she fumbled with the tie of her borrowed apron. She hoped her feet would not prove as clumsy as her fingers had suddenly become.

"It's a good thing you're a horse *trainer* and not a horse *trader,* John Whitefeather. I'm going to come away with by far the better bargain out of all this."

"Why don't you let me be the judge of that?"

One of his long, fluid strides closed the gap between them. Jane stifled a gasp, but this time it was not provoked by fear.

John gave a single deft tug on one of her apron strings and the tie came undone as if by magic. He held out his hand to her, as she had seen so many gentlemen do when inviting their ladies to take the ballroom floor. They drifted out the front door of Brock and Abby's new house just as Harry Talbert struck up a fresh tune.

"'Beautiful Dreamer,'" sighed Jane, as John led her to a shadowy spot beyond the pale of the glowing lanterns. "At least it's a nice slow one."

The sun had finished setting behind the Crazy Mountains while she'd been inside doing dishes. Now a cool night breeze stirred the prairie grass and the leaves of the cottonwoods. A new moon hung in the vast darkened sky like a silver sickle.

If there was a more perfect place in the whole world to dance to this sweet, poignant melody of Stephen Foster's, Jane could not imagine it.

John took her right hand in his, placing his left firmly

around her waist. She brought her left hand up to rest on his arm and they began to sway and swirl.

"Beautiful dreamer, wake unto me,
Starlight and dewdrops are waiting for thee."

Had Jane been told that dancing was a most difficult art to master, requiring endless hours of tuition and practice? Whoever had told her that nonsense must be a left-footed fool!

John moved with such agile, masculine grace it was impossible not to fall in step with him. Perhaps he took some of her weight in his powerful arms, for Jane felt as light as a milkweed floss, or perhaps like "Jeanie with the light brown hair, borne like a vapor, on the soft summer air."

For no earthly reason she could think of, Jane felt warm tears begin to trickle down her cheeks. She had never enjoyed such exquisite happiness in her whole life as she tasted at this moment.

And it scared her worse than Emery Endicott's fists ever had.

Chapter Nine

For the first time in his long career gentling wild creatures, John Whitefeather wondered if he had finally met one whose trust he could not win.

Better to stick with horses.

Why, he'd even made progress with that unsociable little filly, Cactus Heart. As John worked her around the corral at the end of a well-seasoned rawhide lariat, his thoughts kept slipping back to Saturday night's party.

He'd believed his gentling of Jane Harris had been going so well. After he'd coaxed her out of hiding with the children, she'd appeared to enjoy the supper. John knew he'd had a much more pleasant time than at any past Kincaid gathering. Perhaps having to focus on drawing Jane out had made him less mindful of the invisible barrier between himself and the others. Having her by his side might have made him feel more a part of the group.

Or could it be that he was so blasted happy in her company he forgot about being an outsider?

Cactus Heart cantered around the enclosure, sometimes resisting his gentle pressure on the lead rope, mostly going along with it. John kept up a reassuring murmur of Cheyenne words, telling her she was a beauty, that she had spirit, and what a fine buffalo horse she'd make.

How he wished he could convince Jane Harris that *she* was a beauty. That she had spirit, if only she could overcome her fears and cultivate it. That she would make as good a wife as any of the Kincaid women, once she found a husband worthy of her.

He'd been so heartened by his progress the other night. When he'd lured her away from the dish tub, she'd shown a spark of humor. Maybe even gentle flirtation? And when they'd begun to dance, an echo of her joy had resonated in his own heart. She'd seemed to know where his feet were headed before he did, moving hers in an instinctive harmony.

It had brought to his mind a vision of the *other* dance a man and woman might share. The one whose only music was the quickening drumbeat of two hearts, the soft whistle of ragged breathing and the primal refrain of sighs and moans of pleasure. Mounting to a fevered pitch and tempo and crowning in a cry or throaty growl of release.

His body had stirred to those tempting images like a rogue stallion scenting a willing mare. He'd wanted Jane with a sudden gnawing ferocity that nearly drove him to his knees. Even recalling it after three restless nights spurred him.

Perhaps he'd clutched her tighter to him. Through the cloister of her skirts and petticoats, she might still have felt the surge of his need. Or had he been reckless enough to angle his lips toward hers?

Shameful to admit, he'd been too lost in a whirlwind of bewildering desire to trust his memory.

He did recall, with harsh clarity, how she'd wrenched herself out of his arms as the final strains of music died away. This time she'd hidden herself too well for him to find. Or maybe he hadn't searched as hard as he might have, fearing Jane Harris would pummel his heart with a force as violent as the children's kicks of that battered old tin can.

Certain Ruth and Caleb would bring her home with them, John had driven back to the ranch alone. As his buggy cleared Brock and Abby's lane, distant music and bantering laughter from the party had mocked him.

Jane's voice outside the corral fence, soft and hesitant, brought his thoughts back to the present with a jolt.

"Good morning, John. Ruth told me to come ask if you wanted any breakfast."

Jane looked at him with only slightly less dread than on that first day they'd met in the Double Deuce. If she'd been a mare, her head would have been thrown back for sure and her hooves stepping high in retreat. He'd spoiled his approach to her the other night, unnerving her.

Horses were so much easier. With them he never had to worry about his own emotions rearing up to cause trouble.

"I'm not real hungry." At least not in a way that a bowl of oatmeal or a plate of bacon and eggs would satisfy.

With deliberate steps he approached Cactus Heart, slipping the light rope from around her neck. "I was glad to see you got home from the party all right. I couldn't find you after our dance."

They'd hardly exchanged a glance at mealtimes since then, let alone words.

Jane shifted her weight from foot to foot as if the ground had suddenly grown hot beneath her. "I—I'm sorry about that. I had to run off to the...outhouse. I guess I must've drunk too much cider with my supper."

She blushed a violent shade of red. Because of the immodesty of what she'd just said? John wondered. Or because it was such a blatant falsehood?

Steadily he walked toward her, making no sudden moves, keeping his voice temperate. "It's all right. You don't have to invent excuses if you didn't want to dance with me again. Or if you didn't want to drive home with me, alone in the dark."

"I don't?" She made it sound like astonishing information.

John shook his head slowly. "You don't have to suffer my company just because you think you owe it to my sister. Or because I told Brock and Abby that present was from both of us."

Her gaze didn't waver, though John suspected it took some will on her part.

Jane inhaled like a diver about to plunge into a river of uncertain depth from the edge of a high cliff. "What if I just enjoy being around you?"

Well, now... John rocked back on his heels. Had Jane's deep breath sucked up all the air hereabouts?

"Nothing wrong with that, I reckon." He managed to speak the words in a casual tone, but it took some doing.

She nodded her head, backing toward the house. "Well...fine. Then, I guess, if you don't want any breakfast...I ought to...get back to work."

"Me, too."

"John?" She stopped, arms rigid at her sides, fists balled tight.

"Yeah?"

"Would you teach me how to ride a horse? I mean, really ride? Not that walk around the corral we took with Barton."

If things had gone better the night of the party, he'd been planning to suggest that to her. "I don't see why not."

"And how to shoot a gun?"

He tried not to look as surprised as he felt. Would an eagle come asking for swimming lessons next?

"I reckon so, if you've a mind to learn."

"Thanks. I think I need to." She flashed him a quick, bashful smile that might have been thanks. Or maybe something more. "Did Caleb tell you he got word the lady from Bismarck has been delayed a while longer?"

"Not that I recollect." Maybe his brother-in-law hadn't wanted to see the eager hope that would have lit his eyes at the news.

"She'll be here soon enough, though. You said I needed to learn a few things if I'm going to make it here in Montana. I decided it's time I pursued some instruction instead of shutting my eyes and hoping everything will work out on its own."

Just then it appeared to John as though Jane Harris had grown a bit taller. Or perhaps she was only standing straighter.

It wasn't easy to throw her shoulders back and stand tall, Jane reflected as she prepared to go off for an afternoon, riding and shooting with John. For so many years she'd tried to make herself small and inconspicuous. Drawing notice had too often meant drawing criticism. Or violence.

But she must change if she wanted to stay in Montana, and Jane did want to stay—desperately. Not just because it was thousands of miles away from Emery Endicott, but because she'd enjoyed more moments of happiness here in the past weeks than she had experienced in all the years since the death of her family.

She'd woken the morning after the party heartily ashamed of herself for running away from John. What kind of pathetic little mouse turned tail from fear of pleasure and happiness?

New Year's Day was months away, but that didn't stop Jane from making a resolution. Never again would she bolt from the prospect of pleasure. Instead, she would seize and relish every opportunity for enjoyment that presented itself.

What had persuaded her she was capable of change? Possibly the knowledge that she had already taken her first fumbling steps along that path. Since her arrival at the Kincaid ranch, she'd learned many new things, shouldered responsibilities. Gradually she'd begun to take pride and find fulfillment in her modest accomplishments—a clean house, a tasty supper, a contented baby.

Jane cast a longing look over her shoulder at the Kincaid ranch house. On this bold, sweeping frontier, a woman couldn't huddle inside her snug, civilized sanctuary forever. Hopefully, being able to ride and shoot would help her feel less vulnerable.

John finished tightening the cinch on her saddle. "I'll teach you how to do all this for yourself before we're through. First, though, we just need to get you comfortable on horseback. If you don't mind, I'll carry the rifle and ammunition along with me."

"Be my guest." She tried not to sound too anxious, but it didn't work.

"John, Jane!" They turned in perfect unison at the sound of Ruth's voice.

Ruth strode over the hard-packed earth between the house and the corral, her trailing buckskin skirt sending up a faint billow of dust. She held out a cloth-covered basket.

"Don't be in any hurry to get back on my account. With Caleb off to his meeting of the Stock Growers Association in Miles City, and Zeke gone to visit his mother's folks in

Texas, there's little enough to do around here. I packed you some leftovers from the party in case you get hungry out on the range. Nothing like fresh air to give you an appetite.''

"Thank you, Ruth." Jane took the basket. "I guess I'll have to carry this, since John will have his hands full with the gun.''

"Let Ruth hang on to the basket until you're mounted," said John. "If I recollect, you had some trouble with that last time.''

She remembered, all right. Falling back into the arms of that awful Cobbs fellow. How could one man manage to be smarmy and uncouth at the same time?

It went much better today. With John hovering behind her, Jane knew she would never hit the hard ground even if she did slip. That certainty begat a heady sense of confidence. Before she knew it, she was securely mounted, in possession of the lunch basket and riding west with John Whitefeather.

"You're doing well, Jane." He sounded so surprised, and just a little admiring.

Jane sat taller in her saddle.

"Try to let your body move a little *with* the motion of your horse." John exaggerated his own graceful sway to give her the idea. "It's almost like a dance, and your mount always leads.''

He chuckled, and so did she.

Recalling the magical moments of their dance at Brock and Abby's party, Jane listened for the rhythm of her mare's gait and began to rock ever so gently in time with it.

"That's the way." John's tone was as warm as the late morning sun.

Jane felt like a shy wildflower coaxed to grow and blossom by its golden rays.

"Can I make her go a little faster?" Jane could scarcely believe those words had come out of *her* mouth.

"Don't get too cocky now." He chuckled; a sound like brook water gurgling over a rocky stream bed.

After so many arid years, her spirit was parched for the moisture of a friend's quiet laughter.

"Just give your mare a soft little nudge with your knees and she'll quicken her pace."

"Oh!" Jane squealed as the change in speed unsettled her balance.

"It's all right," John reassured her. "You just have to adjust your movements to match her new stride. Keep practicing, and soon you'll be doing it without even thinking."

If she sat on a horse every day for the rest of her life, Jane doubted she would ever ride with John's natural grace. He reminded her of a centaur she'd read about in one of Mrs. Endicott's books. With the torsos of men and the bodies of horses, most of those mythical creatures had been wild and lawless. One, however, had been a wise, honorable teacher to many of the great Greek heroes.

While she certainly wasn't hero material, Jane reflected, John Whitefeather had proved himself a natural teacher.

They'd been riding for more than an hour when John nodded toward a low bluff. "We're almost there. When you want to stop, pull back gently on the reins."

To her surprise, Jane managed to rein her mare to a halt without being pitched over the creature's neck. She also survived her dismount, though her legs quivered a little when her feet hit the ground. As she reached out to clutch her stirrup for support, she felt John's powerful arms wrap around her.

"Guess I should have known better than to bring you so far when this was only your second time in the saddle. You were riding so well, I clean forgot."

Jane allowed herself to wilt against John for just an instant, savoring the scent of leather and sweet hay he always carried about him.

"Please don't apologize for bringing me here." The moment her legs grew steady, she eased herself out of John's arms. With some reluctance. "Even if the riding had been difficult, it would have been worth it to see this place."

She gazed around the high meadow. Brilliant green grass waved in a breeze perfumed with wildflowers. A narrow creek wound around the base of the gentle rise, its banks shaded with clusters of cottonwood and aspen. As far as the eye could see in any direction, not a single man-made structure challenged the sovereignty of nature.

The power and beauty of it took Jane's breath away.

"I used to come here a lot." John tilted his face to the sun. "It's a great place to forget your troubles."

Jane had no difficulty believing that. Human cares shrank into insignificance out here. The natural splendor of the place would surely nourish the most famished soul.

"You've had plenty of troubles to forget, haven't you?"

A choking lump rose in Jane's throat as the words left her mouth. They had not spoken of his painful past, or hers, since that evening when he'd carried her up to bed. Might her intrusive question blight the fragile budding of trust between them?

A weighty sigh billowed out of John. It reminded Jane of a distant breaking wave.

"Still do by times." His voice sounded hushed and weary.

Another question occurred to Jane. She wondered if she dared ask it.

"Is this the first time you've brought someone else here with you?" How she wished his answer was not so important to her.

"Yeah, I suppose it is." He sounded as surprised as she felt.

Jane took a step closer and slipped her hand into his. "Thank you, John."

She wasn't certain which gift was more precious to her—the fact that he'd brought her here, or the fact that he'd never brought anyone else.

If he'd ever guessed that sharing his special place with another person would heighten his own enjoyment of it, John might have brought someone with him long ago. But he was glad he'd waited until now.

Until Jane.

John doubted anyone born and bred under the Big Sky could adequately prize the natural grandeur of this spot. And that included him.

Perhaps being an outsider had its advantages, after all.

Today, John saw his special place through Jane's fresh eyes. Supped deeply from the shared cup of her newfound delight. And got dead drunk with simple happiness.

They let the horses wander to graze while they sat on the crest of the hill and helped themselves to the contents of Ruth's basket. Stuffing slices of cold meat and cheese into bread rolls for improvised sandwiches, John and Jane washed them down with a single shared bottle of sarsaparilla.

They talked about the party, Jane coaxing John to tell her more colorful stories about the Kincaids. Afterward they nibbled on Mrs. Dillard's justly famous cherry turn-overs.

"Would you mind very much if we postponed teaching me to shoot until another day?" Jane brushed the crumbs of pastry from her skirt.

"I guess not. Why?"

"This may sound silly to you, but it seems to me as though gunfire would be sort of an…abomination out here. You know—like screaming cuss words at the top of your lungs inside some great cathedral."

"I don't reckon that's silly at all." John stared off toward the Crazy Mountains. "Anyplace this beautiful has to be a little bit sacred. I know I feel the Great Spirit here, more than I do anywhere else. And there is something blasphemous about the sound of gunfire."

Jane seemed to read his unspoken thoughts. "How long have you been coming here?"

He sensed her gaze upon him, but he could not turn and meet it. Surely it was enough that he answer her question. "Since I was a boy. Not long after my family was killed. I reckon I found peace here."

"I think I have, too," whispered Jane.

Was it being in this place that made it less painful for him to speak of his family? John wondered. Or did it just get a little easier every time? Like a tainted wound painfully pierced, the poison could now seep out.

What canker gnawed at Jane's soul? If he pushed to find out, John feared he might push her away forever. Yet if he failed to purge the poison, any changes he prompted in Jane would have no more substance than an early morning mist. They would burn away as soon as the harsh sun beat down on them.

"What do you say we wander down to the creek?" He

nodded in its direction. "We can give the horses a drink and wash Mrs. Dillard's cherry filling off our fingers."

Jane broke off a cluster of pink sand verbena and inhaled the perfume of its tiny flowerlets. "That sounds like a fine idea."

After leading their horses down to the creek, they shed their boots and bathed their feet in the cold, clear water. John tried to teach Jane to skip smooth, flattened stones across the surface, but she preferred to toss fat round ones in a high arc and laugh at the wet plop they made when they hit.

John found himself laughing, too. There was something contagiously ticklish about the sound.

By and by, they ambled back up to the crest of the hill and sat listening to a concert of meadowlarks.

"Don't they have a beautiful song?" Jane sighed.

"Ha!" John's laughter burst out of him. "The Cheyenne say meadowlarks mock people with their song. 'Boogeyman, big nose!'"

Jane grinned. "I suppose it does sound a bit cheeky."

"Look. Red-tailed hawks." John pointed up with one hand, while the other rested on the grass between him and Jane, inviting her touch.

They watched a pair of the great birds soar in big, easy arcs across the wide tracts of western sky. When John felt the cool, smooth touch of Jane's hand on his, he did not look down at first. In case he had only imagined it.

Her hand grew warmer as it rested against his, until he could deny the sensation no longer. An odd lightness swelled in his chest—fulfillment like the kind he felt whenever a wild maverick gave him its trust. No question, he had made great strides today in the gentling of Jane. Ruth would be pleased.

John couldn't quite decide if he was.

Perhaps the combination of their breathtaking surroundings and his progress in winning Jane's confidence were enough to account for the way he felt. Yet when John remembered that he was only readying her for another man, he tasted a worm in his golden apple where none should be.

Much as he enjoyed her company, she was not the woman for him any more than he was the man for her. Maybe if fewer responsibilities had weighed on him, he could have tried to become the kind of fellow she needed—settled, civilized, a pillar of the white community. He did have responsibilities, though. Here, of all places, he must not forget them.

He might have shaken off her timid touch and stalked away. Only he couldn't bear to spoil the progress he'd made with her.

"We should be getting back."

That broke the spell, but not too harshly.

Jane stirred, but her hand didn't budge. "I suppose we have to sometime."

Though he tried not to, John found himself savoring the reluctance in her voice. She wanted to stay here, with him, far away from the world. Even at the risk of night closing in around them.

Beads of sweat, as cold as the water of a high meadow creek, broke on his brow. He had to get Jane ready to spread her wings and fly away with someone else before he started entertaining even more foolish fancies about the two of them. And he had to remind himself why they had no future together.

"If you'd like some more practice riding, I'm heading out to Sweetgrass for a little visit the day after tomorrow. Care to join me?"

"Sweetgrass—my, that sounds beautiful. Your Cheyenne family live there, don't they?"

John almost choked on a swallowed laugh. He'd see how beautiful Jane found the place if the women were dressing a buffalo carcass or scraping hides. He hoped they would be. Jane's aversion to the Cheyenne way of life might prove a strong antidote to the unwelcome feelings she roused in him.

In the meantime, he'd promised Ruth he would prepare Jane for another man's courting, and he would keep his promise. No matter how much he enjoyed it.

He looked down at their hands. Hers like flawless carved ivory. His like supple, well-tanned moosehide.

"Before we go, I reckon only one thing could make this day better."

"What might that be?" A slight hitch in her breath betrayed Jane's uncertainty, but her hand did not waver from his.

"If you let me kiss you." Damn! He hadn't meant to say that. He was only going to ask her to walk around the meadow with him one more time. The word *kiss* had dropped out of his mouth somehow, and he couldn't bring himself to recall it.

"I...don't think I could do that." Her voice trembled.

Disappointment slammed into John, a treacherous sneak attack by his heart on his reason. It counted big coup.

Then Jane's dainty little tongue flickered out, pink as the verbena flowers, and made a rapid circle of her lips. Like a skittish mare ready to try what John was asking of her.

Maybe she just needed a different approach.

"How about if I hold still and let you kiss me?" When good sense tried to assert its authority over him, passion bound and gagged it.

After a long, breathless pause that stretched his patience almost to the breaking point, Jane whispered, "I think I could manage that, if you promise to close your eyes and not move a muscle."

Joy showered over him like a mountain waterfall. His heart sang as if he had won some rare honor.

"You have my word."

John closed his eyes, wishing she hadn't made that a condition. He wanted to watch her approach.

Angling his head, he parted his lips just a little. If Jane was willing to try this, he wanted to make it easy for her. And for himself? His thoughts didn't dare venture too far in that direction.

Skirts and underclothes rustled as Jane gathered her courage for the attempt. Her hand parted from his with the merest suggestion of a squeeze.

Where her skin had rested against his, the late spring breeze now drifted over it, chilling him. Was that how his life would feel when she'd gone off to marry some respectable Whitehorn businessman? Colder for having experienced the warmth of her company?

She gave him no time to dwell on that disturbing thought, much to his surprise. He'd expected her to dither, approach, then retreat before finally making contact—if she did at all.

The sudden whisper of her breath on his face and the delicate pressure of her lips against his left John scrambling to rally his composure. He kept his promise to remain still, but it was a near thing.

Her hands found their way to either side of his face, their smoothness so provocative against the bristle of shaved whiskers on the crisp lines of his jaw. Her lips parted slightly and moved against his in a timid invitation.

John prayed that his promise to stay still didn't extend to his mouth.

He let the tip of his tongue drift lazily out and glide over her lower lip. She froze for an instant, and John heard a subtle catch in her breath, but she did not back away. If anything, her grip on his face grew firmer and their kiss deepened. John tasted the tang of sarsaparilla, mingled with the ripe sweetness of cherry preserves and the subtle flavor of Jane.

Though he had kissed a number of women over the years, receiving one like this was completely new in his experience. As new and wondrous as this foothills meadow had been to her.

His other senses sharpened and his spirit rose to soar with the red-tailed hawks. His hands ached to touch Jane. His body ached to become one with hers. Pleasure whetted a keen edge on that pang of desire.

One of Jane's hands crept higher and higher up the side of his face, grazing his ear before plunging into his hair. A sound rose unbidden in John's throat. Deep, soft and feral, it mingled a cougar's rich purr with a wolf's menacing growl. He was one with all the male creatures of the Big Sky—the stag, the pronghorn ram, the mighty buffalo bull scenting a desirable mate.

Without warning, Jane jerked away from him. Later John would understand that his growl of arousal had spooked her—like a doe sensing the approach of a predator. At that instant he only felt the unpleasant shock of his body slamming into icy water from a great height.

Promises and control fell before a surging stampede of passion.

He groped for Jane, capturing her in a powerful, insistent embrace. His lips sought hers, true as an arrow from the bow of a skilled hunter. One hand closed around the sweet curve of her hip, the other tore away her bonnet and liberated her hair from its prison of pins.

As those honeyed brown waves rippled through his fingers, he moaned with delight. He had never touched anything to match the texture of Jane's hair. Soft as brushed fleece, but smooth and luxurious as a mink pelt at the end of a cold winter.

Intent on sating his senses with the woman in his arms, John did not immediately notice her struggle. Her hands fluttered against his shoulders in the mildest of token protests. Only when he surrendered her lips for the conquest of her tempting ivory neck did she gasp out his name and two words.

"Please. No." They sounded more like wavering reluctance than true resistance.

For a moment his Cheyenne ears refused to make sense of the English words, just as they strained to hear Jane sigh his true name in the language of his father's people.

In the end, no harsh moral teachings from the residential school made John Whitefeather rein in his renegade desire. For he had seen again and again how the teachings of the white men often differed sharply from their practice. The deeply held honor code of the Cheyenne did not allow for such hypocrisy. A man who forced his attentions on a woman brought untold shame upon himself.

John thrust the woman away with greater force than he had clutched her to him. "I'm sorry, Jane! That was wrong."

He couldn't bring himself to meet her eyes, for fear of what he would see reflected there. He would not look at her at all, in case the sight of her kiss-swollen lips and tumbled hair prove too tempting even for the honor of a warrior.

Instead he marched down the hill and plunged into the frigid waters of the creek, purging himself of the demon lust.

For now.

Chapter Ten

Jane felt as though she'd been consumed by a white-hot flame, then doused with a bucket of cold water to put the fire out. As she readied herself for bed that night, she sensed embers still glowing among the sodden ashes, ready to blaze again at the slightest stirring.

If John's formidable silence on their ride home was any sign, he had no intention of rousing more trouble. His absence at supper had confirmed it. Living all his life on the Montana frontier, maybe he had never heard of Miss Pandora and her box. If he had, he might understand the futility of trying to dam the flood of emotions his kisses had unleashed in Jane, or pretending they would slow to a trickle if he ignored them.

The very first night she'd arrived at the ranch, Jane had noticed her bedroom window looked out over the foreman's cabin. Tonight, as the Big Sky gradually ripened from indigo to purple to black, she perched on Marie Kincaid's trunk and watched jealously for a glimpse of John.

Had she been wrong to kiss him? Jane asked the evening star glittering just above the horizon. Better than most women, she knew a man's control over his passions was tenuous at best. How often had Emery repented striking her, claiming he'd been driven to it by some behavior of hers? Since coming to Whitehorn and making the acquaintance of John Whitefeather and Caleb Kincaid, Jane had grown skeptical of Emery's excuses.

Today with John had been different. She could accept a measure of the blame for his behavior. What she couldn't decide was whether there'd been anything so very wrong with it.

It wasn't as though she'd never been kissed by a man. Emery had kissed her even before they'd become engaged, and many times after. They had all been pretty much alike, though perhaps becoming less gallant and more demanding as time went on. None had been anything like the two very different kisses she'd shared with John this afternoon.

She had enjoyed the first one so much. Scouting unexplored terrain in her newfound spirit of adventure. Taking fresh delight in each discovery.

But her reckless exploration had wakened a slumbering wild creature. He had overwhelmed her, intent on sating his hunger. That was not what had frightened Jane, though.

What *had* made her gasp out that protest? The one that had stopped John as surely as a bullet and sent him hurtling down the hill to throw himself into the icy creek. Had it been the feral she-creature within herself, stretching sleek-muscled limbs and snarling a challenge to her mating partner?

Now that dangerous but beautiful beast prowled restlessly within Jane, vigilant and hungry.

A light flickered on in the foreman's cabin, and Jane thought she saw a rustle of movement through the window. Grabbing a candle and the ewer from her washstand before she had time to think better of the impulse, she dashed down the stairs to fetch hot water from the kettle Ruth always kept simmering on the back of the stove.

Ruth glanced up from her evening beadwork as Jane surged into the kitchen. "I thought you'd gone to bed hours ago, dear. Is anything the matter?"

"Matter? No." Jane hoped the wavering candlelight would obscure the guilty blush that flamed in her cheeks. And that Ruth would attribute her breathless voice to the rapid descent she'd made from upstairs. "I just felt the need of a sponge bath after my ride today in the hot sun."

"Go ahead." Ruth bent her dark head over her beadwork. "There's plenty of water."

For some reason, her bland words sounded charged with cryptic meaning.

"Thank you for letting your brother teach me to ride." Jane half filled her ewer with steaming water from the kettle, then topped it up with cold from the hand pump at the sink. "I hope you won't mind if he takes me out to Sweetgrass the day after tomorrow."

She hoped John's invitation still held, for she was curious to see this other side of his life. Not to mention braving new experiences. Ever since the death of her parents and her brother, she had sought a refuge. She'd endured her engagement to Emery in the hope that she would not lose another home when Mrs. Endicott finally passed on. Looking back, Jane could see that her sanctuary had been little better than a prison. Few of the terrors from which she'd hidden could have been worse than the one locked with her behind those protective, restraining walls.

"Of course you can go to Sweetgrass." Ruth set her beadwork aside. "In fact, I have a few things I want to send with you. I'm glad to see you willing to get out more these days. I know this place must seem mighty different than where you came from, but it's tamer than it used to be. It'll keep getting more so as the years go by, I reckon."

As Jane left the kitchen, clutching the heavy water-filled

ewer to her chest with one hand and balancing her candle in the other, she heard herself say the oddest thing.

"I hope it stays a little wild, at least."

Back in her bedroom, she set the candle and her basin on top of the clothes trunk. Then she filled the basin with warm water, pushed her curtains wide open and began to strip off her clothes in front of the window.

New England propriety protested as Jane carefully unfastened every button down the front of her blouse. In hopes of deterring her, it raised the specter of Mrs. Endicott's face if she could see what Jane was doing. But the imagined look of scandalized horror only made her giggle.

What if Floyd Cobbs or one of the other cowboys should see her? That loathsome possibility made Jane pause and shoot a furtive glance out her window.

No. Two big barns and a grain silo hid the cowboys' bunkhouse from her window. The only man who might see her was probably mending harness or dealing himself cards in a solitary, monotonous game of patience. Never once sparing a glance out his window at the woman he'd made achingly aware of her own body for the very first time.

The white blouse slipped from her shoulders, and Jane suddenly remembered the scars on her shoulders. From this distance, John would not be able to see them...if he was watching. As she reached behind to unhook her skirt, her bosom strained against the confines of her tight corset, two creamy mounds swelling over the top of it. Not certain why she felt compelled to do so, Jane swayed her hips to send her skirt sliding over the bleached knoll of petticoats and puddling in a wide circle around her ankles.

As she bent forward to pick it up, she stole a glance through her eyelashes at the foreman's cabin. Was it only her wishful imagination, or was someone staring up at her through its window?

Untying her petticoats, Jane let them sink over the curve of her hips and down to the floor under their own starched weight. Then, with sinful deliberation, she unfastened each hook down the front of her corset, letting the fullness of her bosom push the two sides farther and farther apart. When only a single hook at the base remained secure, she reached both hands up to the back of her head and began pulling out the pins she'd so hastily shoved into her hair while John had plunged into the creek.

She remembered a story she'd read many years ago in a richly illustrated picture book, about a princess in a tower. She'd often envied the princess her safe tower. Now she wasn't so sure.

Was John watching her now, as the prince had watched Rapunzel? Remembering how he had liberated her hair only a few hours ago? Did he see how her bosom strained against its confinement? And did he yearn to scale the timbers of the ranch house so he could free it, too?

That thought provoked a quick flutter of panic. Or was it excitement?

Tossing her hairpins on top of the trunk, Jane lazily shook out her light brown hair until it cascaded over her shoulders, veiling her bosom. Then she loosed the lowest hook on her corset and let it fall away.

No one could see her below the hips, but if he was watching, she wanted her intended audience left in no doubt that she was fully unclothed. Untying the ribbon that held up her fancy laced drawers, she lowered them with a shimmy of her hips. Then she kicked off her shoes and stockings and began to wash herself with warm water from the basin.

Closing her eyes, she imagined John standing behind her

wielding the washcloth. Letting rivulets of warm water course over her breasts, down her neck. Grazing the sensitive flesh on the inside of her upper arms, across her shoulders. Though the temperature of water was quite warm, goose bumps rippled over Jane's skin where the wet cloth had passed. The pink crest of each bosom grew firm and thrust itself out.

Once or twice, when the full implications of her performance struck home, she barely restrained the urge to jerk her curtains closed. Then she reminded herself she was perfectly safe. John could not touch her, except with his eyes.

More important, he could not pull away from her.

True, he might stop watching, but she didn't have to know that. And if he had seen every garment removed, every intimate swipe of the washcloth, he might understand this was her strange way of expressing repentance.

She was sorry she'd asked him to stop kissing her.

"I reckon Jane's ready to get married now." John stared into the black, bitter well of his coffee cup and saw his future.

Ruth stopped sweeping the floor of his cabin. She insisted on giving the place a thorough cleaning every now and then, usually when she felt she had reason to corner and question him. His absence from supper last night and breakfast this morning had likely brought on this domestic fit.

About all John did in the place was sleep, or in the case of last night, *not* sleep. The endless hours he'd spent in his lonely bed, writhing and burning with a need he dared not satisfy, had given him a grim foretaste of hell.

"So soon?" his sister asked in surprise. John scowled and shrugged. "That lady from Bismarck could be coming anyday, right? Except for a few hard cases, I can't take weeks to gentle the mustangs. If I did, Caleb would soon go back to letting the cowboys bust them the hard way.''

"You must have potent medicine, *hestatanemo.*'' Ruth pulled a handful of dried sweetgrass from her apron pocket, strewed it around the floor, then swept it into a pile. "To make such a highstrung creature ready to marry after only one party and a horseback ride."

He wasn't certain what to make of Jane's mysterious transformation, either. Not that he planned to admit it to his busybody little sister.

"I didn't claim it was all my doing. I reckon Jane's always had more spunk than any of us gave her credit for. With or without me, she might have been ready for courting now if you hadn't thrown those first three suitors at her head so fast."

"I suppose…." Ruth didn't sound convinced.

John wasn't sure how much he believed his own explanations. He had spent half the night trying to fathom that sensuous performance of Jane's. And the other half hotter than the inside of a sweat lodge as he recalled every inviting movement. Every button unbuttoned. Every hook unhooked. Every pin unpinned. Even calling it to mind hours later made his loins ache in his tight denim trousers.

All this time he'd thought Jane's nervousness around strange men was on account of too much prudish modesty about her body. He'd sure ciphered that wrong.

Now he wondered if an old fusspot like Amos Carlton might be man enough to handle a woman like Jane.

"Well." Ruth whisked a small mound of sweetgrass and dirt into her dustpan. "When Caleb gets back from Miles City and you and Jane have made your visit out to Sweetgrass, I'll see if we can set Amos to start courting her. Maybe she could stay with Brock and Abby for a spell once Mrs. Muldoon gets here. That way she'd be closer to town for Amos to come calling.''

Hearing Ruth talk so casually about Amos courting and marrying Jane gave John a tormenting headache.

''Who said we're going to Sweetgrass?''

He wasn't sure he could look Jane Harris in the eye again. Much less make that long ride by her side. Then be her sole companion and interpreter for a whole day with his people.

''Sounded to me like Jane's got her heart set on going.''

Ruth shoveled ashes out of the rugged stone hearth that took up most of the west wall of the cabin. Her tone told John that Jane wouldn't be the only one upset if he canceled their plans.

''Besides, I have some cloth and needles and beads I wanted to send to Walks on Ice. And a tonic I brewed for the children who were sick.''

''Why don't *you* go, then?''

And leave him alone in the ranch house with Jane for meals? That, or go eat in the bunkhouse. Neither of those choices appealed to John, either.

Ruth shook her head. Not just a busybody, but stubborn too.

''Caleb's been away a few days and I'm anxious to see him when he gets back. Someday you'll meet a woman who's special for you. Then you'll understand.''

John got up from his little table by the window. The one he'd been sitting at last night when he'd spotted Jane removing her clothes. He couldn't bear listening to his sister go on about a ''special woman.'' The Kincaid men had enjoyed more than their share of luck in love. John knew better than to expect the same for himself.

''Is this place clean enough for you yet?'' he snapped, jamming on his hat. ''I can't sit around all day. I have to go see if those shiftless *ve'ho'e* cowboys are getting any chores done while Caleb's away. Then I have horses to work."

"What's got the devil hanging over you this morning, Night Horse?" grumbled his sister, rolling up the fleece rug John kept in the middle of the floor. "This needs to be aired and beaten. I'll send Jane out in a while to wash your window."

"Don't bother." John stalked out the door, muttering to himself. "It's plenty clean to see through."

Never one to pass up a chance at having the last word, Ruth called after him, "Can I tell Jane you still plan on taking her out to Sweetgrass tomorrow?"

He knew his sister too well to believe he had any real choice. Besides, the bedeviling Miss Harris would soon be out of his life for good, taking her dual spirits of blushing virgin and brazen temptress with her. Which was the real Jane? He thought he'd known, but she was clearly a trickster of confusing subtlety. Perhaps Caleb had been right about her in the first place.

Over his shoulder John growled, "Tell her whatever you want."

"John's looking forward to your trip out to Sweetgrass tomorrow." Ruth beat the fleece rug from her brother's cabin with vigorous strokes.

"He is?" Jane gnawed at her lower lip as she hung one of John's shirts to dry.

When she'd seen it in the wash basket this morning, she'd had the scandalous urge to smuggle it up to her bedroom so she could wrap herself in it to sleep that night. What had possessed her? Something at once foreign and familiar. A curious power that terrified and thrilled her by turns.

Maybe she didn't have Lizzie Kincaid's golden appeal, nor Abby's strong, striking beauty, but she had still made a potently attractive man like John Whitefeather burn with desire for her. Burn so hot it had taken a creekful of icy water to quench his ardor. So hot it had incinerated the massive barricade of his honor.

When a woman had been so vulnerable all her life, how could she help but let this kind of power go to her head?

Giving the fleece rug one last swat, Ruth nodded. "I talked to John about it just this morning." Something in her voice didn't sound entirely candid. What was John's sister *not* saying?

Ruth dropped her rug beater and scooped her young son up from the ground. "What have you got in your mouth now, Thundercloud? Clover. I don't reckon that'll kill you. One of these days, I'm afraid you're going to take a bite out of a rattlesnake."

The child gave an infectious chuckle, drooling a cascade of pink clover buds out of his mouth. He held out his arms to Jane. "Na-na-na!"

"Yes, you can go to Nana." Ruth passed her son to Jane. "Just like a man. He knows when he has a lady's heart wrapped around his finger. I hope you'll have many children of your own, Jane—you're so good with them."

Trying to ignore the intense, contrary feelings Ruth's words kindled in her, Jane wiped Barton's mouth with the corner of her apron. "I think this young warrior has a new tooth."

She nuzzled his ticklish neck. "Have you cut a big sharp tooth?"

The baby chortled and crowed with glee, and Jane hugged him tight, dreading the day she would hold him for the last time.

"Aren't you putting the cart before the horse, Ruth?"

She tried to sound flippant, but the thickness in her voice hit a discordant note. "I don't have a husband. I'm not sure I want one."

Those last words gushed out, unbidden. A week ago, she'd have vowed solid certainty she didn't want a man in her life again. What had caused this sudden waver in her beliefs and plans?

"I know they seem like more bother than they're worth sometimes." Ruth made a face. "But they probably think the same of us. It's often hard to believe men and women aren't two different orders of creature altogether."

Ruth did understand. Until coming to Montana, Jane hadn't realized how deeply she craved sympathetic female companionship. Barton wouldn't be the only one she'd miss when the time came for her to leave the Kincaid household.

The humor left Ruth's striking face, displaced by ardent sincerity. "There's strong magic in the balance of opposites, Jane. In the Big Sky, we need all the balance magic we can get. This land can be hard on its women and worse on a woman alone. You've only seen it in a pleasant humor."

For the first time since stealing out of Boston, Jane thought about marriage with sentiments other than nauseating dread. In the past month she'd cultivated unexpected talents that a prospective husband might prize.

After an uncertain beginning, she'd become a pretty fair cook. Instinct tempered by trial and error had ripened her love of children into a true knack for managing them. To her amazement, she had come to enjoy all the little chores that made a home clean, warm and snug for a family.

Her acquaintance with Caleb Kincaid had shown her the vital importance of a settled home life to a man who daily wrested his living from this sometimes grudging land.

Zeke had spoken of the messy, haphazard domestic arrangements he and his father had endured before Ruth took the Kincaid ranch house in hand. Might Jane, too, feather a cosy nest for the right man and their young?

While it had come as a surprise to her how much men on the frontier needed a woman's softness in their lives, she didn't for a moment doubt the truth of Ruth's words. A woman of the Big Sky could use a strong, canny man to fight for her and provide for her.

"What if you pick the wrong man, Ruth?" Jane shuddered, thinking of Emery Endicott. She'd been so pathetically certain she needed him to survive, and instead he'd almost killed her. "Wouldn't a bad man be worse than none at all?"

Ruth flashed her a probing look, then grabbed a pair of Caleb's trousers and pinned them to the clothesline. "You're right, of course. Some women haven't much sense about the men they pick. Often I wonder if they choose for the wrong reasons."

"Like…?" Jane prompted her.

"Like thinking nobody else will have them and the man who will is doing them some kind of favor. Like thinking they can reform an incurable outlaw. Like wanting a man for the things she thinks he can give her, instead of for who he is."

No wonder her relationship with Emery had gone so disastrously wrong, Jane reflected, hearing herself declared guilty on all counts.

Barton began to fuss, bouncing up and down in Jane's arms.

"I'll finish hanging out these clothes," said Ruth, "if you want to take him for a walk. John might not be too busy to take him for a little ride."

"Go see *unka?*" Jane asked Barton, unsure whether she was ready to see John Whitefeather.

"Unka-unk!" the baby shrieked, wriggling to reach the ground.

"I reckon that settles it." Ruth laughed.

Jane managed only a tepid smile in reply. One look into John's deep-set blue eyes and she would know whether he'd been watching her last night.

She wasn't sure which would dismay her more—discovering he had or finding out he hadn't.

"Okay, Bronco Bart, away we go." Jane let him latch on to her hands for balance as he tottered off in search of his favorite uncle.

As it happened, Barton's leg power gave out long before they managed to track John down. They found no sign of him around the corral or the stable. Jane even stole a curious peek into the foreman's cabin with the excuse of looking for him.

The place was tidier than she'd expected of bachelor quarters, though she knew Ruth had been in to clean for her brother just that morning. A long narrow bed occupied one corner, with a low chest standing sentinel at its foot. The only other pieces of furniture were a small table and two chairs in front of the window.

One of Ruth's patchwork quilts and a wall hanging of beaded leather and feathers dangling beside the bed were the only splashes of color or personality about the place. The oversize stone fireplace drew Jane, as she imagined its hearth aglow with an inviting fire. This afternoon, it looked as cold and bare as the rest of the cabin, compared to the bright summer sunshine outside.

"Unk's not around, Barton." A mixture of relief and disappointment swirled deep in Jane's belly. "Guess we'll just have to try to catch him later."

Two precious dark eyes crinkled up and one plump lower lip began to quiver.

"It's all right." Jane lowered him to the ground again. "We'll walk some more. Walking always soothes your feelings."

Sucking back a tearful sigh, Barton staggered off, towing Jane away from the part of the ranch with which she'd become familiar. They hadn't gone far when she heard a male voice from behind a shed.

"Big Chief's on the warpath, today, Clel. Mind you stay out of his way or he'll scalp you good with that tomahawk tongue of his."

Several men broke into harsh, scornful laughter. Jane felt something foreign and frightening brewing inside her. How dare they talk about John this way? Why, he was worth a dozen of them!

"He's a fine one to talk about us not pulling our weight around here." The bitter words spat out like a disgusting gob of chewing tobacco, and Jane recognized the voice of Floyd Cobbs. "Lazing around the corral petting those wild mustangs instead of busting 'em like a real man."

"Shucks, Floyd," joshed a third fellow. "You're just sore on account of Kincaid made his brother-in-law ranch foreman over you. Or is it 'cause Big Chief rode off with that pretty little Boston filly yesterday? I reckon *that's* what put him on the warpath today. Got a whiff of her and now he's all hot and bothered like a stallion in rut."

"I reckon you got a damn big mouth, Clel Harding!"

Jane grabbed Barton as the sound of a scuffle broke out. Twelve years of life in Beacon Hill told her to run the other way, but six life-changing weeks in Montana propelled her forward.

The flabbergasted looks on those leathery, unshaven faces as she rounded the corner of the outbuilding might have been comical, if Jane had been the tiniest bit disposed to laugh. She wasn't.

"M-may I assume Mr. Kincaid pays you gentlemen to do something besides fighting and gossiping?" Jane couldn't believe she was scolding a bunch of Montana ranch hands like they were so many schoolboys, still wet behind the ears.

"Now, ma'am, no need to get riled." Floyd Cobbs winked, as though telling his cronies he could handle her. "We was just funning is all."

He took a step toward her, and it was everything Jane could do not to turn tail. They wouldn't dare lay a finger on her while she was holding their boss's son, she tried to reassure herself as her mouth went dry and her heart raced. Besides, the house was within screaming distance.

"Y-you'll think it's a good deal less funny if you're run off this ranch on the barrel of a smoking gun, Mr. Cobbs. And I imagine that's just what Mr. Kincaid would do if he heard you'd been speaking of his wife's brother with such disrespect."

"Now, ma'am—"

A sharp elbow in the ribs stopped Floyd. "Shut up, now, before you land us up to our necks in fresh cow pies!"

"An admirable suggestion, sir." The combustible mixture of fear and anger inside Jane almost exploded in hysterical laughter. What a pungent image the cowboy's words conjured up!

She hadn't been on the receiving end of Mrs. Endicott's haughty stares for nothing. Now she mimicked one for the benefit of Floyd Cobbs and company.

"If I hear one of you so much as whisper your disgusting insinuations about Mr. Whitefeather and me again, I will take the matter directly to Caleb Kincaid. Is that understood?"

"Loud and clear, ma'am. Loud and clear."

They vanished like so many nasty insects confronted by a bright light.

Jane let Barton slide to the ground. She wasn't sure she could sustain her own weight, let alone his, on legs that felt like twin columns of mashed potatoes.

Just then, John Whitefeather came charging around from the other side of the smokehouse. "Jane, are you all right? I heard your voice and some of the men's. They didn't hurt you or Barton, did they?"

He looked so anxious on her behalf, and maybe a tiny bit...jealous? An urge to swoon almost overcame Jane. She did feel a bit unsteady, and she longed to revisit the sensation of being cradled in John's strong arms.

But she'd finally learned to stand on her own two feet and she wasn't about to let go of that hard-won accomplishment for anything.

She willed her voice not to tremble and her chin not to quiver. "We're both fine. I just told the men they'd better get back to work. By the way, how early will we be heading out for Sweetgrass tomorrow morning?"

Chapter Eleven

Early the next morning, while a mild breeze sighed through the western fringes of a prairie wet with dew, John and Jane prepared to set off for Sweetgrass.

"Are you sure you don't mind us leaving you by yourself again today, Ruth?" John asked as they drank coffee around the kitchen table.

His sister waved her hand as if to sweep them on their way. "Caleb should be back from Miles City by noon. You need to get away before it becomes too hot to travel. Jane, you won't forget to give those sewing supplies to my auntie?"

Jane shook her head. "I'll make sure she gets them. Did you tell me her name means 'Walks on Ice'?"

John spoke up, his voice gruffer than he intended. "I suppose you think that's funny. Well, it happens Auntie is a skilled midwife. Women of my people always call on her when it's a hard birth. One spring when she was young, she crossed a river on thin ice to attend a woman in labor. The ice cracked behind her with each step, but she got to the other side safely. The elders said the Great Spirit made her step light because she was doing a worthy deed."

"I don't think it's funny, at all." Jane looked him

straight in the eye, her voice quiet but uncowed. "How wonderful to have done something so important folks are reminded of the story every time they say your name. I've never done anything that would earn me a name."

Her wistful tone blasted John's conscience. He hadn't meant to hurt her any more than he'd meant to kiss her the other day. Would he regain control of his actions once she was gone from his life? And if he did, would the price be too high?

Ruth patted Jane's shoulder and flashed John a scolding glare. "If you were a Cheyenne girl, your name would likely be Calls to Children. That's a gift, and not everyone has it. Especially not... Ah, listen to me going on when you two should be on your way."

If Ruth was hoping to distract Jane, she failed.

"Especially not...who?" Jane turned her soft hazel eyes on his sister.

John knew from experience the futility of trying to hold anything back from that beseeching gaze. He also knew what Ruth had meant to say.

"Especially not *ve'ho'e,* dear." Ruth sighed over the offensive truth. "Most white folks are much harsher with their young than the *Tsitsistas.*"

"I see. Then I guess I'll fit right in at Sweetgrass, won't I?" On that modestly defiant note, Jane drained the last of her coffee, then carried her dishes to the washtub.

Oh, she'd fit in at Sweetgrass. Suddenly John had a bad feeling about the whole day ahead of him. Jane Harris would fit in at a Cheyenne village...when frogs grew teeth!

"Oonâhá'e mâxhevéesevôtse," said John as they rode north.

"What does *that* one mean?" Jane nudged her horse to a slightly faster pace to keep up with him.

Asking him questions about the Cheyenne language, she'd finally got John talking to her again. She couldn't tell from his manner whether he'd seen her in the window the other night, so she'd made up her mind to behave as if he hadn't.

"It's a saying of my people—'when frogs grow teeth.' It means 'never.'"

Jane laughed. "Back in Boston, we say, 'when pigs fly.' Some folks say 'when hell freezes over.' I guess none of those are too apt to happen, are they?"

"A flying pig would be quite a sight." John appeared to be doing his best to fight off a smile.

Jane wished with all her heart he'd surrender.

"Ruth told me a bit about Sweetgrass, but I don't quite understand. Is it a government reservation?"

Her question averted any threat of a smile from John, and she regretted that. His usual grave countenance was one of the most striking she'd ever seen. But his rare smiles lit up something inside of him. And her.

"A reservation's the one thing Sweetgrass is *not*. I don't want my band living off government charity, overseen by Indian agents like we're children who don't know what's best for us. We *own* every acre of Sweetgrass, and it's a good piece of land. It has water with plenty of fish, woods where we can hunt and trap, tall grass where the buffalo herds still come. William Kincaid approved the loan and a lawyer in Livingston registered the deed."

"That must have cost a lot."

John gave a curt nod. "I reckon if I keep working for Caleb until five years after I'm dead, that should just about pay it back."

"I see."

It did illuminate a number of puzzling questions. Like why a man who so obviously prized his Cheyenne heritage worked as a ranch foreman instead of living among his father's people. Like why he fought so hard against his obvious attraction for her. Did he think he had nothing to offer her compared to men like the doctor and the saloon-keeper?

In terms of Endicott values, perhaps he didn't. No big house in an affluent neighborhood. No fine carriages or jewels or accounts with the best tradespeople.

In terms of the things that really mattered—priceless assets like strength, honor and kindness—John White-feather was a millionaire and Emery Endicott a pauper. What John had just told her proved that he would go to any lengths to protect and care for those he loved.

If she could someday count herself among that number, Jane thought she might be the happiest woman in the world.

"We're riding on Sweetgrass land now." As John looked around at the flourishing land his voice took on a rich note of pride. "We'll come to the camp soon."

He pointed toward the northern horizon. Jane shaded her eyes and peered into the distance. Sure enough, she could make out a cluster of tall, conical dwellings and slender plumes of smoke lofting skyward. It was as though she had stepped into the pages of a Beadles dime novel. With John by her side, she felt a quiver of excited curiosity, but surprisingly little fear.

As they drew closer to the camp, some boys and girls about Zeke's age ran out to meet them, laughing and call-ing to John. The girls wore beaded buckskin dresses and the boys fringed trousers. Several dogs with pointed snouts and curled tails barked at the children's heels.

"What are they saying?" asked Jane, thankful all the cordial commotion didn't upset her placid gelding.

"They say they're happy to see me. The girls ask who

you are. The boys want to know if I brought them any sweets from Whitehorn.''

"Have you?'' Surely a man this much at ease with children wanted sons and daughters of his own.

One corner of John's wide mouth tilted as he reined his mare to a halt. "I know better than to come without.''

He dug in his saddlebag and tossed down a small paper sack bulging with some variety of confection.

"Licorice,'' he told Jane. "They're all crazy about it.''

The children ran away with the bag, calling back words of thanks in their own language.

"Shouldn't you tell them to share it fairly?'' Jane slid from her saddle. She remembered the times she and her brother had fought over treats. Armed with her newfound contentment, she no longer battled to suppress memories of her family.

John shook his head. "It wouldn't occur to them to do anything else. Here at Sweetgrass the hunters bring back game for everyone in the village. The women make fry bread, and when mealtime comes everyone eats.''

Had any of the men who wrote those dime novels about savage, warlike Indians ever been west of the Mississippi? Jane wondered. Might she have grown into a different, stronger woman if she'd been born into a community like this one, where the whole group took responsibility for nurturing all its members?

They left their horses to graze, and John led Jane into a loose circle of tepees. Beside the smoldering embers of a large central fire, a group of older men sat talking. Around the camp, Jane could see four or five grandmotherly women doing chores, with cradleboards strapped to their backs. Two were scraping hair from an animal hide, another stirred something in a big cast-iron pot suspended over a smaller fire. Two more sat together talking over their beadwork. Fascinated, Jane took it all in.

One of the women spotted John and called out to him. He led Jane over to where she sat. He addressed the old woman in the language Jane sometimes heard him speak to Ruth. It had a pleasing staccato rhythm and, from what she could tell, employed a much narrower range of sounds than English. She did not need to understand John's words to recognize the tone of respect and affection in which they were uttered.

"Jane, this is my auntie, Walks on Ice." Was it her imagination, or did he look nervous making this introduction?

She had picked up a few words of Cheyenne from Ruth's conversation, but none of them seemed like an appropriate greeting, so Jane settled for smiling and nodding.

Walks on Ice was a tiny scrap of a woman. Jane doubted she'd needed much divine intervention to cross the thin ice of a thawing stream. John's aunt must have been a beauty, too, for her graying ebony hair was still lustrous and her high-cheeked features gave her a curiously aristocratic look.

The old woman acknowledged Jane with a cool but polite nod, and one dark eyebrow raised in a haughty stare worthy of Mrs. Olivia Endicott herself.

Suddenly Jane remembered the parcel in her hands. She knelt and held it out to Walks on Ice. "Ruth asked me to bring you these. Beads. Needles. Thread." She pointed to the women's handiwork.

A smile softening her features, Walks on Ice patted the ground beside her, inviting Jane to sit.

"Will you be all right here?" John hovered near. "I have to go talk with Bearspeaker and the other elders. The young men are out hunting and the young women are off gathering wood. They'll be back soon. So will the children, once they've eaten all the licorice.''

"I'll be fine.'' The ring of truth in her own words surprised Jane.

For a little while after John moved away to confer with the elders, she felt awkward and out of place. Then a small girl, not long out of the cradleboard, toddled over and plopped herself in Jane's lap. They fell into a game of peekaboo, then patty-cake. After a while more children joined them. Jane pillaged her memory for nursery songs with accompanying actions.

They crowded around her, touching her clothes and her hair. It made her a trifle nervous until she realized that these children might never have seen a woman with clothes and hair like hers. She traded them touch for curious touch, praising the lovely bead and quillwork on their clothing, telling them they were clever, strong, swift and handsome. They might not understand her English any more than she understood their language, but she hoped they would know the tone of a compliment when they heard it.

The sound of feminine laughter heralded the return of the younger women, with bundles of wood strapped to their backs and more in their arms. Some of the children ran to their mothers, talking excitedly and gesturing toward the white visitor. After they had unpacked their burden of fuel, the women came and sat near Jane and Walks on Ice. Pointing to them one by one, John's aunt made the introductions with grave formality, also signaling which of the children belonged to each mother.

Two of the youngest women brought everyone tin mugs full of a steaming beverage. Gingerly, Jane took a sip. It had a mellow sweetish taste, like sassafras tea.

Some of the women took up beadwork; some sewed

together pieces of tanned hide. One young woman suckled a small baby at her breast as Jane had seen Ruth do with Barton before she put him to bed. As they gossiped and laughed together, Jane let the bewitching melody of their language wash over her while she soaked up the novel sounds, smells and sights of the Cheyenne settlement.

She eyed the tall tepees with their frame poles tufted out above patchwork sheaths of stout buffalo hide. Slanted racks with animal skins stretched for tanning. Cosy cradleboards, whose breathtaking beadwork spoke volumes about how the Cheyenne treasured their babies.

As the molten-gold Montana sun made his slow arc across the Big Sky, he seemed to kiss the people of Sweetgrass with his blessing. And Jane wished she never had to leave.

John Whitefeather sat among the council of elders, listening to their warnings and complaints, nodding his head at strategic moments and frowning as if in deep, concerned thought. His true thoughts concerned Jane.

How soon he could steal his next glance across the camp at her without arousing notice. How amazingly well his kinswomen had accepted her. How very much he wanted to kiss her again and make the most intimate acquaintance of the tempting body she'd let him glimpse.

As he'd expected, Walks on Ice had not been very pleased to see him show up with a white woman in tow. She hadn't been bashful about telling him so, either. With a curt word, John had reminded her that he was the son of a white woman. In doing so, he also reminded himself.

Watching Jane sitting among the women, looking more at ease than he'd ever seen her, John recalled another beloved pale face and head of light-colored hair. Strangely, Jane's presence at Sweetgrass made him feel more at one with his band, just as it had made him less alien among the Kincaids. He'd brought her here to convince himself how futile it was to hanker after her. But his plan had misfired badly.

The return of the hunters a few hours after midday brought John a welcome distraction.

"We caught four rabbits in our traps," Red Stone announced, "and we shot an old stag of good size."

A murmur of approval ran through the council, and several of the women went off to help dress the carcasses. As the hunting party took seats among their fathers and uncles and accepted cups of tea, Red Stone shook his head.

"We bring a good kill, but also troubling news. The buffalo have moved north, looking for more plentiful water and greener forage. We must strike camp and follow them, or it will be a hungry winter."

"It is as I said," Bearspeaker reminded John. "We cannot stay in one place. We depend on the herds, at least the pitiful remains of the *ve'ho'e* wasteful slaughter."

John drew a deep breath. How could he make them see the world as the whites did? With property divided into neat parcels and held by individual owners, entitled to keep others off. At the point of a gun, if necessary.

"You told me the old stories yourself, Bearspeaker. How, long ago, the Cheyenne lived far to the east, growing corn and squash, living in permanent lodges. Then times changed. The Sioux came and pushed us west onto the Plains to follow the buffalo. Our people had to make homes of hides and poles that would travel with us. Now times have changed again, and we must change our way of living again."

The men grumbled among themselves and cast him reproachful looks that said *ve'ho'e*.

Part of John Whitefeather wanted to wash his hands of

the whole thing. He was tired of struggling to live between two such different worlds. His head ached from trying to balance two viewpoints, so completely opposed. His heart yearned to belong.

Let his kinsmen chase the herds until they ran into trouble with white settlers, and the government sent soldiers to slaughter them outright or kill them slowly in the prison camps called reservations. John could stop paying most everything he earned to William Kincaid's bank, and let Will foreclose on Sweetgrass. John could work and live just for himself.

Then he glanced up and caught Jane watching him. She did not blush and look away as she had so many times in the past few weeks. Instead she held his gaze and smiled. Her gentle, delicate face radiated admiration and encouragement. John could almost feel his heart melt within him.

He had heard that phrase used, but never understood it until this minute. He wasn't sure most English speakers did, either.

Like all elemental forces of change, melting hurt. It transformed something of solid strength, like ice or iron, into formless liquid that moved, flooded, swallowed. A wise man respected its power.

"Does it matter so much if we change our dwellings or what we eat?" he asked, knowing he had committed himself to their survival and there could be no turning back. "As long as we can keep our dances and our rituals and our language? Don't think of our boundaries as a prison. Think of them as a fortress."

"This is good land," agreed Red Stone. "Better than our brothers on the reservation must make do with. We have game and fish, wood for our fires. Soil that might grow crops. If you can get me seed, Night Horse, next spring I will plant. When the rains come, the buffalo will return.''

Some of the others still looked doubtful.

''Change is a fearful thing,'' John conceded. ''It takes great courage to embrace change, and great wisdom to decide what things we can change and what things we must cling to at any cost.''

If there was one quality his people prized about all others, it was courage. Make planting a seed or building a house sound like an act of bravery and they might be willing to try.

Did he have the courage to risk personal change? John wondered. Did a lone wolf who had spent his life prowling at the edge of the pack dare to seek a mate?

It scared him almost spitless to contemplate. Though not half as much as it scared him to think of handing Jane over to another man.

''What were you and the men talking about?'' Jane asked John as they rode back south, their stomachs full of fry bread and rabbit stew and Juneberry pudding.

''I was preaching the gospel of change.'' John's voice sounded weary and just a little bitter. ''Now I know why some of those Old Testament prophets they taught us about in residential school were so unpopular.''

''It's hard to give up doing what you're used to.'' She wasn't thinking about the Cheyenne, Jane realized, but herself. ''Even when the old ways aren't good for you, or they don't work anymore. It's like that saying, 'better the devil you know.' I saw a play once with Mrs. Endicott where the hero said fear of the unknown is so strong it makes us willing to suffer the troubles we have rather than run away from them and risk landing in something worse. I never forgot that.''

"Yet you left Boston to come all the way out to Montana. Are you really that much braver than you seem, Jane? Or were your troubles back there so bad they made it worth the risk?"

The sun had almost set behind the Crazy Mountains, lighting the horizon in shimmering bands of red and gold as spectacular as everything else in the Big Sky.

Jane wasn't sure she could find the courage to answer John's question. The other night she had flirted with baring her body to him. From a safe distance and completely on her own terms. Did she dare bare her ugly past and risk turning him away forever?

"You know," John murmured as if to himself, "the first time you got me talking about what happened to my folks, it was almost like living it over again. I dreamed about it that night and I was angry at you for making me remember."

She nudged her horse a little closer to his. "I'm sorry."

"Don't be. What I'm trying to say is I've thought about it since. Talked a little about it with Ruth. That's something I could never do before. Each time it gets a little easier, and I never would have found that out if you hadn't made me speak of it that first time."

Jane's heart seemed to swell within her until she wondered how her small body could contain it. Here was something more she could give this man who offered her so much. Not just the mundane things like a clean house and home-cooked meals. Not even the delicious mysteries of physical intimacy. Any woman could supply him with those.

She could give him balm for his wounded heart, because she too had known hurt and bereavement. And perhaps she could give him her trust, confident that he would recognize it for a fragile, precious treasure.

It cost her some effort to raise her voice above the soft beat of the horses' hooves and the intermittent clink of harness.

"John?"

"Yes?"

"I think I'm ready to tell you about Boston. It's more than just losing my family. It's everything that happened after."

"I understand." He sounded like he really did.

"Can it wait until we get back to the ranch?" She still wasn't comfortable enough on horseback that she wanted to risk losing her concentration. Tempting though it was to bare her scars under the comforting veil of darkness.

"Whenever you're ready."

"Could I come to your cabin after Ruth and Caleb have gone to bed?"

Why did a slight tremor of panic seize her as she murmured those words? She'd been alone with John before in the ranch house. Zeke and Barton hardly counted as chaperons. The day John had taken her riding she'd been alone with him, far from another living soul.

The thought of that small, dark cabin bothered her, though—exhuming memories of small dark rooms where Emery had taken her to be alone. Free to kiss her or to strike her, whichever took his fancy. She'd been as powerless against one as the other. And almost as frightened.

Swallowing a hard knot of panic in her throat, Jane heard an echo of that same sound from John before he spoke.

"If that's what you want."

Her fear drained away, like water spilled on parched earth. John had just articulated the key difference.

This would be her choice.

Off in the distance, the lights of the Kincaid homestead beckoned. A queer mixture of brooding, longing and eagerness welled up in Jane's heart.

Was this what homecoming felt like?

Chapter Twelve

From his early years on the move with the Cheyenne, John Whitefeather had a sense of home that didn't attach to any one location. The day he'd returned from residential school, the first whiff of smoke from the fires of his people had almost overwhelmed him. Tonight, for the first time, he felt a sense of homecoming as he approached the hearth lights of the Kincaids' ranch.

Was it because his sister and her family lived here? Or had his trickster heart adopted Jane as its new lodestar? He glanced over at her, admiring the fragile beauty of her silhouette, gilded by the light of a waxing midsummer moon.

From his cabin window, he had watched her let down her soft sorrel hair and strip away her clothing piece by piece. Tonight she would come to his cabin, let down her quivering defenses and strip away her secrets one by one. Then he would hold her and comfort her and begin courting her for himself.

Just the thought of it made him dizzy with delight and dread. What if she didn't come? What if he frightened her away again? What if she made it plain she didn't want him?

When they reached the stable, Jane made no move to dismount on her own, waiting patiently for John to lift her down. She felt so light in his arms, her waist so slender beneath the broad reach of his hands. By sweet, lingering degrees, he lowered her to the ground, savoring the subtle rub of her clothing against his. The closeness and the warmth. The delicacy of her scent, not completely overpowered by the familiar musk of horse and leather.

It was everything he could do not to press his face into the inviting swell of her bosom. Particularly when she canted into his embrace. He had no self-control left to resist when her lips came level with his.

He succumbed to their innocent temptation, pink and soft as bitterroot petals, sweeter than the last ripe clover of summer. Clasping Jane to him, he kissed her with all the tenderness she had called forth in his heart—from the very first minute she'd approached him in the saloon, battered and scared. More than anything in the world, he didn't want to frighten her away now.

So he cradled her close, one arm clasped around her waist, the other crooked beneath her arm, stretching across her back. That hand slipped under the nape of her bonnet to lose itself in her hair.

Barely conscious of a gentle tug at the back of his own head, he felt his hair falling free of the leather cord that bound it. The sensation of Jane's delicate fingers whispering through his mane like a warm Chinook almost drove John to his knees.

Then the pinto gelding shook his head and blew out a long, sighing breath.

Jane chuckled and John felt the delicious ripples of mirth run through her body. "The poor old fellow must be wondering if you're ever going to unharness and water him."

"Maybe he's wishing he was still a stallion." John nuzzled the downy curve of her cheek. "Getting up to all kinds of lusty mischief with a pretty mare."

"Is that what you're planning with me tonight—lusty mischief?" In her voice a light teasing note mingled with the huskiness of desire. But in her velvety hazel eyes, John detected a wistful shadow.

She'd promised him nothing more than to share a piece of her past, after all.

Touching his forehead to hers, he gazed deep into her eyes. "Miss Harris, you have my word as a Cheyenne warrior. My intentions toward you are entirely honorable."

"It's a good thing one of us has honorable intentions, Mr. Whitefeather. I fear it wouldn't take too many of your kisses to turn me quite wanton."

A pair of delicious dimples blossomed on either side of her lips. Had he never been close enough to notice them before—or had he steeled his senses against their appeal? Now his imagination churned like white water, dreaming up a hundred ways to coax them out in the future.

The gelding threw back his head and whinnied.

"All right, I'm coming." John let his precious burden slide the rest of the way to the ground, though his hands ached to tarry beneath her backside and scoop her up again.

Plenty of time for that later.

He enfolded Jane, reaching one hand up to pull her bonnet back. Then he bent forward until his cheek rested against her hair.

"Promise you'll come back?"

Her face nestled against his chest, so his heart heard her reply first. "As soon as Ruth and Caleb go to bed."

"I hope Caleb's good and tired from his trip."

"So do I."

They drifted apart, slow, reluctant inches at a time until one backward step broke the last contact between their fingertips. John held on to a stirrup of the gelding's saddle, letting the horse tow him away from Jane. He wasn't sure he could force his own feet to leave her.

She retreated from him, walking backward so their eyes could continue to play over one another, when hands could not.

When she took that final step out of his view, John shook himself as if waking from a trance. He unsaddled both the horses with fumbling hands, giving them extra oats and water to compensate for his clumsy haste.

For the first time since coming to the Kincaid ranch, his feet itched to get back to the foreman's cabin at the end of the day. He wanted to make it ready for Jane. Kindle a welcoming fire in the hearth. Make sure the fleece rug was spread and everything still tidy from Ruth's cleanup.

A faint aroma of sweetgrass hung in the still, dark air when John entered the cabin and groped his way toward the stone fireplace. After fumbling on the mantel for matches, he struck a light to a small mound of tinder, then added a few thin sticks from the wood box to get the fire going. He made the round of his quarters, smoothing the quilt on his bed, arranging and rearranging the chairs, hanging up his hat.

Perhaps he should run down to the creek for a quick bath? He'd have plenty of time before Jane came, wouldn't he?

John glanced through his window toward hers. No light up there yet. She must still be in the kitchen telling Ruth about their day at Sweetgrass.

Sitting down on the bed, he pried off his boots, then tossed his socks into them. While he added a couple more substantial pieces of wood to the fire, he tugged open the buttons of his shirt.

A firm knock at the door made him jump, and set his heart racing. Jane's bedroom must have been dark because she was on her way here.

"You almost missed me." John pulled open the door. "I was just about to—Caleb, what are you doing here?"

Caleb Kincaid looked his brother-in-law up and down, his eyes lingering longest on John's unbound hair and open shirt. "You expecting somebody else?"

"Yes. No!" John fumbled with his shirt buttons. "Well, I thought Ruth might want to hear the news from Sweet-grass…maybe. How was your trip?"

"Everybody in the Stock Growers Association is worried about this drought, of course. But that's not why I'm here. Do you mind if I come in?"

"Yes…I mean, no." John stepped out of Caleb's way so he could enter. "Can't it wait until tomorrow?"

Caleb hauled one of the wooden chairs out from the table and sat down. "I thought it could, John." He pulled a folded envelope from the breast pocket of his shirt. "Until Jane Harris waltzed into our kitchen all dreamy eyed and looking suspiciously like a gal who'd been kissed real good."

"Now hang on, Caleb. I can explain about—"

"Just have a seat and listen to what I've got to tell you." Caleb drew a piece of paper from the envelope. "Then we can talk about you and Miss Harris…if you still care to, that is."

John didn't like Caleb's tone. Part of him wanted to run out of the cabin, swing Jane up behind him on the back of a horse and ride away from whatever bad news that letter contained. But, as he'd told Bearspeaker and the other elders at this afternoon's council, ignoring trouble never made it go away. Sooner or later it would find a fellow, so he might as well stand and face it.

Jerking the other chair out from the table, he dropped onto the seat. "Let's hear it."

Now that John was ready to listen, Caleb looked reluctant to speak. "I'm sorry about this, old friend." He turned the paper over and over in his hands. "It's best you know, though. It's best we all know."

John wished he could be sure of that. "What is it we should know?"

"I haven't told Ruth yet. She's going to be upset about it, too. You recollect that wire I sent to the police in Boston? Well, I finally got an answer back."

"Where's Caleb off to?" Jane settled into one of the kitchen chairs and took a sip from the cup of tea Ruth had poured for her.

"He wanted to talk to John about something. Business from the Stock Growers Association, most likely." Ruth glanced up from her beadwork. "Men! I don't imagine it's anything they can do much about tonight. How's everybody out at Sweetgrass?"

"The children all seemed well." Jane smiled to herself, remembering the songs and games they'd shared. "Everyone had a good appetite that I could see. Walks on Ice said to thank you for everything you sent. At least I'm pretty sure that's what she said."

Ruth smiled and nodded, but her expression immediately turned serious again. "I worry what will happen if we don't get some rain soon. If the water in their creek gets much lower, I'm afraid it'll turn brackish and folks will start to sicken."

"The elders are worried because the buffalo have moved north off of Sweetgrass land."

"Staying in one place isn't going to be easy for them."
Ruth sighed. "I hope they didn't complain to John too
much."

"For a minute there, I thought he was going to lose his
temper, or just walk away, but he stayed and they talked
some more. I think they're only willing to do what he
suggests because they trust him."

"They should. He's a good man, especially after all he's
been through."

Jane fought the urge to nod. She wasn't sure she wanted
Ruth to guess how much she knew about John's past.

"I just wish…" Ruth stared hard at her beadwork, but
her needle didn't move. "I wish he didn't carry the weight
of the whole band on his shoulders every minute of the
day."

Though she knew Ruth wasn't expecting any response
from her, Jane did nod this time. She didn't like the
thought of John being weighed down by so much responsibility. Then again, if he hadn't proved himself such a
caring man, would she have let him burrow so deeply into
her heart?

Perhaps she could help lighten his cares, if he would let
her.

A yawn tugged Jane's mouth open and she exaggerated
it for Ruth's sake. "All that fresh air makes a person
sleepy. Guess I'd better turn in."

Ruth glanced toward the door. "I hope Caleb won't be
much longer. He'll be tired after being away. He never
sleeps well in a hotel bed. Speaking of hotels, Caleb and
I are planning to go into town later this week, and we'd
like you to come along. We'll have a real fancy meal in
the dining room of the Carlton Hotel. I'm sure it'll make
you feel like you're back home in Boston."

"That's kind of you both." Jane drained the last of her tea. "But, truly, I don't hanker after Boston one bit."

"If you say so." Ruth shook her head. "I can't imagine pulling up stakes and going so far from home, then *not* hankering for it. Anyway, there's somebody in town we'd like you to meet."

"Of course, Ruth. You and Caleb have been so good to me, I'll do anything I can to oblige you." Jane took her teacup over to the washtub and rinsed it out. "Now I'd better get off to bed. Good night."

"Good night, dear. Don't worry about getting up too early tomorrow morning after the long day you've had."

Where would the morning find her? Jane wondered as she climbed the stairs to her bedroom with a light, waltzing step. The way John had kissed her when he'd helped her off her horse made her suspect he'd let her stay with him as long as she wanted.

She searched through Marie's trunk again and found a dress she'd buried at the very bottom. A light, lacy pink confection of a gown, it looked too frivolous for any occasion on the Montana frontier. Imagine wearing such attire to a barn raising or a basket social!

Marie probably would have hankered for the ballrooms of Boston, but the poor silly creature must have been miserable on the Kincaid ranch. Hard as she tried to imagine a woman like that wed to a rugged rancher like Caleb Kincaid, Jane just couldn't picture it.

Remembering Caleb, she glanced out her window to see if he might still be visiting with John. When she caught a glimpse of him walking back to the ranch house, she had to stifle a whoop of glee. Soon the Kincaids would be tucked up in bed and she could go to John.

In a rush, she shed her riding clothes and performed a quick wash with the small puddle of cold water in the bottom of her ewer. As her skin rose in goose bumps and the nipples of her breasts puckered, she wondered if it was due to the water's chill or her anticipation. By the time she had put on Marie's dress and brushed her long hair out, the way John seemed to like it, Jane heard the quiet tread of footsteps on the stairs and the murmur of voices.

She blew out her candle and waited for the footsteps to pass her door. It seemed to take the longest time for Ruth and Caleb to walk down the hall and enter their own room. Once they had, Jane counted to a thousand to give them time to settle. Then she turned her doorknob slowly and softly. Pushing her door ajar inch by inch, she paused anytime the hinges threatened to squeal.

Once out in the darkened hallway, Jane closed the door behind her with the same painstaking care, then tiptoed down the stairs and groped her way to the kitchen. Only when she found herself out in the cool night air beneath a swath of twinkling stars did Jane expel an easy breath. She flew the few steps to the foreman's cabin, lured like a rose-colored moth to the friendly light of his fire.

When she tapped softly on his door, no one answered. Perhaps the crackle from the hearth had drowned her out.

She knocked again, louder this time. Still John did not open to her. Had he gone out after Caleb's departure…to check on a horse or something?

Jane tried the knob. It turned. John wouldn't want her hanging around outside, faintly visible from the house if anyone should look this way.

Pushing the door open, she slipped inside.

For an instant, the dead stillness in the cabin made Jane think it must be empty. Then John raised his head and looked at her.

With a strangled squeak she jumped back, one hand rising instinctively to her thundering heart. Then she laughed at her own foolishness.

"You frightened me. When you didn't answer my knocks, I thought you must have gone out. Did you not hear me?"

He continued to stare at her, as if seeing her for the first time. Was there something wrong with the way she looked? His eyes glittered like the fast-flowing, icy water of that upland stream.

And he didn't answer.

"John, what's wrong? Did Caleb bring bad news from Miles City?"

"Oh, he brought news, all right." John's voice had the harshness of a cracking bullwhip. "A letter from your fiancé back in Boston. Is that what you came here to tell me, Jane? That you wormed your way into a man's heart so you could steal from his family? That you don't want to go back to Boston because you're a thief on the run?"

Jane began to tremble. Emery knew she was here.

But that was not the worst of her troubles.

The worst was that John Whitefeather had learned the truth about her past. And he hated her for it.

"Did you really mean to come here, or did you have to change plans quickly when you lost your loot in that train wreck?" John squirmed a little in his chair, furious with himself that Jane Harris still had the power to rouse him now that he knew the truth about her.

His mind hammered with questions and his heart writhed from the sting of her betrayal. His pride smarted, too, because he'd been so easily deceived.

It wasn't as though there hadn't been plenty of signs if he'd been shrewd enough to read them. Jane's evasiveness about her past and the circumstances of her arrival in

Whitehorn. Her insistence on not returning to Boston. The nagging sense that she was always looking over her shoulder.

Caleb had been wise to her from the beginning. He hadn't been fooled by her fluttering, helpless act. Dr. Gray, Reverend McWhirter and Henry Hill probably would have seen through her soon enough, too. No wonder she'd been so nervous around them.

Here John had been congratulating himself on winning Jane's trust where they'd all failed, when he'd clearly been her target all along—the dumb Indian, too simple to see through her wiles.

Had the brutal lessons of life taught him nothing? *Ve'ho'e* were tricksters, always presenting to the world a face at odds with the heart. They were earnest negotiators of treaties written to be broken. Fatherly Indian agents who stripped children from their families. Self-righteous teachers who corrupted the students they were pretending to *civilize*.

He'd been worse than a fool to accept Jane Harris at face value, especially since that face was so full of contradictions. The timid little mouse who'd braved a solitary journey clear across the country to settle in a place still wild and dangerous by Eastern standards. Desperate for a job to mind children and keep house, when she clearly had little experience with either. Going out of her way to cultivate a friendship with the rancher's half-breed brother-in-law, whom most other whites politely shunned.

If any harm had come to Ruth or her family because he'd failed in proper brotherly vigilance, John knew he would never have forgiven himself.

All these thoughts and emotions scoured through him as he waited for Jane to answer. What could be taking her so long to find her voice? Was she spinning a fresh web of lies to patch the holes he'd blown in her first ones?

"There wasn't any train wreck." This sounded more like the truth.

Had Jane just gotten more cunning, or was he still so deeply in her thrall that he was willing to believe anything?

Her skin had paled, growing as white as the first snow of the Hard Face Moon. In her pink cobweb of a dress, with her hair falling around her shoulders, she looked younger and more vulnerable than ever. John sternly reminded himself it was all a cynical act.

"I lied about it to explain my injuries and having no luggage. I didn't lose anything, because there was nothing to lose."

"So you're saying you never stole anything from this Mrs. Endicott? I'm surprised you told us her real name. Guess you figured a bunch of bumpkins on the frontier would be too dumb to check out your story."

Jane wrapped her arms around herself. "Very well. I did take that brooch of Mrs. Endicott's. I know it was a wicked thing to do, and I never would have done it if I hadn't needed the money for my train ticket. It wasn't one of her most expensive ones, or one she liked best."

Nothing in the letter from Emery Endicott mentioned the extent of Jane's theft, only that she'd stolen jewelry from her former employer. John's sense of fair-mindedness chastised him for jumping to the conclusion that she'd cleaned the old lady out.

He ignored the call of his better nature. Jane Harris had played him for a fool. Made him believe he was the first and only man she'd ever cared about. If he'd been ruthlessly honest with himself, John might have admitted that's what galled him worse than her theft or her lies. The fact that she had already run away from one man who cared about her.

And he'd been ready to lay his heart at her feet so she could trample it into the dust.

"So you admit you did steal from Mrs. Endicott." John crossed his arms in front of his chest, just in case one of those fool winged babies might still be flying around with a quiver full of arrows. "What made you so all-fired desperate to get out of Boston? And what really happened to your face and your luggage?"

She took a step toward him. Then, heeding the threat in his eyes, she retreated again.

"That's what I came here to tell you, tonight." Her voice rose to a brittle pitch and her lower lip began to quiver.

That was the last straw.

He jabbed his forefinger at her. "If I see you dare shed so much as one tear, woman, I swear I'll toss you out that door and let Caleb and Ruth deal with you any way they see fit."

Jane turned her back on him. Her slender frame shook in silence and she drew several shuddering breaths before dragging one hand across her eyes and facing him again.

"I know I haven't given you much reason to believe me, and maybe I shouldn't care if you do or not. I came to Whitehorn with only the clothes on my back because I ran away from the infirmary before I was officially discharged. Mrs. Endicott came to visit me there and I noticed the brooch on her shawl. When she stepped out to talk to the doctor for a minute, she left the shawl hanging on the chair by my bed. I didn't have much time to weigh the rights and wrongs of it. All I knew was that I had to get away from Emery, and I thought I'd have a job with Ruth and Caleb if only I could get to Whitehorn."

He wanted so badly to believe her it was like poisoned honey on his tongue. But she'd reminded him of yet another clumsy lie. Surely she'd had time to concoct a more probable story since then.

"This is all a bit twisted for a poor, ignorant horse trainer to follow. You see, I can't reckon for the life of me how you knew you *had* a letter from Caleb without knowing he and Ruth didn't want to hire you."

The fire had burned low. John strode to the hearth and hurled a couple more logs onto it. A smoldering bit of wood popped, sending sparks flying.

Behind him he heard Jane whisper, "Emery got hold of Caleb's letter. He burned it right in front of me before I had a chance to read it. Then he…beat me. That's how I ended up in the infirmary. I told the doctors I'd fallen down stairs. I'd had lots of practice at lying about my injuries. Once you get used to doing that, it's hard to stop."

John felt as if he'd swallowed a shovelful of red-hot coals from the fire. Slowly he turned to Jane.

"How do I know you *didn't* hurt yourself in a train wreck or falling down stairs?" Especially if that's what he wanted to believe. "How do I know *this* story isn't just another lie?"

Jane swept her hair back. Then she pulled down the short puffy sleeves of her dress to bare her shoulders. As she walked toward him, John found himself retreating until his back pressed against the stones on one side of the fireplace.

"Tell me how I could have gotten these marks by falling down stairs, John."

The haunted look in her eyes told him the truth. But John still forced himself to look at her delicate white flesh marred by two crescent-shaped scars on the front and eight smaller matching ones on the back.

He struggled to breathe.

Even stripped of all her clothes, that night at her bedroom window, she had not looked so completely exposed.

She drew a shuddering breath. ''I suppose you wonder why I didn't tell you about this sooner.''

John shook his head. ''I understand why you kept it a secret.'' He tugged open the buttons on his shirt. ''I reckon I must be the biggest fool in the world for not guessing.''

As he pulled his shirt off, Jane backed away from him. John dropped to his knees to give her a better view.

''I won't touch you, Jane, I swear. Just look. Then you can go if you want. Or stay.''

She took a wary step toward him. Now that he understood what had happened to her, John knew what courage that step took.

Jane raised her hand, pushing a few strands of his long dark hair off his shoulders. With a touch as gentle as a prayer, her fingertips traced the slender white scars on his bronzed skin.

Chapter Thirteen

The thin ridges of scarring on John's shoulders seared Jane's fingertips.

"Who?" The word almost choked her. "Who did this to *you?*"

Kneeling before her, John looked up into her face, his breathtaking eyes truly unmasked to her for the first time. "A teacher at residential school in Saint Louis. The Indian agent sent me there after my parents were killed. Bruises, black eyes, even broken bones healed. This left scars that still show. My Cheyenne friends probably wondered why I always wore a cotton shirt in the summer instead of going bare chested, like them."

Jane expelled a long, quivering breath. No wonder she'd felt such a bond with this man and he with her. On some level deeper than words or actions, even deeper than old hurts and defenses, they had recognized and called to one another. Understood each other as no one else ever had or could.

The helplessness. The secrets. The shame.

"Does anyone else know?" She could not coax her voice above a whisper.

When he shook his head, she was not surprised.

"I told myself it was a test of my courage not to cry out. But in my heart I felt less than a man for not fighting back."

"You weren't a man." She clasped him to her bosom, letting his hair graze her cheek. "You were just a little boy. Not much older than Zeke. I had so much better chance to fight back, but I was too frightened to take it until Emery left me no choice."

John's arms slipped around her waist, strong and warm but infinitely gentle. Through the flimsy fabric of her dress, Jane felt the delicious heat of his bare chest against her belly...and below. The sweetly scalding vapor of his breath against her bosom.

"Oh, Jane. What can I do to make you forgive me for doubting you?" He sounded more grieved about that than about the old, tainted wounds that she'd reopened.

Her body ached and burned with the mystery of what she wanted from him. Did she dare ask for it?

"You can start by...kissing me. And touching me. All over. You can teach me what a man and woman do together. The thing that makes their eyes soften and their lips curve into a sly little smile when they remember it."

She wasn't asking him for promises or protection, though in her heart she yearned for both. Right now all she wanted was to erase the memory of Emery's violent hands with something wondrously different. "Will you do that for me, John?"

"Taa'evâhe'hame."

"What does that mean?"

"It's my Cheyenne name, Night Horse. Do you think you could learn to call me that...sometimes?"

She knew what he meant. At special times. Intimate times. Like tonight would be.

"Taa...?"

They practiced it together as their hands explored and their bodies welcomed the exploration.

Taa'evâhe'hame. Jane said it over and over until she forgot every other word she'd ever known.

She spoke it in a beseeching whisper at first, like a novice rider warily prodding her mount to a walk. He responded by unfastening the hooks of her dress at a deft, deliberate pace until she wanted to scream in anticipation.

She purred it deep in her throat as the lacy garment melted off her body and he pressed his hot, tender lips to her neck, her scarred shoulders and the rounded tops of her breasts. Purging her ugly memories of Emery's violence. Healing less visible wounds.

She gasped it as he lowered her onto the fleece rug. With the firm, bronzed flesh of his torso bathed in flickering firelight and his long dark hair falling free, he was the most magnificent male creature Jane had ever imagined. He silenced her with a deep, potent kiss that set her blood ablaze.

And his. With restraint and patience burned away to ashes, he grappled with the hooks on her corset and feasted on her breasts. She arched to meet his mouth, plunging her hands into his hair. Urging him closer, deeper.

The leaping flames in the hearth consumed the dead wood with a low, sensuous crackle and hiss. The banked fire of their passion purged the lovers' fear and mistrust. It fueled their power and kindled their special gifts. When his lips were free, which was not often, he crooned a continuous Cheyenne litany of her beauties.

And she understood every word.

They shed the rest of their clothes with lazy urgency and reveled in the contrast of her flesh against his. Hers the color of milk warm from a woman's breast. His the hue of juicy roasted meat and bread hot from the fire. Her rounded softness and his taut, lean strength. Her vulnerable delicacy and his fierce, restrained might.

She spread her legs as though astride a horse's broad barrel and keened for something she could not name or imagine. With his fingers, lips and tongue, he set wild pleasure galloping through her. Nostrils flared, silky mane tossing, she bucked beneath him again and again until a high ecstatic cry broke from her.

As she lay there, heavy limbed and sated, he mounted and eased himself into her. When he balked, hovering above her like a ripe, hot summer night, she urged him on.

"I won't, Jane. This is going to hurt you and I don't ever want to do that."

"Will it hurt every time?"

Her body ached for him all over again. Her shattering release had bordered on pain in its intensity. Perhaps *that* was the mystery of this intimate rite. By some blissful alchemy it forged golden pleasure from the dross of pain.

"Only the first. Then maybe a little until you get used to it."

She caressed his face and strained to reach his lips with hers. "Then don't stop. Please. I choose this. I want you."

Like a gathering storm, the muscles of his loins tightened and he bent almost double to clamp his lips on hers. Then he thrust past the flimsy resistance of her virginity and filled her with raw, life-giving energy.

John hadn't lied to her—it hurt. Though Jane gripped a fistful of his hair, she refused to give voice to her pain. What Emery had inflicted on her had robbed Jane of so much—security, confidence, trust. In some mysterious way, John's lovemaking had begun to restore what she'd lost.

When he drew back from their kiss, his gaze searching

hers, Jane swiftly covered his lips with her hand. She could not let him spoil this wonder with foolish words of regret.

"Some things are worth the hurt, *Taa'evâhe'hame,*" she murmured. "And this is one of them."

Taa'evâhe'hame. Night Horse. John Whitefeather. He was no longer sure of his name, or the time of day, or whether his heart and lungs still worked.

Nor did he care.

He only knew he had a willing woman beneath him. A woman who set his body on fire. A woman who helped him unravel the baffling riddle of his heart. A woman who gave him his first true taste of belonging—to their very own nation of two.

When she tensed against his entry and stifled a cry, his heart begged him to stop, as fiercely as his body urged him to continue. Her husky murmur of reassurance roused him all over again. Cautiously he drew back, then pressed ahead, the exquisite friction whetting his desire to a pitch sharper than Spanish spurs.

He wanted to lose himself in a tangle of limbs, questing mouths and mingled breath. Jane wriggled beneath him and her lips grazed his chest, mouthing his name. Together they moved to the rapid drumroll of their hearts. Harder. Faster.

A stampede of unbridled pleasure overtook them. Plunging. Wheeling. Rearing. They were borne to the stars by the elemental forces they had given free rein.

John clung to the saddle horn of consciousness just long enough to roll onto his back, taking Jane with him. Then his body stopped obeying him and his heart knew true peace for the first time in many long years. His thoughts wandered, almost in a dream vision, aware of little in the earth world but the comforting warmth and weight of Jane draped over him.

Later, as dawn began to break over the Big Sky, she stirred. Lifted her face to his, like a prairie flower to the rising sun, for the morning kiss that would bring her to life.

She ran her smooth white hand over the dark stubble on his cheek and gazed at him with those enormous hazel eyes. Eyes the rich brown of earth and bread, mingled with the vital green of forest and prairie. This morning, frets of shimmering gold danced in them, too. Splinters of magic, left from last night?

"How do the Cheyenne say 'thank you'?"

"*Néá'ese.* Why?"

"*Néá'ese, Taa'evâhe'hame.* For giving me what I asked, and so much more."

In the sweet hours of flame-kissed darkness, when he and Jane had become a nation of two, his Cheyenne name had been a sort of mystic incantation. Now, in the cool light of morning, it held the shadowy power of a curse. What would the elders say if they knew what he'd done?

His father's people did not consider the mating of a man and woman dirty or shameful, as many whites seemed to. For the Cheyenne it was a select activity, reserved exclusively for marriage. They prized chastity in unwed girls, encouraged long, modest courtships and expected husbands and wives to be faithful all their lives. None of that had entered John's mind last night. Proof, perhaps, that his heart was not as truly Cheyenne as he'd always claimed.

Jane had not demanded any commitment from him when she'd offered herself. Though she had been engaged to that cowardly monster back in Boston, John knew beyond a doubt that he was her first and only partner.

That left only one honorable course open to him.

His heart welcomed it, eager to charge ahead. His reason shied from taking a risk he'd flirted with embracing just last night. The letter from Boston, and all that had followed it, had sown poisonous doubts in his heart.

Marriage to Jane would be like trying to ford a surging, swollen river. So many dangerous currents pulling at them. So many sharp rocks on which swift-moving events might dash them. Contrary as it seemed, if he cared for her *less*, he might have been more willing to risk it.

He kissed her again, stalling for time so he could think. And so she would not see the dark clouds of doubt gathering in his eyes. Oh, but when he kissed her and wrapped her in his arms, he *couldn't* think. Nor could he remember any of the reasons why a union between them would be doomed from the start.

Jane subsided against him. "You're the most comfortable bed I've ever slept on." She chuckled and the vibration of her body on his made him dizzy with delight.

"Well, I reckon you're the warmest blanket I've ever slept under." He'd spent his whole life being sober and serious. Why had no one ever told him how good it felt to spout fond nonsense like this?

From outside came the first distant sounds of the ranch waking to a new day. A dog barking. Someone splitting kindling for the stoves. Cookie banging on the bell to call the ranch hands for breakfast. The real world threatened the borders of his and Jane's tiny private nation.

She shivered for the first time all night. "How am I going to get back into the house without Ruth and Caleb knowing I've been here all night?"

"Don't worry." Was he talking to her or to himself? "Caleb's probably gone by now, and I can keep Ruth busy in the kitchen while you slip in the door by the parlor."

What would his sister say when she found out about this? John's warrior courage almost deserted him at the thought.

"It won't likely matter much." Jane sighed. "After Emery's letter, I expect they'll turn me out today, anyhow."

She burrowed deeper into John's embrace and her voice took on a scared, hunted note. "Could Caleb show that letter to the sheriff and make him send me back to Boston to face charges?"

"Hush, now, hush." John stroked her hair. No wonder she'd been so skittish when she'd arrived in Whitehorn, wary of trusting anyone. "I'll talk to Ruth and Caleb about that letter. I'll tell them what you told me. Some of it, anyhow. When they stop for a minute and think, I know they'll take your word over that bast—that *ve'ho'e* back East."

"Emery!" Jane looked up into John's eyes. He could feel her heart racing, but not the exciting way it had raced last night. "Now that he knows I'm here, what if he takes it into his head to come after me?"

How desperately she needed someone to protect her. That urge swelled in John's heart, almost overpowering him. But at the same time a poisonous suggestion of doubt hissed in the back of his mind.

Had Jane offered him her body last night in hopes of snaring herself a protector?

All her old fears threatened to overwhelm Jane, but they didn't quite manage to. Even Emery lost some of his power to intimidate her when she rested in the charmed circle of John Whitefeather's protective arms.

If only she could stay here forever.

"Shh." John's voice comforted her as no sound ever had. "Don't worry. I'll get Caleb to wire Endicott that you've already moved on. I won't let him hurt you ever again."

How could John promise her such a thing? Unless...he

meant to be a part of her life forever? The blissful possibility left Jane breathless.

She hadn't thought of it last night. She hadn't thought of anything past her astonished recognition of their common bond and her undeniable desire for this man. In the cold light of day, it seemed the perfect solution to all her problems.

By some miraculous providence, she had found a man she could trust never to hurt her. One who was also strong enough to protect her from the rest of the world. If she was his wife, an entire regiment of Bismarck widows couldn't displace her from the Kincaid ranch. She'd be part of the family she had come to love. A sister to Ruth. A doting aunt to Barton and Zeke.

It wouldn't be a completely lopsided partnership, either, with John giving her so much and gaining nothing in return. She would look after him, feather the kind of cosy nest this wild hawk craved in his deepest heart. Give him the children he'd been destined to father. Soothe his darkest wounds and share his most secret joys.

And when the sun faded from the Big Sky and the ghost lights of a million stars glittered in the Montana heavens, she would make him tremble and sweat and cry in ecstasy. As he had done during their very first mating.

Wouldn't that be a more than fair exchange?

As he continued to stroke her hair, Jane vowed she'd never pin it up again.

John's body tensed ever so slightly beneath her. "Maybe you ought to tell me a little bit more about how you came to Mrs. Endicott's house and got yourself engaged to Emery—so I can convince Ruth and Caleb not to believe the things he wrote in his letter."

Jane didn't want to talk about her past. Didn't want to befoul her tongue by speaking Emery Endicott's name. But if it would keep her lying here in John's arms, lulled by the strong, steady beat of his heart, she would say or do just about anything.

"Mrs. Endicott was Mama's godmother. Like the rest of the family, she cut Mama off when Mama married a man they considered unsuitable. They were wrong, though. Papa wasn't rich but he was a good man. And when he was home, he made Mama very happy."

"And when he wasn't home?"

Jane hesitated. "That was harder. Mama had been looked after all her life. She found it hard to manage when he was at sea. After his ship was lost, she sort of gave up on life. I tried to help her and so did Ches, my brother, but I guess we couldn't make up for Papa being gone."

All her life she'd never quite measured up. First being a girl, who could never follow Papa to sea, like Ches would one day. Then watching her mother fade away, and feeling guilty that she hadn't been an important enough reason for Emily Harris to keep on living.

"After Ches died and she got sick, Mama wrote Mrs. Endicott, begging her to give me a home."

"I guess I didn't understand." John's voice rumbled through his chest, where Jane's head rested. "I thought you worked for this Mrs. Endicott."

"I did, from the very first. I guess legally I was her ward, but she treated me more like a servant. An unpaid companion and nurse. I suppose it's ungrateful of me to complain. Who knows where I'd have ended up if Mrs. Endicott hadn't taken me in? I always had enough to eat and warm clothes and a roof over my head."

"I had those at the residential school, too." John *did* understand—everything. "That didn't stop me from stealing a horse and running away after three years. That's how

I earned my name. Because I rode west at night and hid during the day.''

He'd stolen a horse and she'd stolen a brooch, both to escape an intolerable life and search for something better in the West. Another strong link had been forged in the invisible chain that bound them together.

"I didn't have the gumption to run away." If she'd been standing, Jane would have hung her head. "I used to worry a lot about what would happen to me if Mrs. Endicott died. She had so many complaints and ailments, I expected it almost daily. I guess that's what made me accept Emery when he proposed. I thought it might be the only way I could stay there. I did love that house—most of it, at least. And the neighborhood and the servants. It had been my home for a good many years."

"Did you love him? Before he started to hurt you, I mean." John's voice had a threatening edge. Could he be jealous?

The idea seemed ludicrous to Jane, but it also gave her hope for a future with him. Then again, Emery had been insanely jealous of her interest in other men. It hadn't meant he'd loved her.

Jane shook her head, ashamed to admit she'd been ready to marry a man she didn't love, just to keep a roof over her head. "I thought I did, in the beginning. He was the first man—the first *person* to show much of an interest in me. And I didn't know any other men to compare him with. I barely remembered what Papa had been like, and I couldn't bring myself to think much about him."

She fought against the tightness in her throat to continue. "Emery and I had to keep our engagement a secret because Mrs. Endicott wanted her nephew to marry a better sort of girl. It seemed romantic to me that he was willing to marry me in spite of his aunt—though, of course, we knew we'd have to wait until after she passed on, or she'd disinherit him.''

Jane lofted a swift glance at John's face. Could he understand why she'd promised herself to someone like Emery Endicott, when she could scarcely fathom it herself?

"Last night, you told me you'd had lots of practice lying about your injuries. Did Endicott…hurt you often?" John's jaw tightened and his eyes gleamed like the strange blue light at the heart of a flame.

Jane gave a bitter laugh. "I guess that depends on what you mean by 'often.' Not every week—sometimes a month or more would go by. There were times I wished he'd strike me with his hands instead of his words. Bruises on your skin heal so much faster. I just knew if I said anything to Mrs. Endicott, she'd believe Emery instead of me. He was her own nephew, after all, and I was only…''

Cold, severe, fault-finding Mrs. Endicott. Though subtler than her nephew, she'd managed to erode Jane's sense of self-worth to the point where she was grateful for the attentions of a man bent on destroying her.

Unearthing these memories hurt far more than when John had thrust into her that first time, but Jane forced herself to continue. John would need every scrap of ammunition she could give him to convince Ruth…and especially Caleb.

"I don't remember quite when I decided to run away. I had a little money, but not enough to live on, so I knew I needed a job. I started checking the employment notices in the papers Mrs. Endicott's cousin sent us from Saint Louis. I sent off several letters, but I never heard back from any of them…until one came from Whitehorn. The mail was late that day and Emery saw the letter. He flew into a rage and burned it before I could read it. I thought he was going to kill me. I could hardly believe it when I woke up in the infirmary. I knew I couldn't go back to that house, for the next time I might not be so lucky."

"So you took the brooch off Mrs. Endicott's shawl and sold it for train fare?"

Jane nodded. "I was so worried that someone here would find out about what I'd done, or that Emery might come after me. But as I got to know you and Ruth, I felt so wicked for deceiving you. I planned to tell you…some of this last night, even before you saw Emery's letter. You'd been so kind to me the past while, I figured you might understand."

"Bet you never thought I'd understand *this* well." John held her tight and drew a deep breath. "I reckon there's only one more matter to settle before we get up and face the day."

He sounded so solemn.

Jane mouth went dry as ashes. "What matter?"

"The matter of you and me." His voice sounded strange. Hesitant…fearful? "Lord knows, I don't have much to offer a wife. Pretty well everything I make goes to William's bank to pay off the mortgage on Sweetgrass. If you don't mind sharing what's left, I promise I'll always look after you and make sure no one ever hurts you again. If you'll be my…wife?"

Had she heard right?

"You mean it?" She looked him full in the face, praying she hadn't imagined his proposal.

John nodded. "Every word."

He hadn't said anything about love, and the majestic blue of his eyes seemed strangely clouded. What did that matter? Perhaps the Cheyenne didn't think of love in the same terms white folks did. What they felt in their hearts was still the same. Who could blame the man if he entertained a little uncertainty? Events had propelled them toward this moment so swiftly, it might take a little getting used to.

He'd waited a long time to take a wife. Perhaps he'd never intended to. *She* had made this handsome, wise, courageous man ready to commit the rest of his life to her. Jane glowed with the wonder of it. For the first time in her life, she had not only measured up, but eclipsed every other woman John Whitefeather had ever known.

She shoved aside the doubts that threatened to steal her joy. "I'd be honored."

They kissed to seal their pledge.

Their lips refused to disengage. Longer and deeper they kissed, breathing fresh ardor over the glowing coals of last night's passion. Jane sensed the heat and need building between her thighs and felt the straining evidence of John's desire pressing against them.

Parting her legs, she lowered herself onto him. True to John's promise, it didn't hurt at all this time. It felt wonderful.

A cry, something between a gasp and groan, broke from his lips. "Mmm, what are you up to, woman?"

Jane grinned. Never had she felt so light of spirit and yet so powerful, holding a large, vigorous man captive beneath her.

"I'm not *up* to anything," she purred with mock innocence. "I'm just trying to learn how to read a person's body movements the way you do. I had a silly notion your body was inviting me to do this. Maybe I misunderstood."

She raised her hips, then eased them down again, savoring the delicious sensations that skittered through her.

"No...I reckon...you understood just fine."

"That's good." She began a leisurely, rhythmic thrust of her hips. "I also wanted to make sure if...oh...this was the kind of, mmm, activity you could…ah…tolerate on a regular basis.''

Her husband-to-be didn't reply. At least not in words that meant anything in either English or Cheyenne. But as he writhed beneath her and they shuddered together in blissful waves of release, Jane got the answer she'd been hoping for.

Chapter Fourteen

"Answer me, *hestatanemo.*" Ruth's dark eyes glowed like live coals. "Did Jane spend last night here with you?"

Hearing Jane's name, Barton began bouncing in his mother's arms, chanting, "Na-na-na-na-na."

John sighed and nodded. What was the good of lying?

The flattened state of his fleece rug might have told the tale, even without the flecks of dried blood. Besides, he and Jane were going to be married. He might go into Whitehorn for a license this very day, just in case Caleb refused to accept the truth about Jane. By the sound of it, Barton would be pleased, at least.

"How could you do something so foolish?" Ruth transferred the baby to her other hip. "Now the girl's ruined for Amos Carlton! I never would have asked you to get her ready for his courting if I'd thought you'd turn into a lovesick calf and then a rutting bull."

"It wasn't like that, Ruth."

It hadn't been, had it? Sure, he'd wanted Jane so badly he'd feared he might burst into flame. But *she'd* been the one to ask, the one to take it each step further until they'd plunged off the lip of a canyon together.

His sister shot him a scornful look. "What *was* it like,

then? And what's this letter Caleb got from some man in Boston? Foolishness about Jane being some kind of jewel thief—honestly! If I wasn't crazy in love with that man, I'd clout him with a frying pan.''

John would sooner have tried to bag a wolverine with his bare hands than mess with Ruth when her temper was up. Thank goodness there weren't any frying pans or rolling pins handy in his cabin.

He avoided her first question by answering the second. ''That letter is nothing but a pack of lies. Jane pawned one little piece of Mrs. Endicott's jewelry to buy her train ticket out here, so she could get away from the old lady's miserable snake of a nephew. Remember what her face looked like when she got here? He did that to Jane when he saw the letter you and Caleb sent to her. And it wasn't the first time, either.''

Ruth's sun-kissed cheeks paled and she held Barton tighter to her. ''I knew there was something not right about that. And the train wreck?''

''Never happened. She didn't want folks knowing why she'd come here with nothing but the clothes on her back.''

''That's foolishness. She could have told us.''

John shook his head. ''Not at first, Ruth. How could she know we weren't every bit as bad as the Endicotts? Would you have hired her, even for a short spell, if you knew she'd run off from her last job?''

Ruth opened her mouth to protest, then looked at her little son and appeared to reconsider. ''But later—''

''Later she was ashamed to admit she'd lied to us in the first place.''

''The poor thing. No wonder she was so nervous around strangers.'' Ruth grimaced. ''And me shoving all those suitors at her. Henry Hill—it's a wonder he didn't end up with worse than creamed peas.''

"It's all right. You didn't know."

Ruth had nothing to apologize for. She'd dismissed that confounded letter from Emery Endicott, trusting Jane, while he'd been quick to believe the worst. How could he be a good husband to a white woman, when his suspicion and hostility toward her whole race could blaze out of control so quickly?

Ruth pulled a handkerchief from her pocket and wiped the drool sliding down Barton's chin. "You still should have let her be, *hestatanemo*. I asked you to get her ready for Amos Carlton to court. This business of her past is all the more reason Amos would have made a good husband for Jane. Now, thanks to your...meddling, there'll be no chance of that."

"Don't fret yourself." John threw back his shoulders, accepting his responsibility, though the prospect of it tied his stomach in knots. "She may not have Amos Carlton for a husband, but she'll have me. I'll take care of Jane."

Ruth's graceful black brows drew together in a worried frown. "I suppose it's the only honorable thing to do, now that you've taken Jane into your..." she stared at the fleece rug "...*bed*."

Hot shame seared John's face.

His sister shook her head. "I can't help fretting for both of you when I look into the future. Jane is a dear soul, and taking account of her past, she's done well since she came out here. You and I both know the spirits of the Great Sky haven't shown off their strength lately. A girl as delicate and sensitive as Jane Harris needs a different kind of looking after than a half-Cheyenne ranch foreman can give her."

John wanted to shut his ears to Ruth's words, but he couldn't. He'd entertained those same misgivings, until the power of his attraction for Jane had hog-tied his reason.

"Besides," his sister reminded him, "you have responsibilities to our people. I worry that if you're a good chief to them, you won't have anything left for Jane, and if you're a good husband to her, you won't have anything left for the band."

"Will you stop chewing on me if I admit you're right?" John paced the short length of his cabin like a wild creature caught in a trap of his own making. "I was crazy last night. Jane and I are wrong for each other in more ways than I can name. Even if she was a pretty little Cheyenne girl and I tugged on her dress, our families would object to the match."

Ruth lowered herself onto one of the chairs, letting Barton balance on her knees. "I used to think our people's way of courtship was too formal. Too strict." She ran a hand over the baby's dark hair. "Now that I have a child of my own, I see things differently. A man and a woman feel that pull to each other and it makes them simpleminded. How can they tell if it has the makings of a good, strong match that will last for life?"

She gazed up at John with the same anxious fondness she lavished on her son. "That's my biggest worry for you, John. I'm afraid after this first glow of craziness wears off, Jane will find life here too hard for her and she'll run away from you. Like she ran from that Endicott man in Boston."

John flinched. Maybe he'd rather take his chances with a frying pan, after all. If he'd been certain Jane felt about him the way he felt about her, the fear of her leaving him would not have loomed so great. But if she'd only bartered her body in exchange for his protection…

Shaking her head, Ruth continued. "Better if she did leave outright than stay and hurt you the way Caleb's first wife hurt him. I feel so bad for putting you both in the way of temptation like this. You just never paid much attention to other women, and you've always been so wise and steady, I never thought of you taking a notion of Jane for yourself.''

''This isn't your fault, Ruth.'' It was his fault—all of it. Jane had asked him to show her the ways of mating, but she hadn't put a gun to his head. ''I'm a grown man, even if I have been acting more like a calf-eyed boy lately. I made my choices, and even if some of them weren't very wise, I'm going to stand by them. I'll do everything I can to take care of Jane and make her happy.''

Jamming on his hat, he fled outdoors, hoping it might ease the sense of confinement strangling him every time he thought about his doomed future with Jane.

To himself he muttered, ''I hope it'll be enough.''

The vast spaces of the Big Sky were suddenly closing in on her and she couldn't get enough air. Jane backed away from John's cabin, wishing she could scour her memory clean of the words she'd just heard.

''…*throwing all those suitors at her.*''

''…*get her ready for Amos Carlton to court.*''

''…*the only honorable thing to do…*''

''*Jane and I are wrong for each other in more ways than I can name.*''

The faster she gulped in air, the more her head spun and the higher her panic mounted. She'd felt like this the evening Dr. Gray had come to dinner.

Dr. Gray! A hiccup of mirthless laughter shuddered out of Jane. What a perfect idiot she'd been, not to have seen how desperately the Kincaids had been trying to find her a husband. Desperate enough to recruit their resident horse trainer to domesticate the troublesome mare. Well, they'd all gotten a whole lot more than they'd bargained for!

After she and John had finally managed to pry themselves apart that morning, Jane had tried to sneak into the ranch house to wash and change clothes. Instead, she'd found Ruth waiting in her bedroom.

"I worried when you were so late getting up this morning. But it looks as if you haven't been to bed at all."

Glancing down at the wreck of her lacy pink dress, Jane blushed to a similar shade. "It's all right, Ruth. I'll just wash and change and get to work."

"I'm not anxious about you missing work. I'm anxious about *you,* Jane. Do you want to tell me where you spent the night?" Ruth didn't look any more inclined to accept evasions than her formidable aunt, Walks on Ice.

Suddenly Jane felt ashamed of what she'd done. Asking, practically begging, a man to teach her the mysterious ways of married folk, when they weren't married and he didn't even love her. Why, the ladies of the Boston Temperance Society would keel over in a dead swoon if they knew!

Now all she wanted was a few private minutes to make herself *appear* respectable again. "May-maybe you should ask your brother about that."

"My...brother?"

Why did Ruth sound so shocked? Hadn't she seen the attraction between them? She'd been the one pushing them to attend Brock and Abby's party together. The one who'd urged Jane to go off riding with John and visiting Sweetgrass. She'd even lectured Jane on all the reasons a woman in Montana needed a husband.

Backing up to the window, Jane glanced out at the foreman's cabin. The sight heartened her a little. Would it be her home soon? Or might Caleb offer her and John a place in the big house?

"I'm sure if you talk to John, he can explain everything."

Ruth sighed. "I hope he can, because I've got plenty of questions that want answers."

She'd left Jane to change clothes, shutting the door behind her with barely restrained force.

Wishing she could enjoy a nice long soak in a tub of hot water, or even a brisk dip in the creek, Jane had settled for a quick change of clothes. Then she went looking for Barton.

Her search put her right outside the foreman's cabin. She knew John and Ruth would be talking about her, and for a moment, she considered joining the discussion. After all, she was going to be part of the family soon.

What she overheard sent her stumbling away, dizzy with renewed fear for the future and a pain in her heart as big as the Montana sky. Emery had battered her body and her spirit, but because she hadn't truly cared for him, he hadn't been able to inflict any lasting damage on her heart.

John Whitefeather, with his genuine attraction, kind heart and fierce honor, had hurt her far worse than Emery ever could. Making her love him when he was only doing a favor for his sister. Letting her seduce him when he didn't love her. Proposing to her simply to satisfy his idea of Cheyenne honor. What distressed Jane most was that she had forged his weapons herself. She had placed them in his hands and bared her heart for his assault.

Looking back, she realized that Emery's violence and Mrs. Endicott's unspoken censure had hurt less than Papa's long absences and Ches and Mama's deaths. No wonder writers referred to love as "losing one's heart."

Somehow, Jane managed to calm herself enough to march back up to her bedroom and put on the clothes she'd come to Whitehorn wearing.

She'd lost her heart to John Whitefeather, but she was

going to get it back. And once it was safely in her possession again, she'd never surrender it to anyone.

It was suppertime before John finally surrendered to hunger and weariness.

Though he shrank from admitting it to himself, he'd been doing his level best to avoid Jane. Part of him longed to see her again. Feast his eyes on her beauty. Talk to her and touch her as only a husband had the right to do.

And yet he worried what he would say to her in the bald light of day, with the ordinary routine of the ranch going on around them. What if the magic of their night together had vanished like the early morning mist?

Without friendly shadows to shroud his eyes, Jane might spy the regret and the uncertainty that brooded in his heart, ready to ambush those defenseless pioneers—happiness and contentment. Strange how one slender waif of a woman could turn a Cheyenne warrior into such a yelping coward.

He began to eat supper with Ruth, Caleb and Barton, eyeing Jane's empty chair for a while until it became obvious she wouldn't be joining them.

"Where's Jane?" He nodded toward the place Ruth had set for her, struggling to keep his tone casual.

Ruth shrugged. "I haven't seen her since this morning, *hestatanemo.* I knocked on her door to tell her supper was ready, but she didn't answer. Maybe you'd better go up and talk to her."

Swallowing the mouthful of food that had kept him from answering sooner, Caleb shook his head. "Did you not know? Jane's gone. Came to me and asked if I'd give her a lift into town. Under the circumstances, I figured it was the best thing."

Seeing the looks on the faces of his wife and brother-in-law, he added, "I paid her handsomely for the time she's been with us. Most handsomely, considering she got room and board and even clothes from us. What are you looking at me like that for?"

John rose abruptly and strode to the door. He felt as if someone had pulled a plug in each of his hips, allowing his internal organs to seep down into his feet.

"Where are *you* going?" Caleb barked. "The last time I talked to you, I got the impression you never wanted to lay eyes on Jane Harris again. I reckoned I was doing you a favor getting her away from here without a big fuss."

How could he fault his brother-in-law's perception? John asked himself as he grabbed his hat. If he hadn't been so quick to swallow all the lies in Emery Endicott's letter, Caleb would never have spirited Jane away. And if John hadn't been so yellow-bellied scared to risk a daylight encounter with Jane, he'd have missed her long before this.

He wasn't sure what frightened him worse, the notion of Jane alone and defenseless in Whitehorn, or the thought of her boarding a train bound far away from him.

"Caleb…" He swung the door open. "The next time you want to do me a favor, would you ask me first?"

Dashing to the stable, he threw a saddle and harness on Hawkwing with the kind of sloppy haste that would have made him chew out the ranch hands.

He had just mounted when Caleb appeared at the stable door looking well chastened. "Jane's not headed out of town, if that's what you're worried about. I asked her if she wanted me to drive her into Big Timber to catch the train, but she said to let her off at the hardware store."

John curbed a wave of relief that surged through him. "I'd like to check that out for myself, if you don't mind."

Caleb shrugged. "Do what you want, John. You're a big boy. But on your ride into town, maybe you ought to think about leaving well enough alone. Jane Harris landed on us from out of nowhere, and she's managed to keep life around here in a bit of commotion ever since. We didn't ask for her to come, but we tried to treat her decent while she was here. Maybe we'd all be better off if she moved on.''

"Speak for yourself, Caleb." John nudged Hawkwing.

The horse's hooves tapped across the rough wooden floor of the stable. Once they were outside and pointed down the long lane to the main road, Hawkwing rapidly sped up to a strong, mile-eating gallop.

Hard as John tried to leave Caleb's words of warning behind him, they dogged Hawkwing's hoofprints.

John had been worried about Jane running off, and sure enough, she was all set to abandon him when life was going along smoothly. That didn't exactly bode well for their first hard winter, or a bout of illness, or a hundred other hard certainties of Montana life. Maybe he *would* be better off saying goodbye now than later, when Jane had worked herself so deeply into his heart that he couldn't dislodge her without cutting himself to pieces.

But what if the seed he'd sown in Jane bore fruit? Like a low-hanging bough, the thought almost knocked John off his horse.

Last night, as he'd been rocked by wave after wave of conflicting emotions, he'd deliberately blinded himself to the consequences of what he and Jane were doing. This morning he'd worried only about satisfying Cheyenne honor. A woman's chastity had high value among his people, whether or not a child resulted from her first mating.

Though he couldn't bring himself to regret the most blissful night of his life, John wondered if he was destined to pay a very dear price for that intense but fleeting pleasure.

When he reached Watson Hardware and asked after Jane, Sam Roland nodded.

"Pretty little thing." He cast a nervous glance back to see if his own pretty little wife happened to be within earshot. "Mrs. Kincaid was in here looking over the books this afternoon. She and Miss Harris talked for a while, then they went off in Mrs. Kincaid's buggy. If Miss Harris comes back, should I tell her you're looking for her?"

"No." John tried to smile to cover his abruptness. "That's all right. I'll find her, I'm sure. Thanks for your help, Sam."

Dusk was beginning to gather by the time John back-tracked out of town to Brock and Abby's place. The fading light and the odor of sawdust put him in mind of the night he'd danced here with Jane, under the stars. In his imagination, he could hear a faint echo of Harry Talbert's fiddle crooning "Beautiful Dreamer."

His empty arms ached for Jane.

A dog barked, summoning Brock to the door. "Oh, John, it's just you. What can I do for you?"

Caleb's brother relaxed from his wary stance. John wondered if he was armed. Perhaps Brock Kincaid hadn't entirely shaken off his exciting, shadowy past, but he seemed well satisfied with his new life. He was clearly a more contented, happier man than the one who'd shown up at the ranch a few months back.

"Is Jane Harris staying with you folks, by any chance? I'd like to talk to her."

Brock sauntered down his front steps, shaking his head as he approached. "She's not here, John. You're welcome to check, if you like."

"No. If you say she isn't here, that's good enough for me."

If Jane *was* taking refuge in this house, Brock might

hold him off at gunpoint if necessary, but he wouldn't lie about it. Dealing with men was so much more straightforward than trying to cipher the contrary riddles of women. Jane wasn't at the hardware store. She wasn't at Brock and Abby's. Where had she gone?

"Could I talk to your wife for a minute, then? Sam Roland told me she spoke to Jane earlier today."

Brock swiped his knuckles back and forth across his chin. "I reckon that'd be all right. I'll tell you what, John. Abby did ask me if maybe we could hire Miss Harris to help her around the house so she'd be free to supervise the store a little closer. Can't say I cared for the idea. That gal kinda gives me the creeps, she's so on edge all the time. Did that widow woman finally show up to work for Ruth and Caleb? Is that why Miss Harris is looking for a new job?"

"No." John wondered how much he could safely tell Caleb's brother. Best to keep his own counsel for the moment, he decided. Considering he didn't know all the ins and outs of what was going on. If Jane ended up staying in Whitehorn, he didn't want folks gossiping about her.

"Mrs. Muldoon should be here before long, though. Maybe Jane thought she ought to get something else lined up."

Brock chuckled. "If she wasn't so dadblamed jumpy, she might've landed a husband by now and not needed to look for work."

"Just between you and me..." John lowered his voice "...Jane's got good reason to be jumpy, just like you've got good reason to be cautious when a stranger rides up to your door at sunset. Once she finds out folks aren't going to hurt her or make fun of her, she'll settle down."

"I see." Brock ran a hand through his tawny hair.

"Maybe if she can't find anything else, we could reconsider giving her a place."

He called back over his shoulder, "Abby! John Whitefeather's here trying to track down Miss Harris. You want to come and talk to him for a minute?"

Abby Kincaid emerged from the house carrying a lantern. The light from it flickered over her coppery hair.

"I know where Jane is and I know she's safe." Abby spoke with the confidence of a woman who'd looked after herself and her son before Brock Kincaid came back into her life. "What I don't know is whether she'd welcome a visit from you tonight, John."

Abby would probably have said the same thing to Emery Endicott if he'd shown up in Whitehorn looking for Jane. That thought struck John like a physical blow. Why was Jane hiding from him? He'd never done anything to hurt her and he never would.

"I *have* to talk to her. Please, Abby. It's important."

Her reply was regretful, but firm. "I give you my word she's safe. Anything else you need to discuss with her can wait the night. I'll go see her and get her permission to let you know her whereabouts. If you come back here after noon tomorrow, I'll have her answer for you."

What if Jane took it into her head to leave town in the meantime? Caleb had paid her enough to buy a train ticket just about anywhere. John couldn't let her slip out of his life without understanding why.

"Whitehorn isn't *that* big a town." His voice came out sharper than he meant it to. "And some folks don't have much else to do with their time but find out everybody else's business. I reckon Mrs. Dillard must have some idea where Jane is by this time. Or old man Waverly. It'd be quicker if you'd just tell me. For Pete's sake, Abby, you and Ruth are sisters-in-law. That makes us almost family."

Urgency seethed inside him like the sulphurous water that periodically gushed up out of the ground hereabouts. He slid out of his saddle, the better to confront Abby.

"Or do you think just because I have Cheyenne blood that I'd harm Jane? Let me tell you something, ma'am. My father's people prize courage above every other virtue, and we know it doesn't take courage to harm a weaker opponent. The greatest bravery a Cheyenne warrior can show is to face an armed enemy with nothing but his bare hands. To hurt a woman, a child or an elder is the mark of a coward."

Reacting to John's fierce outburst, Brock took up a defensive stance.

His wife didn't flinch a muscle. "I didn't know that and I thank you for telling me. It doesn't change anything, though. It never occurred to me that you might mean Jane harm. Not because of who your folks are, but because I've known *you* a while and I count myself a pretty fair judge of character. Prove I'm right about you, John. Please. Go back to the ranch, let your temper cool and get a good night's sleep. I don't think Jane'll thank you for hunting her down at this time of night."

"Damnation, Abby!" John's shoulders slumped. "Do you *have* to spout such good sense?"

Brock gave a sympathetic chuckle. "Morning'll come soon enough."

"You can spend the night here, if you like," Abby offered, gracious in victory. "Save you that long ride out to Caleb's place and back."

"Thanks, but I'd better not. Ruth'll be worried if I don't come home. Besides, I do my best thinking in the saddle and I reckon I need to think some more. If you'll just let me water Hawkwing, here, I'll be on my way."

"Oh, sure." Brock took the lantern from Abby and walked toward the barn. "Trough's right this way."

As if the horse understood, Hawkwing followed Brock's bobbing light. John lingered behind.

"Will you promise me one thing, Abby?"

"That depends what."

Suddenly he was glad Jane had made a woman friend who had this kind of quiet strength.

"Please don't help Jane leave town until I've had a chance to talk to her."

"I don't believe she plans to leave Whitehorn anytime soon."

In spite of the warm summer night, John shivered. "I wish *I* could be sure of that."

Chapter Fifteen

"Are you sure there's nothing else I can get you, Jane?" asked Lizzie Kincaid. "A mug of warm milk to help you sleep, maybe?"

Jane looked around the dainty little room with its rose-bud paper and white enameled bed frame. In her heart she yearned for her rustic gabled room back at Ruth and Caleb's ranch.

"You and your husband have been too good to me already, Mrs. Kincaid. Trusting me with a job, even after I told you about taking that brooch from Mrs. Endicott. Giving me this lovely room and even one of your own nightdresses."

A girlish giggle reminded Jane that her new employer was actually several years her junior. "Do call me Lizzie, instead of Mrs. Kincaid. Between Kate, Abby, Haley and me, it's so hard to keep us straight unless we go by first names. I hate it when folks call me Mrs. William, as if I didn't have a name of my own. As for the other," declared Lizzie, "don't you dare feel one bit beholden. You'll be doing me a great favor by staying to help when the baby comes."

She ran a hand over her bulging midsection with a sweet, brooding smile Jane envied with all her heart.

"Ruth told me what a wonder you were with little Barton. You might not think it to look at me now, but I was down on my luck once and ready to do a desperate deed just to survive."

Lizzie was right, Jane did find it hard to believe that a girl of such obvious refinement had ever contemplated theft…or worse.

"Somebody gave me a helping hand." The fond, faraway look in Lizzie's pretty blue eyes left Jane in no doubt that "somebody" was William Kincaid. "Now I'm happy I can pass along that kindness."

"I appreciate it and I'll do everything in my power to justify your trust in me." Jane knew better than to think she could be indispensable…to anyone. But she was still determined to work hard for the banker and his young wife.

Lizzie beamed. "I'm sure you will. Now, how about that warm milk?"

"Not tonight, thank you." It would take a mug of warm milk the size of Boston harbor to insure her a restful sleep tonight. And then only if she drowned herself in it.

"In that case, I'll let you settle in and get to bed. Oh! I think I just felt the baby kick. I must go tell Will. Good night." Lizzie pulled the door closed behind her and pattered off.

Jane sank down onto the crocheted bedspread and hugged herself around the waist. The moment Abby Kincaid had ushered her into Lizzie's presence, the fear that she might be carrying John Whitefeather's baby settled in Jane's heart like an early frost. Before last night she'd been pretty much ignorant of what went on between a man and a woman. She did know it had something to do with the creation of babies.

Did folks only engage in such activity when they wanted to start a baby? Was a baby the inevitable result of every mating?

In that case, she might have twins!

Why hadn't she given this some thought last night, before she'd thrown herself at John?

Because she wouldn't have cared then, Jane sternly informed herself as she undressed and put on Lizzie's nightgown. Last night she'd believed John cared about her. This morning she'd been convinced of it. Now she understood that he'd only pretended to court her so she wouldn't be nervous around genuine suitors.

He'd coupled with her because she'd begged him to. And perhaps because his body hankered for hers in a way his heart never would. It had been a mistake; he'd admitted as much to his sister. No matter how dire the consequences, Jane could never look back on the one night of her life when she'd felt beautiful and powerful and cherished, and think it a mistake.

Turning out the lamp, she lay down on yet another strange bed and pined for the delicious resting place where she'd slept so peacefully the night before. Now she discovered the meaning of the old saying, "No rest for the wicked."

Ever since she'd overheard John and Ruth, Jane had forced herself to keep moving, keep talking. First to Caleb, then to Abby, then to Lizzie. Troubling thoughts had prowled around the edges of her consciousness, ready to pounce whenever she stopped or fell silent. Now, in the quiet of William and Lizzie Kincaid's spare room, they moved in for the kill.

In the first agonies of hurt and betrayal, Jane had wanted

to get as far away from the Kincaid ranch as Caleb's money would take her. That wasn't very practical, though. She certainly couldn't return to Boston, and she didn't have friends anywhere else. Though she'd been fortunate to fall among kind strangers when she'd arrived penniless in Whitehorn, Jane knew better than to suppose she might be so lucky in another town.

Besides, she *liked* Whitehorn. The place was small enough for a person to get to know everyone. From what she'd heard or guessed, most folks here were refugees of some kind from farther east. Whether fleeing poverty, social disgrace or just plain boredom, they'd washed up in the lee of the Crazy Mountains, just like she had. They'd forged new lives for themselves, just like she wanted to. Damned if she would let John Whitefeather take that away from her, the way he'd taken her fragile trust and dreams!

Staying in Whitehorn, with the brother of his brother-in-law, meant she'd have to face him sooner or later. Jane's reasonable self hoped it would be later. She needed time for the caustic offense of his actions to corrode her lingering fascination with him.

Some pathetic part of her longed to accept John on any terms, whether he loved her or not. However, her budding sense of confidence and self-worth refused to settle for less than his heavily defended heart.

John's head ached worse than his heart. So perhaps the sleepless night he'd spent *had* been worth something.

"Here." Ruth slammed a bowl of oatmeal onto the kitchen table between her brother and his lifesaving cup of coffee. "Make yourself useful by feeding Barton while I see to breakfast."

She'd made no secret of her opinion that he was to blame for Jane's leaving. He couldn't convince her that

Jane had been a more-than-willing partner in their love-making. John found it hard to believe himself, come to that. So much so that he'd begun to question the trustworthiness of his memory.

Had Jane invited him to do *everything* he'd done? Had his attentions pleased her? He'd been so certain at the time. Now he wondered if he'd only seen and heard what he'd wanted to be true. Absolving him from ultimate disgrace in his own eyes and the eyes of his people.

"Here you go, little dogie." John tried to distract himself from that impossibly disturbing thought by loading the spoon with oatmeal and aiming it at Barton's mouth. "Chuck wagon's coming."

Barton banged on the tray of his high chair. "Na-na-na-*Na!*"

Did his nephew also blame him for Jane's unexplained disappearance?

"Sorry, you have to settle for Unka today, Thundercloud."

Barton pursed his lips and blew out a hail of soggy oats. "Na-*Na!*"

"Stubborn little cuss," John muttered, wiping his face. "You must take after the Kincaids."

Like a good herd dog responding to a cowboy's whistle, Caleb pushed open the kitchen door and strode in to breakfast.

Pouring himself a cup of coffee from the pot on the back of the stove, he announced, "I don't give a hang what the other stockmen are doing. I want to round up my cattle early, before they lose any more meat on account of this drought. We'll get organized today and ride at first light tomorrow morning."

John had thought nothing could make his headache worse. Then along came Caleb to prove him wrong.

"The drought could break soon," he protested. "Got a few likely looking clouds up there today."

"The other stockmen are pinning their hopes on the drought breaking, but I say after this long a dry spell one storm'll barely wet the ground."

Caleb tucked into a plate of steak and eggs, almost before Ruth got it properly set down in front of him. "More likely a lightning strike will start a range fire and then what'll we have? One great big barbecue."

"You know we don't have enough hands for a roundup," John warned his brother-in-law. And boss.

Ordinarily, in the fall, the ranches in an area would send their cowboys out to round up all the cattle and drive them to a central point. Once there, they'd sort them out by brand and cull the stock to be shipped East for slaughter. If the other ranchers hereabouts were content to leave their cattle out on the range, it'd mean the Kincaid cowboys would have to check the brand on every blessed cow they came across and only collect their own.

Caleb shrugged. "Then it'll just take us a little longer, is all."

"What's the harm in waiting a week to see what happens?" John offered Barton another bite of porridge. This time the little fellow grabbed the spoon away from him and sent oatmeal flying in all directions.

"I'm tired of playing wait and see." Caleb's tone brooked no opposition. With his fork, he pushed aside a gob of Barton's porridge that had landed beside his eggs. "Every day the cattle are losing flesh, or at least not gaining. More get sick and die. I want to bring them in where we can water them and feed them up and have good stock to send East when everybody else's are barely fit food for the buzzards. It's thinking ahead like this and being willing to risk what the rest are too timid to try that's made my ranch what it is today.''

John glanced at Ruth. They both knew it was useless trying to dissuade Caleb Kincaid from a course of action he'd decided on.

''If you're set on doing this, I'll go into town and see if I can hire us some extra hands for the roundup.''

''Tarnation!'' Caleb slammed down his coffee mug. ''That's what this is all about. You want to hang around Whitehorn on account of Jane Harris.''

''Abby wouldn't tell me where she was staying. I have to talk to her.'' Did he sound as anxious as he felt? John wondered.

''If you've got a lick of sense, you'll leave her be and put her clean out of your mind. That gal's been nothing but trouble since the day she landed here.''

Stroking a rogue lock of hair off her husband's brow, Ruth asked softly, ''Like you put me out of *your* mind all those years ago?''

Caleb tried to scowl, but couldn't quite manage it. ''Oh, all right! Go see if you can hire any extra hands in Whitehorn. I've got a half-dollar says you can't scare up a single one. Check with Cookie and see if there's anything he needs from the mercantile for his chuck wagon. And if you've got any *other* business in town, get it seen to and make sure you're here and ready to ride come sunup.''

John was on his feet and out the kitchen door almost before Caleb finished speaking. He drove into Whitehorn, hired one warm body that could sit a horse, and went to fill Cookie's order at Dillard's Mercantile. He was just loading his purchases onto the wagon when he caught sight of Abby riding up Main Street.

When he hailed her, she pulled up beside him.

''I haven't got time for a lot of foolishness, Abby.

Caleb's going to have us hit the range tomorrow to round up his stock. Don't know how long I might be gone. I *have* to talk to Jane before I leave. Now will you please tell me where I can find her?''

''I just spoke to her and she told me the same as you did, last night.'' Abby still didn't seem anxious to betray Jane's whereabouts. ''Said she couldn't hide from you in Whitehorn for more than five minutes if you had a mind to track her down. She's over at Will and Lizzie's place. She's going to look after Lizzie and help her with the baby when it comes.''

When John vaulted onto the seat of the wagon and grabbed the reins, Abby warned him, ''You go easy on her, you hear? I know there's more to this than just Jane needing a new job. Somebody's hurt her, and the way you've been carrying on, well...''

He wanted to assure Abby that he hadn't done anything to hurt Jane and he never would, but his own doubts wouldn't let him. ''I just want to *talk* to her, and I don't have much time.''

Abby didn't hold him up with any more chatter, but her green eyes glittered a warning, hard as emeralds.

Fortunately, Abby's sister-in-law proved a good deal more sympathetic when John showed up on her doorstep.

''Jane's out back watering my garden.'' Lizzie ushered him inside. ''This dry summer has been so hard on the flowers. I could fetch her in so the two of you could talk in the parlor, but the garden's so much more romant—I mean, more private.''

In spite of all the conflicting emotions raging inside him, John could hardly resist smiling. This little porcelain princess was the last woman he'd have expected a cool-headed banker like Will Kincaid to take for a wife. Come to that, a plain, no-nonsense schoolmarm like Kate Elliott had been a surprising choice for a black sheep gambler like Will's cousin, James. It had been the making of him, though, just as Will's marriage had turned him more friendly and approachable.

Was it possible, John wondered, that the sharp contrasts between him and Jane *didn't* spell disaster for a future together?

"Thank you, ma'am. The garden'll do fine."

Toying with the brim of his hat as he walked, John followed Lizzie Kincaid through the house. He couldn't help noticing what a fine job she'd done fixing up the old Tanner place. Wood, brass and glass gleamed. Each piece of furniture looked at home with the others. Rugs, mirrors, pictures and cushions provided just enough decoration to brighten the place and make it welcoming.

Like a heavy hoof in the belly, John realized *this* was the kind of home that suited Jane. The kind of home she deserved. The kind of home he could never hope to give her.

"Right that way." Lizzie pointed to a screen door, through which John could see the garden. "I'd love to keep Jane here with me, but I don't believe her heart's in it. I have no idea what's between the two of you, but take my advice and tell her exactly how you feel."

How did he feel? Confused. Forsaken. Angry. Anxious. The list ran on and on. If he ever got it all sorted out, maybe he could explain it to Jane. John fanned his face with his hat. Now that he'd finally found her, he wasn't sure what he'd say.

Jane's tongue turned to stone.

Hearing the screen door open and close, she'd glanced up, expecting Lizzie to join her in the garden. Instead, John Whitefeather's towering frame cast a long shadow across the grass. She'd known she couldn't avoid him forever, but Abby had left only a few moments ago. Jane wasn't prepared to confront him so soon.

A knot of fear tightened in her stomach for a moment as his stormy gaze ran over her. Jane ignored her body's instinctive reaction. She knew John was nothing like Emery. He would never raise a hand to her, no matter how hot his anger burned. All the same, she set her watering can down in case her hand might shake.

"Why'd you run off on me, Jane?" Montana men didn't believe in beating around the bush, apparently. "When you promised you'd marry me, were you lying to buy yourself time to get away? What did you think I'd do if you said no?"

His voice sounded hoarse. And hurt. What right did he have to be grieved, when all she'd done was absolve him of responsibility for her?

For the first time in her life, Jane allowed herself the dangerous luxury of venting her outrage at someone who'd done her wrong. "I guess I was as sincere in accepting your proposal as you were in asking. Probably a whole lot more."

It was hard to stand there and say what needed to be said. Part of her longed to throw herself into his arms and savor the illusion of safety she'd found in his embrace. Another part just wanted to run away and hide.

"Don't go talking riddles, Jane." He took a few steps toward her—reluctantly, as though his legs were dragging him in a direction he didn't want to go. "I wouldn't have asked you if I hadn't meant it."

How tempting it was to believe him. The way his long, brown fingers moved over the brim of his hat seduced Jane with the memory of his tender touch. The lost, bewildered look in those heavenly eyes made her yearn to hold him close. She steeled herself against the terrifying power he wielded over her heart.

"I'm sure you would have made yourself go through with it. Cheyenne honor and all." Every fragrant flower in Lizzie Kincaid's garden couldn't have sweetened the bitterness of Jane's tone. "Please don't insult my intelligence by pretending you're sorry I've let you off the hook."

"Cheyenne honor?" His deep-set eyes widened. "You heard Ruth and me talking?"

Jane hesitated a moment, until the pointless urge to weep passed. "You weren't exactly whispering."

His wide-brimmed hat fell on Lizzie's neatly clipped grass. One long stride brought him within reach of Jane. And reach he did, grasping her shoulders. "How much did you hear?"

She held her gaze steady, and for a wonder, neither her lower lip nor her chin trembled. "Kindly take your hands off me."

For a moment he looked at his large, powerful hands as though they didn't belong to him. Then, as if by force of will, he lifted them off Jane's shoulders and let them fall to his sides.

Jane tried to take another step back, but Lizzie's rose trellis blocked any further retreat. "I heard enough to know I was a fool to think you cared about me. Any more than those horses you gentle for Caleb."

He opened his mouth to speak, but before he could get a word out, Jane's indignation ran away with her. "Your technique is very good, I must say. Took me in completely, fool that I am. Perhaps you should advertise in the papers—'Domesticates bashful virgins for matrimony. Satisfaction guaranteed.'"

John winced hard and raked a hand through his hair.

"Sure, it started out like that, but…tarnation, I'm sorry, Jane!"

"Sorry you led me on or sorry you got caught?" She hated to admit it, but there was something heady about calling a man to account for his actions.

"Sorry for everything."

Though it sounded like surrender, his words brought Jane no satisfaction. He was sorry for everything. For making her care about him far more than she'd ever wanted to. For succumbing to the intensity of their mutual need and making love to her. For feeling pressured to "make an honest woman of her." Jane had always wondered what that phrase meant. Now she wished she didn't know.

"I'm sorry, too. I should have known better than to believe you could fall in love with someone who's wrong for you in more ways than you can name. I'm sorry I threw myself at you. I'm sorry I didn't recognize your offer of marriage for what it was."

When he raised his hand, Jane flinched. But he only reached past her to pluck one pale pink rosebud from Lizzie's trellis.

"Are you sorry for what we did together?" He offered her the rose.

A strangely vulnerable look came over his rugged, handsome features, as though her answer mattered to him more than anything in the world.

Jane wanted to lie.

After the way he'd deceived her, she certainly didn't owe him the truth. It might only give him another weapon to turn against her.

Before she'd made up her mind exactly what to say, she found herself shaking her head. Accepting the rose, she bent to inhale its perfume. "Are you?"

"Hell, no!" The force of his reply ruffled a tendril of

hair that curled over her ear. Softening his voice, he continued, "I never knew it could be like that with a woman, Jane. I swear. Whatever happens, I won't be sorry."

The warm moisture of his breath caressed her face. As did the melting blue of his eyes. His words and his nearness intoxicated her. Jane found herself wondering what it would be like to lie with him under the stars in a fragrant garden.

But there were harder truths she must face. "You don't love me, though. Do you, John?"

If he did, the words would have come easily. Of their own accord. Instead, Jane sensed a fierce tension within him.

"I don't know," he admitted at last. "I know I want you. I know I enjoy being with you. I know I worry about you and want to keep you safe. But I also know my feelings for you make me reckless. With my responsibilities I can't risk being wild and foolish. I have to consider what's best for everyone."

What he described sounded perilously close to love. Could she accept this much for now and hope for more?

John stepped back from her, as if he feared her nearness might overpower his reason. "I'm not certain you're best for me and I doubt like hell I'm best for you, Jane. While we're being honest here, you'd better look into your heart, too. Can you swear you really love me? That you're not just looking for a man you can feel safe with?"

Jane tried to speak. The ringing assurance she wanted to give him stuck in her throat. In one way, John Whitefeather seemed to offer her security and protection. But she had discovered the grave threat he posed to her heart.

He scooped his hat back up off the grass. "That's what I thought. I don't know what the answer is for us, Jane. I'm scared you'll run off if life gets tough, or that we'll make each other miserable, like Caleb and his first wife. The trouble is, we may have somebody to consider in all this besides ourselves.''

He averted his gaze from hers, and his mahogany skin suddenly looked badly sunburned.

''You mean...a baby?'' Jane's fingers fumbled on the stem of the rose, and one impaled itself on a sharp thorn. ''Ouch!''

She pressed the wounded finger between her lips.

''What will you do?'' John's eyes pleaded and challenged with the same look. ''If you are?''

''I don't know,'' she admitted. ''I don't want you to marry me out of pity or obligation, but...''

His straight, dark brows raised in a wordless question.

''...I also wouldn't want to keep you from your child.''

The way the Indian agents took you from your family. Jane didn't say it. Perhaps she didn't have to.

''I have to go away for a spell. Caleb wants us to round up all his cattle, and I don't know how long it might take us. Will you promise me you won't leave Whitehorn until I get back and we can talk some more? By then you should know....''

She had planned to stay, anyway. That still didn't make it easy to comply with his request. What if Emery arrived in town while John was on this cattle roundup? What if some other kind of trouble reared its head? Could she surrender the choice to leave if she felt the need?

Lifting her chin and straightening her shoulders, Jane tried to look resolute. ''I'll be here when you get back.''

John acknowledged her pledge with a nod and turned to go.

''Be careful on that roundup.'' The words were out of her mouth before she could stop them.

He froze in midstride as though jerked back by a lasso.

Then he pivoted to face her again. "Don't suppose you could spare me a kiss goodbye?"

The question set her insides wriggling. Or maybe it was just the mellow caress of his voice.

"My feelings for you make me reckless, too, *Taa'evâhe'hame*." She approached him half eagerly, half warily and lifted her face. "I can't afford it, either. And I don't like it any better than you do."

Their faces moved toward one another. Then hesitated and veered apart. Then tried another advance.

With a maximum of awkwardness and self-consciousness, they met. Afraid to seem overeager. Reluctant to forfeit control. Cautious of demanding what the other might not be able to give.

It was not a very satisfactory kiss.

Yet, when the screen door swung closed behind John Whitefeather's retreating form, Jane pressed her eyes shut and tried to recapture the unsettling magic of it.

Chapter Sixteen

"Tarnation, John, quit your woolgathering!" Caleb pulled his black mare alongside Hawkwing. "At the rate we're going, it will be fall by the time we get this damn stock rounded up."

John knew his brother-in-law too well to risk saying "I told you so." He took considerable satisfaction in thinking it, though.

They'd decided to make a wide circular sweep of the eastern range, sending individual cowboys riding out each morning to round up as many Kincaid cattle as they could find by midday, then driving them back to a rendezvous point before sundown.

"We need more manpower, Caleb, that's all there is to it." John surveyed the pitiful number of cows they'd collected together on their first day's ride. "It's liable to get worse the farther on we go, because we'll need to keep more of the hands with us to drive the big herd."

Caleb unstopped his canteen and took a long swig from it. He looked as though he wished it held something stronger than water. "You got any bright ideas?"

That was as close as he was apt to come to admitting John had been right in the first place.

Partly to keep his mind off the perplexing riddle of himself and Jane, John had been forcing himself to mull over this cowboy shortage problem.

"You may not like it," he warned Caleb, "and the hands sure won't."

"Out with it." Caleb veered his horse away from the trail of rising dust thrown up by Cookie's chuck wagon. "You might be surprised what I'm prepared to abide to save this year's herd. The hands can like it or lump it."

"I might be able to recruit some of the men from Sweetgrass to help us with the roundup. They're good riders and they're used to tracking and driving buffalo."

Caleb considered the idea for so long John was certain he meant to reject it. Finally he spoke. "Do you think they'd come?"

"Maybe. If we make it worth their while. They'll be losing time away from their hunting. We'd need to compensate them for that, somehow."

John paused to take a drink from his own canteen. He had an idea, but he hoped Caleb would come up with something similar on his own.

"What if we give them some of the cattle?" asked Caleb after a while. "All the old and sickly ones. They've still got meat and hides on 'em, just like buffalo. A mite less dangerous to kill, too. Maybe the Cheyenne at Sweetgrass should think about trying a little ranching."

"They might go for that." John pulled up his neckerchief, less to keep the dust out of his face than to mask his grin. If his plan worked out, not only would Sweetgrass be a step closer to supporting itself, but he could get back to Whitehorn and Jane all the sooner.

"I'll tell the fellows tonight," said Caleb. "Then you can ride off to Sweetgrass first thing in the morning. As many Cheyenne as you can bring, come and meet up with us at the first creek that feeds into the Musselshell.''

Nothing more was said about recruiting Cheyenne hunters to help with the roundup until after sundown, while all the men sat around the campfire.

As the last strains of the ''Red River Valley'' quavered from Clel Harding's harmonica, John heard a couple of the cowboys telling some wild story about a fortune in gold hidden in Whitehorn.

''True as your life. I got it straight from Miz Cilla at the Double Deuce. Or was it Miz Lulubel?''

Abruptly, Caleb scrambled to his feet and silence fell around the campfire. ''I wouldn't pay much mind to any foolishness you hear from a saloon gal, boys. We've got to keep our minds on the job we have to do. You've been working hard, but I reckon you all know a few more hands would make this roundup go a lot faster.''

A murmur of agreement traveled around the circle.

One voice, a bit louder than the rest, quipped, ''Where are we gonna find more hands out here? Set prairie dogs on horseback?''

All the men laughed, including Caleb. ''We aren't that hard up, boys. In fact, I know a bunch of fine riders who might be willing to lend us a hand if John can talk them into it.''

''Injuns herding cattle?'' a voice challenged. Then came a sound like spit, followed by ominous muttering.

John started to his feet, but his brother-in-law restrained him with a firm hand on his shoulder.

''I guess any man who can go after a buffalo with no more than a blanket tossed over his pony's back for a saddle isn't going to have too much trouble with my cows.''

Most of the men laughed. John got the feeling they

might be willing to give his Cheyenne friends a chance. From a few spots around the fire, he still caught a dark mutter or two, and in other places sullen silence. Would his plan solve one problem for Caleb only to spawn others?

As the men retrieved their bedrolls from a covered cart hitched behind Cookie's wagon, John overheard Floyd Cobbs grumble to Clel Harding. "Mark my words, them Cheyenne are gonna make off with two steers for every one they rustle up."

In the flickering shadows of the campfire, Floyd might not have realized John was close enough to hear. Or maybe he did and was hoping to provoke a reaction. If so, he was about to get more than he bargained for.

"Why don't you say that a little louder, Cobbs, and let the boss know what you think of his idea?" John suggested, in a tone of muted menace.

Judging by how the mouthy cowboy jumped and gasped, he hadn't reckoned with Kincaid's foreman being so near.

"It's still a free country, ain't it?" he snapped. "No law against a feller speaking his mind."

"The trouble is, you don't *speak* your mind, Cobbs. You gossip behind folks' backs and hint at things without coming right out and saying what you mean."

"Yeah?" Floyd yanked out his bedroll, while Clel backed away, perhaps hoping to distance himself from the trouble to come. "Well, how's this for coming right out and speaking my piece? That pretty little Miss Harris up and left the ranch 'cause the foreman wouldn't keep his hands off her."

Red-hot coals exploded inside John's head and his fist went racing toward Floyd's jaw before his natural prudence could stop it. His knuckles collided with something solid, but in the shifting shadows, John wasn't sure what.

A balled fist found his belly, driving the air out of him. The next thing he knew, they were rolling on the ground, whaling away at one another with fists, knees and elbows, each trying to gain the advantage of height.

"What the hell's going on?" Caleb's voice rang out.

John blinked against the bright glow of the lantern in his brother-in-law's hand as the other cowboys pulled him and Floyd apart.

"Cobbs, I've had as much of your shenanigans as I can stomach!" Caleb bellowed. "At first light, you hightail your sorry rump back to Whitehorn and collect your pay from my brother William. Anybody else want to go with him?"

John shook off the restraining hands of three men and wiped a trickle of blood from the corner of his mouth. "It was my fault, Caleb. I threw the first punch. If you're going to fire anybody, it had better be me."

He cast a baleful glare at Floyd Cobbs. Sure he'd been provoked, but he should have kept a cooler head. A good foreman didn't go around clobbering his cowboys. Besides, it would only prove to the men what many of them believed already—that Indians and whites couldn't live in peace.

"Good enough, then—you're fired," said Caleb.

The range froze in a breathless hush.

John shook his head. Surely he hadn't heard his brother-in-law right? What would become of Sweetgrass if he lost his job at the ranch? How could he possibly persuade Jane to marry him?

"Mr. Kincaid, sir." Floyd Cobbs shook off the men holding him. "I reckon I had that punch coming on account of I said something about Whitefeather and Miss Harris. You can't hold it against a feller for defending a lady's honor."

Had he taken a harder blow to the head than he thought? John wondered. Floyd sticking up for him sounded even more unlikely than Caleb giving him the sack.

Sharp shadows cast by the lantern made Caleb's rugged features look hard and ornery.

Slowly, he looked from Floyd to John and back again. "If you pair of fools insist you're equally to blame, I suppose I'll have to keep you both on, at least till we get the stock rounded up. But I'm warning you, and all the rest of you, too. I can't afford to lose good hands on account of they're beating each other senseless. The next one I catch or hear of fighting will be fired on the spot. Or we may just hang him on a charge of assault. Is that clear?"

He bellowed the last words. Off in the distance a cow bawled back.

"Hell yes, boss."

"Real clear."

"Yep."

The bedroll cart emptied in record time.

"Listen, Caleb." Bedroll tucked under his arm, John strode after his brother-in-law. "I'm sorry about that. I should have known better—"

Caleb chuckled under his breath. "Don't know how I'd have backed out of that if Floyd Cobbs hadn't done the right thing for once in his life."

"But..." John's mouth fell open.

"I reckon we won't have any trouble between my cowboys and your Indians on this roundup, now." Caleb sounded in better humor than John had heard him since the roundup started. "Guess I owe Jane Harris a little something for provoking that fight between you and Cobbs. Remind me to buy her a new dress when we get back to Whitehorn."

* * *

"We'd like to look at some dress goods, Mrs. Dillard." Lizzie pulled Jane up to the main counter of Whitehorn Mercantile. "Something serviceable, but pretty."

Mrs. Dillard swept a glance over Jane. Had the woman heard some gossip and wondered about her abrupt change of employment? Jane forced herself to stare right back with a confident smile. At least, she hoped it looked confident.

"I got a real nice calico print in last week, direct from Saint Louis." Mrs. Dillard rummaged beneath the counter for the bolt of yard goods.

The bell above the door tinkled as new customers entered the shop.

"Na-na-na!"

Jane spun around. "Barton!" It had been only a few days, but she was so glad to see his dear little face her heart hurt.

"Na-na!"

He wriggled and kicked in the arms of a stout, motherly woman until she passed him to Jane with a smile. "We'll have no peace until he's said howdy-do. You must be the girl who was filling in for me. I'm Peggy Muldoon."

"Pleased to meet you, Mrs. Muldoon. I'm Jane Harris, and this is Caleb and Ruth's sister-in-law, Lizzie Kincaid."

A queer mixture of feelings churned inside Jane as she held Barton close and planted kiss after kiss on his plump brown cheeks. She was glad to know Mrs. Muldoon had finally arrived from Bismarck. Now Jane could stop feeling so guilty for deserting Ruth. A dismaying stab of jealousy marred her sense of relief. She didn't want someone else taking her place at the Kincaid ranch and in Barton's life.

Like an arrow piercing her chest, the truth hit her.

She wanted a dark-haired baby all her own. One who

wouldn't call her Nana, but Mama. Even if it meant all
the complications and potential heartbreak of marrying
John Whitefeather.

Especially if it meant marrying John Whitefeather.

Maybe he had started out courting her for the wrong
reasons, but the way he'd touched and treasured her during
their night together told Jane his feelings for her went beyond lust and even beyond duty.

In Lizzie Kincaid's garden, he'd confessed himself as
frightened of getting hurt as Jane was, if their relationship
went wrong. For some baffling reason, John's fear soothed
hers. It meant she wasn't the only one made vulnerable by
love.

"What do you think of this, Jane?" Lizzie unrolled a
length of calico off the bolt.

"It's pretty," said Jane. "Don't you think it's pretty,
Barton?"

More important, would Barton's uncle find her attractive
in a dress made from that cloth? The pale blue flowers on
a cream-colored background reminded Jane of Mrs. Endicott's china pattern. For the first time since coming to
Whitehorn, she thought of Boston and Mrs. Endicott's
house without a qualm of panic.

The bell on the door jingled again and Lizzie flashed a
smile over Jane's shoulder. "Hello, Ruth! I'm so glad to
see you've got Mrs. Muldoon here at last. Now I don't
have to feel so bad for poaching Jane from you."

Ruth addressed her reply to Lizzie, but her eyes locked
with Jane's. "I'm happy she found such a good position
to keep her in Whitehorn."

While Lizzie ordered the yard goods and Mrs. Muldoon
took Barton to look at all the colorful wares around the
mercantile, Ruth drew Jane off to a quiet corner.

"John told me you overheard us talking and that's why
you left the ranch so suddenly. I'm sorry I made such a

mess of this. All I wanted was for you to be happy and to have the kind of life you deserve. I should have been more forthright about it, I reckon. Please don't blame my brother.''

Taking Ruth's slender, bronzed hand, Jane gave it a re-assuring squeeze and whispered, ''It was kind of you to want me looked after. I hope *you* won't blame John for what happened between us. He wasn't responsible—at least no more than I was. I know you think I'd make John a pretty poor wife, but I do care about him. Very much.''

''I believe you do, Jane.'' Ruth's tone sounded sympathetic. And regretful. ''Sometimes that isn't enough, though. Out in a place like this, especially. I don't want to see you hurt any more than my brother.''

How could she persuade Ruth that she was strong enough to stick with a marriage even through tough times? Jane asked herself. And how could she persuade John?

Those questions gnawed at her thoughts long after she and Lizzie had returned from the mercantile and begun making up her new dress. They haunted her when she went to bed at night, and stalked her through the next few days as she helped Lizzie prepare for the baby.

Then one night she happened to look in the reticule she'd brought from Boston. The instant she spied the pawn ticket, she knew. If she was ever to convince John, and herself, that she wasn't the same quivering bundle of fears who'd washed up in Whitehorn two months ago, she would have to confront her past. That would mean com-pensating Mrs. Endicott for the theft of the brooch and explaining why she'd taken it.

Jane tried to think of some other way. Communicating with her former employer would mean alerting Emery to her whereabouts. And what if Mrs. Endicott did decide to press charges? Could a theft in Boston get her arrested out here in Montana? The very fact that she was afraid of doing it made Jane realize no other test of her precarious courage would serve.

"Mr. Kincaid?" she asked William at supper that night. "Can you tell me how I'd go about sending a sum of money back East?"

"Come by the bank tomorrow and we'll arrange it for you, Jane," replied Will Kincaid. "If you need funds, I'll be glad to make you an advance of your salary."

"Thank you, but I believe I have enough from what your brother paid me."

Fearing her letter might fall into Emery's hands, Jane addressed it to Mrs. Endicott's solicitor instead. Writing the letter itself proved the most difficult part of the whole task. She sat up late one night at Lizzie's writing desk composing her message.

Revealing the shameful secret of Emery's abuse to his aunt made Jane relive the dark, stifling atmosphere of that house. At times she had to lay down her pen because her hand trembled too badly to write. Then she thought of John. Of his strength and bravery. Of how he'd encouraged her in every tottering step she'd taken toward self-reliance.

Jane forced herself to pick up the pen and keep on writing.

Once it was despatched to Boston, however, a curious lightness of spirit came over her. As though, by writing about what had happened to her, she had trapped all her demons on the paper and mailed them out of her life. She could picture John standing behind her, appreciating the effort it had cost her, and radiating quiet pride in this modest feat.

"A storm's brewing, I think." Lizzie looked up from her rocking chair when Jane returned to the Kincaids' after posting her letter. "I hope we'll get some rain to dampen that dust the wind is whipping around."

Jane's thoughts flew immediately to John, out riding the range. Would Caleb call off the roundup if rain came? Might John's experience with the harsh life of the trail further convince him she was too soft and spineless a creature to make him a good wife?

"Lizzie?" she asked. "Would you mind answering a question...well...of a rather intimate nature?"

Lowering the soft white baby blanket she was knitting, Lizzie flashed a mischievous grin. "Well, you *have* got my attention! As far as I'm concerned, there are few more amusing pastimes than talking over intimate matters with my lady friends." She giggled. "Except enjoying them with my husband."

If she hadn't liked this lively, generous girl so much, Jane feared she would have been eaten alive with envy of Lizzie. Not of her elegant home or her pretty clothes or her social standing in town, but of the way William doted on her. The sweet sly smiles they exchanged over the supper table that betrayed their anticipation of bedtime. Their joyful excitement over the tiny product of their love that was growing inside Lizzie.

"I was wondering..." Jane's cheeks tingled with a hot blush. Where had all the frank wantonness with which she'd seduced John Whitefeather gone? "How soon can a woman tell if she's going to have a baby?"

"Bless my soul." Lizzie's sparkling eyes widened. "You and...Ruth's brother?" She fanned her face with her hand. "He *is* a handsome fellow. I've often thought what a criminal waste it is for him to stay a bachelor... Ooh!" She twitched in her rocking chair and laid a hand over her belly. "I don't know whether I've got a baby in there or a bucking bronco! I have my doubts this rambunctious young fellow will be content to follow his papa into banking.''

Jane began to wonder if Lizzie would ever give her an answer.

"Oh, yes. About babies. Haley told me all sorts of interesting things. She's a midwife, you know. I wish she lived handy enough to deliver my baby. Mind you, Dr. Gray is awfully nice. I wonder if he'll ever get married?''

Lizzie fell silent for a moment, perhaps weighing the local prospects of a match for the doctor. Then she remembered Jane's question again. "Sometimes it can take a while to be certain you *are* going to have a baby, especially if...your courses don't follow the moon too regularly.''

Jane digested this information, wondering what exactly to make of it.

"Mind you, it's dead easy to tell if you *aren't* expecting," added Lizzie.

Beckoning Jane to come closer, Lizzie whispered the secret in her ear.

"Oh," breathed Jane as understanding dawned on her.

If she was going to have his baby, she knew John would put aside his misgivings and marry her. Then she would have a chance to prove her constancy and to make him love her. She didn't want to hope too hard, though. She had known too much disappointment in her life for that.

But there could no denying she was several days late.

"It is too late," Night Horse, son of Whitefeather, told the Sweetgrass Cheyenne around the council fire. "*Ve'ho'e* are here to stay. They are the new masters of this land. We are not prairie dogs who can hide in our burrows. We must seize this chance to help ourselves. Cows may not be as big as buffalo and their hides are not as rugged, but their meat makes good eating and they are not so dangerous. The buffalo herds are dwindling and they move where they will. We cannot follow them anymore. Cattle we can keep on our land.''

John sensed their resistance. They wanted no more part of this than Caleb's ranch hands did. Even if their combined efforts would yield benefits for both, they had lived too long in a climate of mutual fear and suspicion to suddenly embrace cooperation.

''May I speak?'' asked Ravencrest, one of the youngest and most recklessly courageous of the hunters.

Bearspeaker nodded.

''Haven't we settled here in Sweetgrass to keep our people away from the whites?'' Ravencrest challenged the council. ''To protect our language and our beliefs, which they would steal from our children? For us to go and work with them might bring bad ideas among us, the way smallpox comes.''

John wanted to stand and refute the young man's fears, but a warning look from his friend Red Stone kept him silent.

''I have met these cow herders,'' Red Stone chuckled. ''They don't have many ideas, good or bad.''

After the quiet laughter died, he added in a more serious tone, ''Except perhaps the foolish idea that Cheyenne are killers and thieves. Maybe we can change this idea, a little, if we ride with them. Maybe if we open our hearts, we will learn more about them, too.''

Bearspeaker nodded. ''Learning is a slow way to overcome enmity. But there is no fast road. There can be no learning if there is no contact. Besides, cow meat is easy on my old tapeworks.''

''One more thing we must consider.'' Red Stone looked around the circle at each one in turn. ''Think of all Night

Horse has done for us. Without him and Caleb Kincaid, we would be on a reservation now. If they ask this of us, we would be ungrateful to refuse."

They continued to talk until everyone had his say, but John could tell Red Stone and Bearspeaker had turned the tide. John was wise enough to realize his closed mouth would draw no flies.

Instead, as he looked through the rippling air above the fire, he pictured Jane sitting among the women, as she had on his last visit to Sweetgrass. Would she find the strength to keep her promise and wait in Whitehorn for his return? Had his seed taken root in her womb and begun to grow? And when he concluded that it must be so, was the bewildering feeling that pulsed in his veins elation, or terror?

Bearspeaker seemed to sense his mood. When the council finally broke up with an agreement to Caleb's proposal, the old man beckoned John away from the tepees.

"Come walk with me, *Taa'evâhe'hame*. A devil hangs over you, I think. Tonight, the wind pushes the clouds and they hide the stars. Tell me what troubles you and hides the truth?"

All his life John had kept his own counsel, dealt with his own problems. Who among the whites or the Cheyenne could understand more than half of anything that troubled him? Then he had bared his dark memories with Jane. She had shared his old pain and eased it in ways he could not have foreseen.

"Tell me, old one, can a single woman be both completely right for a man and completely wrong?"

Bearspeaker gave a gravelly chuckle. *"Seheso?"* he asked. *The little snowbird?*

John's reply caught in his throat. He had used exactly that endearment in a tender moment.

As if catching his answer in John's silence, Bearspeaker

continued, "Who can say when two people will suit for life? Never tell Walks on Ice, but I only asked for her when my friend Whitefeather beat me to my first choice. But after so many years, her heart beats in my chest and mine in hers."

John stopped in his tracks. "You wanted...my mother?"

"No, no." Bearspeaker's voice moved away from him and John followed, stumbling on the uneven ground. "Your mother was not Whitefeather's first wife, remember. Running Doe was killed with their two daughters at Sand Creek. When I saw how Whitefeather mourned them, I was happy the Great Spirit had denied me the woman I'd first wanted. Then Little Wolf led us north, back to our old lands, and on the way we found your mother. She had killed her evil coward of a husband when he was beating her, and she feared the white soldiers would hang her for his death. So she came with us and in time she healed Whitefeather's heart."

So his Norwegian mother had battled her own Emery Endicott. Had John heard this story when he was too young to understand? Was that why Jane Harris had drawn him so?

"I told Whitefeather he was crazy to take the white woman for his wife," continued Bearspeaker. "But they were happy together and from their union our band gained you and your sister. You have both been a great blessing to us. Again I was wrong. Love is a trickster, *Taa'evâhe'hame.* Even wise men cannot fathom his riddles."

John clapped an arm around his uncle's shoulder, partly to turn him back toward the camp, partly in fondness and jest. "For a wise elder, you haven't been much help, Bearspeaker."

"Your doubts are like howling coyotes, Nephew. Throw a piece of meat to quiet them. Once they are silent, listen for the whisper of your heart and follow it."

"And if that whisper lures me away from my people and my duty?"

"Are you so sure it will?"

"I'm only one man, Bearspeaker. Some of what I give to the band now, I would owe to my family."

In silence they walked back toward the dying fire within the circle of tepees. At last the old man spoke again. "When a tall tree falls in the forest, saplings that were starved for sun in his shadow may rise to take his place. Maybe you have done *too much* for us, *Taa'evâhe'hame,* when we need to do more for ourselves. Don't blame our people if you lack the courage to risk your heart."

An angry retort rose to John's lips and died there. Could Bearspeaker be right? Could all his doubts about Jane and his duty to the Cheyenne simply be a self-righteous mask for the cowardice of his own heart?

Chapter Seventeen

"Chin up, Jane. No Cheyenne warrior wants a coward for a wife."

If she thought or muttered those words to herself once over the next week, Jane thought or muttered them a hundred times. Lizzie's belly had expanded to such a size that she didn't feel much like stirring outside her own house. She also had a touch of dropsy that swelled her delicate ankles and hands, and made Dr. Gray look anxious.

So Jane had to run many errands around town. Daily trips to Mr. Lundburg's meat market and Whitehorn Mercantile. To the little Chinese fish market built of oil cans. Into the post office to fetch the mail. Once to summon the doctor on account of false labor.

When she'd first come to Whitehorn, such duties would have sent Jane into a swooning fit. Since she'd gotten to know so many folks in town, it had become much less of an ordeal.

"Good morning, Mrs. Dillard. A pound of coffee, please, and a tin of baking powder. No sign of the baby yet, though Mrs. Kincaid sent for the doctor yesterday. Both Mr. and Mrs. Kincaid said to thank you for the chicken and dumplings you sent over last night. I don't know when you get the time to cook with the mercantile so busy. Good morning, Mrs. Fairfax. No, the stork hasn't arrived at the Kincaids' yet. I hope your mother-in-law's improving. Summer colds are the worst.''

Leaving the mercantile with her purchases stowed in her basket, Jane savored a sense of belonging unlike any she'd ever known. She enjoyed recognizing faces and being able to call so many people by name. Having them take a neighborly interest in the Kincaids and in her.

There was still one fly in the ointment, however. Jane had yet to discover a route for running her errands that did not take her past at least one saloon, and often more. The Double Deuce, where she'd first met John Whitefeather, was easily the largest and busiest. Gamblers congregated at the Four Kings, which belonged to Mr. Hill, the man she'd baptized with creamed peas.

The circuit judge held court in the Gribble and Warren Saloon. Jane had once heard a gunshot fired from inside that establishment. The Centennial catered to a somewhat better crowd. Even Will Kincaid went there now and then for a drink and a game of billiards. Big Mike's Music Hall and Opera House, for all its fine-sounding name, was actually no more than a saloon with a stage, a banjo player and a few hard-faced dancing girls.

Jane never walked past one of these places without her stomach seething and her palms breaking out in cold moisture. Between the fumes of alcohol and the frequent clamor of raised voices, they always seemed poised to erupt in violence. Each time she had to pass a saloon, she reminded herself that the Cheyenne prized courage above all virtues. Like some magical incantation, it always heartened her.

Then one day, when she'd just left the butcher's with a brown paper parcel of pork chops, the swinging doors of Gribble and Warren crashed open and two cowboys came flying out, fists flailing. Jane let out a terrified squeak and stumbled back.

One of the combatants saw her and froze. The other glanced her way and his fist fell to his side.

"Aw, Jeb, ye done scared the lady."

The two of them hung their heads like naughty schoolboys. On closer inspection, Jane guessed neither of them had ever seen the business end of a razor.

"Sorry about that, ma'am."

"Like he said, ma'am."

Jane's hammering heart slowed a little. A queer bubble of ironic humor swelled inside her.

She shook her head in gentle reproach. "Gentlemen, what would your dear mamas think if they knew you were frequenting a saloon at this hour?"

The one named Jeb looked ready to cry. They stammered an almost incoherent mix of excuses and apologies until she bid them goodday and walked on. Later, when she shared the story with Lizzie, they both laughed until their sides ached. Jane concluded that the Boston Ladies' Temperance Society would have been proud of her.

"What's all this frivolity?" William Kincaid affected a stern, bankerish frown that couldn't mask the glow of love in his eyes for Lizzie.

"See if you don't laugh, too, when you hear." Lizzie grasped her husband's hand and held it against her cheek. "Tell it again, Jane."

She repeated the story, though with a little less sparkle than her first telling. The sweet bond between the banker and his young wife was so intense, Jane fancied she could taste it, like tangy, refreshing lemonade on a hot day. This was what she wanted with John, and she couldn't bring herself to settle for anything less.

At times she would remember their night together and

glow with blissful certainty. Then she would recall what John had said to Ruth, and what he'd confessed to her in Lizzie's garden. Brooding over the tragedies of his past, she wondered if he was capable of loving her as she needed to be loved.

When the familiar ache started deep in the pit of her belly and she knew John had not sown a baby inside her, after all, she feared he might not even want to try.

"I'm getting soft, John." Gingerly, Caleb Kincaid lowered himself onto a wide flat rock beside his brother-in-law. "Soft and old. Why, I used to love nothing better than going on a cattle drive down to Texas with my pa. Sleeping on the hard ground every night under the stars. Wearing the same clothes for days on end. Eating out of the back of a chuck wagon and never seeing a face prettier than a heifer's."

His mouth full of beans and fry bread, John cocked an eyebrow to ask Caleb how he liked riding the range these days.

Caleb chuckled. "Can you imagine anything so danged foolish?"

"We're on the home swing now." John glanced around, his senses alert to any sign of trouble.

During the past week, he'd felt like he was treading on eggshells, as the cowboys and the Cheyenne began working together. They'd exchanged dark, wary looks and camped apart every night.

Walks on Ice had volunteered to come along and prepare food for the hunters. By the end of the second day, she and Cookie were swapping recipes, even though neither could speak a word of the other's language. A few of the cowboys grumbled when Cookie declared he was done messing with sourdough till they got back to the ranch. After their first taste of fry bread, they quit complaining.

Caleb seemed to read John's thoughts. "This wasn't such a bad idea, after all. I'm surprised everything's gone as smoothly as it has. Who'd have thought Floyd Cobbs and that Ravencrest boy would have taken such a shine to one another?"

John licked molasses off his spoon. "Not me, that's for sure."

The first day Caleb had paired the two biggest potential troublemakers, John had braced for all-out war. When they'd been late getting back to camp, he'd feared perhaps they'd killed one another. But they'd finally appeared with the largest roundup of cattle yet to join the herd, grinning like a pair of fools. Something had happened out on the range and John didn't want to know what. Perhaps they'd saved one another's hides, or maybe they'd just taken the measure of each other's skills and come away impressed. Whatever it was, John was grateful for it.

"I wasn't happy about going on this roundup," he admitted to Caleb. "But seeing what shape the stock's in, I think it's a good thing you went ahead with it."

"If we ever see the rain that's been threatening all week, I may look like a darn fool in front of the Stock Growers Association." Caleb took a swig of coffee to wash down his supper. "You still sore at me for dragging you away from Jane Harris?"

Jane. Caleb might have dragged John away from her in body, but not in heart. Through the past weeks, she'd never been more than a thought away. Sometimes he almost fancied he could feel her perched on Hawkwing's hindquarters, clinging to his waist, the way she had on their first ride from Whitehorn.

He shrugged. "I miss her. Like Zeke used to say, it feels

like my heart has a toothache. But I needed some time to think, and I reckon she did, too. I'm scared of rushing into something…and twice as scared of losing her.''

''I hear what you're saying.'' Caleb stared off into the fire. ''You know, John, I reckon I owe your Jane an apology, sending that fool wire off to Boston. Ruth told me what was what about Jane taking that pin of the old lady's. Wish I could get my hands on that varmint who beat her. I'd hog-tie him to the belly of a longhorn steer.''

''No way you could have known about that, Caleb.'' His own blindness to Jane's problems still haunted John. She needed a man who could shelter her and help her heal, not one too busy wrestling his own demons to care about hers.

Caleb scuffed the dust with the heel of his boot. ''I hope you didn't take too much to heart those things I said about Jane being like Marie. I like to blame all the troubles of my first marriage on Marie not being suited for life in Montana. The fact is, she probably wouldn't have been half so discontented if I'd loved her.''

Sipping Cookie's bitter coffee in silence, John felt the healing balm of Caleb's words sinking into his aching heart. He wondered what it had cost his proud brother-in-law to take responsibility for the failure of his first marriage. Caleb had wed Marie against the inclination of his heart, because he'd believed Ruth was lost to him and because Marie had tricked him into her bed and gotten pregnant.

It was different for John and Jane. No other woman had ever touched him as she had, and he was certain none ever would. How he hoped he would find her waiting for him back in Whitehorn. If she was carrying his child, he might convince her to marry him. If he worked as hard to prove his love as he had worked to prove his loyalty to the Cheyenne, it might be enough to keep her with him.

A bright flash in the sky backlit the Crazy Mountains.

"What was that?" Cicero Price called out.

"If it ain't lightning, we're in trouble," quipped Floyd Cobbs.

"And if it is?" the young fellow asked.

That sobered Floyd right up. "Then we could be in even worse trouble."

Beside John, Caleb hauled off his hat and slapped it against his knee. "Damn, I'm tired of being wrong," he muttered. Then he raised his voice. "Break out the canvas, boys! You may not get dry again until we're back in Whitehorn."

He barely got the words out when the first fat drops of rain came plummeting to earth and embedded themselves in the parched Montana soil.

"Is that rain at last?" Lizzie glanced toward the window.

As Jane got up to check, a jagged fork of lightning spiked the evening sky. The abruptness of it made her jump back.

"That's rain, all right. I'll go make sure the windows are shut." Though she braced herself for the following roll of thunder, it still made her heart jump into her throat.

She ran to the west-facing side of the house first, where the wind lashed rain hardest against the windowpanes. Later, when she peered out her own east-facing window, Jane looked toward the rolling rangeland outside town. Would John have any shelter tonight? Might Caleb abandon the roundup once some rain fell?

A blinding flash of lightning shattered the darkness of the Big Sky, followed by a deafening clap of thunder.

None of the storms she'd experienced in Boston had ever seemed as violent as this one promised to be. Was it possible John could be in danger out on the range? A tight chill crept into Jane's stomach and lodged there.

"I wish William hadn't needed to stay late at the bank this evening," said Lizzie when Jane returned to the sitting room. "He'll get drenched to the bone coming home in this downpour."

"Do you still want to wait supper for him, or should we go ahead and eat?" Jane stifled a yelp as another clap of thunder rumbled overhead.

"Hmm. I don't feel very hungry. Knowing Will, he may decide to stay put at the bank until the rain eases. And who knows when that's likely to be?"

As Lizzie struggled to rise from the rocking chair, she let out a squeak of surprise and sat down again, hard. "Oh dear. I'm wet."

"Wet?" Jane glanced at the ceiling, expecting to see rain leaking through.

"From the baby." Lizzie's creamy complexion paled to the bluish cast of skim milk. "Haley told me this might happen, so I'd be prepared. It means the baby's going to come soon. Can you help me up to the bedroom, Jane, then go fetch Will?"

Jane's glance skittered toward the windows, where the rain hammered. "Y-yes, of course."

She knelt by Lizzie's chair. "Put your arms around my neck and lean all your weight on me when we stand up. There."

They walked slowly to the stairs and began to mount them. Halfway up to the first landing, Lizzie clenched the banister and sucked a raspy breath in through her teeth. Jane could scarcely believe the force with which her tiny friend clutched her hand. It almost brought tears to Jane's eyes.

After a minute or two, Lizzie's grip eased and she let out a shaky sigh. "That was much worse than anything from the other day. Jane, I haven't told Will, because I don't want to worry him, but I'm scared."

In spite of her bulging middle, Lizzie suddenly looked so very young and vulnerable.

Jane wrapped her in a swift embrace. "That's all right. I'm scared most of the time, with a lot less reason. Let's get you to bed, so I can go tell William to bring the doctor. Once they're here, I'm sure you'll feel better. And just think, Lizzie, very soon you'll have a beautiful little son or daughter in your arms."

In spite of the frightening ordeal ahead of Lizzie, Jane would have changed places with her friend in a heartbeat. How she wished she'd conceived John's child that night in the foreman's cabin.

"I—I will, won't I?" Lizzie caught her quivering lower lip between her teeth. "I wonder which it will be and who it'll take after in its looks?"

"Your little one's pretty sure to be blond." Jane coaxed Lizzie up the rest of the stairs. "Have you and William settled on any names yet?"

"I'm partial to Dixon for a boy, but William has a fancy to call him Washington. Can you imagine that? What would you call the poor little fellow for short—Wash?"

As they talked, Jane sensed Lizzie calming. Could that be the secret of conquering fear—to concentrate on the future, once the trial was past?

"What about a girl?" she prompted, as she helped Lizzie change into her nightgown. "Would William like to name her after old Queen Victoria in England?"

"Oh my!" Lizzie grabbed the bedpost and whimpered

until the pain passed. "That wasn't very long between spells. Haley told me it'd likely be longer than this, at first. Can you go get Will and Dr. Gray for me, Jane?"

"Sure, I will. You just get into bed and relax. Maybe once you're off your feet it'll slow down a little," said Jane, as if she knew a fool thing about the delivery of babies. "I'll try to get back with them before your next...in a jiffy. Now you just keep your mind on that little baby, won't you?"

If it came to a choice between venturing out in the storm or staying alone with Lizzie, to watch her suffer, Jane was willing to take her chances with the rain and the lightning. Sucking in a deep breath, as if she was about to jump into a river, she ventured out to meet the storm. The wind almost blasted the door out of her grip, but Jane held on, slamming it behind her to make sure the latch caught. She gasped as the rain instantly drenched her clothes.

The world seemed to be engulfed in one great river, Jane decided as the wind buffeted her like a treacherous current, one second stealing her breath and the next lashing rain into her face. She could barely see an arm's length in front of her. The dusty, hard-packed dirt of the road had turned to slippery mud.

From William and Lizzie's place, a mile outside of town, Jane could walk to Whitehorn in less than half an hour. Tonight it took her nearly twice that long to reach the bank. All that time, part of her mind fixed on Lizzie, alone, afraid and in pain. Another part fretted over John. Where was he and how was he faring?

A strong capable man like John could take care of himself, her reason insisted. Papa had been a strong, capable man, too, she remembered as the fear grew colder and heavier in her belly.

When Jane stumbled up to the door of the bank, she

found it locked, though a faint light glowed within. Pounding on the door, she yelled, "Mr. Kincaid!" at the top of her lungs, until it opened abruptly. She staggered inside.

"Jane, good heavens, what is it?" demanded William Kincaid as she gasped for breath to speak. "Lizzie? Is the baby coming?"

Jane nodded. "The...pains came...on her quite...suddenly."

"I'll go fetch my rig from the livery stable, then we can swing by Dr. Gray's place to fetch him."

"Lizzie needs...you with her...as soon as you can get there. I'll go find the doctor."

The banker blanched. "Are you sure?"

Nodding, Jane fought down a smile. William was every bit as scared as she and Lizzie. Maybe more.

"Just hold her...hand and talk to her. Take her...mind off it. Keep her think...ing about the baby."

"Very well. You go on. I'll put out the lamp and lock up here."

He opened the door just wide enough for Jane to slip out, then banged it shut behind her.

She hesitated for a moment, trying to orient herself with almost no visual landmarks. If she crossed the street, she could hug the front of those buildings and be shielded from the worst of the wind and rain. Jane plunged out into the darkness. Moving from building to building, she managed to reach the doctor's house at last.

"Dr. Gray!" Even as she hammered on his door, Jane could tell it was useless. Not a glimmer of light showed from any of the windows. The doctor must have been out calling on another patient when the storm broke.

But which patient?

Jane racked her brains. Old Mrs. Fairfax, the Methodist

minister's mother? The manse wasn't too far off. At least it would be a place to start.

The minister's wife gave Jane a very sour look when she stepped into the manse entry, dripping rain all over the carpet. Her disapproval rapidly changed to solicitous concern when she discovered Jane's errand on that wild night.

"Dr. Gray did come to see Mother Fairfax a while before the storm started. Then he got called away. A brawl at one of the saloons, I believe." She shook her head reproachfully. "Broken bottles, if you please. Stitches needed, I understand."

"Do you…recollect…which saloon?"

"Oh my. I suppose it makes quite a difference, doesn't it? I can never keep them straight. Dens of iniquity, every one."

Mrs. Endicott would get along swimmingly with Mrs. Mead Fairfax, Jane decided.

"Was it Gribble and Warren, where the circuit judge holds court? Or Big Mike's?"

"It's no use, I can't recall." The minister's wife shook her head. "You certainly do seem to know their names real well, Miss Harris."

"I guess I'll just have to go look until I find him," said Jane. Not wanting to shock Mrs. Fairfax senseless, she didn't add what she was thinking—that poking her nose into one saloon after another was her idea of hell.

"God bless you, I'm sure. If Dr. Gray shows up back here, I'll tell him to get right out to William Kincaid's." With that, Mrs. Fairfax held the door for Jane to slip out.

At least the saloons were all ranged along Main Street in pretty close proximity. She'd just begin at one end and work her way up, Jane decided, starting with the Centennial. As the rain beat down on her, she made her way there.

At the threshold, Jane hesitated. The noise coming from

inside the saloon was loud enough to compete with the howling wind and the distant thunder. Remembering Lizzie, she squared her shoulders and pushed the door open.

None of the Centennial patrons even turned to look at her. They were all craning their necks and standing on chairs to get a better view of the boxing match going on in the middle of the saloon. Yelling encouragement to the favorite, booing and heckling his opponent, they didn't even notice Jane's arrival.

She almost burst into tears of relief when she recognized Harry Talbert, the town barber, at the back of the crowd.

"Mr. Talbert!" she hollered, tugging on his coat. "Has the doctor been here? We need him out at the Kincaids'."

After recovering from the shock of seeing her there, Harry Talbert tapped on several shoulders and bawled inquiries about Dr. Gray.

"Somebody heard there was a fight at the Four Kings!" he shouted above the roar of the crowd. "Try there!"

One down, Jane thought as she let herself out.

Compared to the Centennial, the Four Kings was silent as a tomb. Jane would have preferred it noisy. From the various poker games, every eye seemed to train on her as she staggered in. Henry Hill rose from one of the tables. He cast an insolent, lingering glance over Jane from the crest of her sodden bonnet to the toes of her shoes.

"To what do we owe the pleasure of your visit this evening, Miss Harris?"

By now Jane was too frantic about Lizzie to care about herself at all. She couldn't even work up a blush. "I'm looking for Dr. Gray and I was told I might find him here."

The proprietor of the Four Kings shook his head and flashed a smile that showed his gold tooth. "The good doctor isn't much of a gambling man, I'm afraid. He only comes here when one of my girls needs...seeing to. Will you stay and have a little drink to warm you up, Miss Harris?''

"No, thank you." Jane shot him the kind of withering look she'd often watched Mrs. Endicott dispense.

The saloonkeeper's smarmy smile faded. "You might try the Double Deuce. I hear Dr. Gray sometimes stops there for a drink."

Jane didn't stop to explain that the doctor was out in his professional capacity. With a curt nod to Mr. Hill, she set off again. What if Lizzie's baby had already come? Could infants be born without a doctor in attendance?

Gribble and Warren was practically deserted. But when Jane saw the overturned chairs and broken glass, she almost broke into a cheer. *This* must be the place.

A dark-haired man turned from the bar. "Miss Harris, what are you doing out on a night like this?" asked James Kincaid, the sheriff.

Jane spotted Dr. Gray, packing his satchel. "Looking for him. Lizzie's having her baby. We have to get out there right away."

The doctor ran a hand through his hair. "I swear babies have an affinity for storms and the middle of the night. I'll go fetch my buggy from the livery stable."

"Don't bother." The sheriff glanced over at two men who had obviously just received medical attention. "I brought a wagon to cart this pair back to my lockup. I think a little ride out to Will's place and back would do them both a world of good."

Almost before she knew it, Jane found herself seated between the doctor and the sheriff, with the two prisoners huddled miserably in the back of the wagon. They hurtled toward the Kincaids' place with reckless disregard for the darkness, the rain and the muddy road. One second Jane wished the sheriff would slow down so they wouldn't all be killed, the next she thought of Lizzie and wished they could go faster.

Their noisy entry into the house brought William Kincaid hurtling down the stairs. "Dr. Gray, thank God! I've got lots of hot water boiling."

"Good." The doctor peeled off his sopping coat and hat and handed them to Jane. "I could use a cup of coffee."

After removing his muddy boots, he hefted his satchel and headed upstairs. Jane wandered into the kitchen and collapsed onto one of the chairs. The cast-iron stove fairly glowed with heat, and steam poured from a dozen pots and kettles crowded on top of it. Jane longed to jump into one of them. Then maybe she could warm up.

"The doctor wants coffee," she reminded herself, scarcely aware that she was speaking out loud. "He'll need dry clothes, too, poor man. I suppose I could do with a change myself. I wonder if Mr. Kincaid's had anything to eat?"

Rising from the chair, Jane tried to ignore her own shivering as she brewed a pot of coffee and heated some soup.

An hour later, the doctor banished William downstairs to calm his nerves with a hefty tot of brandy. Jane thought she'd never seen anyone quite as miserable and frightened as William Kincaid looked just then.

"What's taking so long?" he demanded every time he heard Lizzie cry out.

He raised a pair of haunted eyes to Jane. "I can't lose her. I can't. What would I do without her?"

Such an impassioned outburst from a man usually so calm and composed brought a lump to Jane's throat. She managed to soothe him with reassurances she scarcely believed herself. Before the night was over, though, she

watched William Kincaid twist on the rack of his love for
Lizzie. And she recalled with wrenching clarity her
mother's anguish as days had stretched into weeks with no
news of her father's ship.

When dawn broke over the Big Sky, the wind suddenly
eased, though the rain still beat a steady tattoo. A deathly
hush fell over the Kincaid house.

William froze and Jane held her breath.

Then a lusty infant wail shattered the silence. The cool,
reserved banker bent his head to his knees and sobbed.
Jane stole away to the kitchen so William could vent his
feelings in privacy.

Later, while Lizzie slept and William made the acquaintance of his new son, Jane served Dr. Gray an enormous
breakfast.

"I hope you won't take offense at what I'm about to
say, Miss Harris." The doctor leveled a look at her over
the rim of his coffee mug.

"That depends on what it is, Dr. Gray." Jane wilted
onto the chair opposite him. She was too tired and spent
of emotion to summon up a proper sense of outrage.

One corner of his mouth crinkled in a sardonic smile.
"I can hardly believe you're the same young woman who
fainted dead away when I tried to make conversation with
you in Caleb Kincaid's parlor."

Jane thought about it before answering. "Maybe I'm not
that girl anymore."

"You showed a lot of pluck last night, hunting me up
at that saloon in the teeth of the storm."

If she hadn't been so tired, Jane might have smiled. Dr.
Gray didn't know the half of what she'd gone through to
find him.

"When I first met you," the doctor continued, "I

doubted you had the necessary strength for life here in the West. I'm pleased to be proved wrong.''

Though she acknowledged his compliment with a nod, in her heart of hearts Jane knew it wasn't so. Oh, she'd managed to prevail over her fear of physical threats to herself. But watching Will Kincaid last night, she'd witnessed the test of a different kind of strength.

Would William have given Lizzie his heart if he'd understood how deeply any threat to *her* would threaten him? Probably.

As she thought about John out on the range in such a terrible storm, Jane wasn't sure she'd ever be able to muster that kind of courage.

Chapter Eighteen

The rain they'd prayed for all summer slammed into the Kincaid roundup with the force of a stampede. Wind seemed to rage from every direction at once. Thunder and lightning spooked the horses. In all his years under the Big Sky, John Whitefeather couldn't recollect a worse storm.

The first night passed in a violent blur. One fierce gust ripped the canvas off Cookie's chuck wagon. Lightning struck a tree, killing a cow and calf huddled nearby. A couple of the horses bolted.

Fortunately, the tepee Walks on Ice had brought from Sweetwater on a travois remained standing. Most of the Cheyenne and a number of Caleb's men crowded inside to snatch a few minutes sleep sitting up, leaning against each other. When a sullen gray morning dawned to a steady downpour, the old Cheyenne woman still had a small fire and dry supplies with which to brew tea and fry bread for everyone's breakfast.

"We've got the lion's share of our stock collected," Caleb told his crew. "And who knows how long this'll keep up? I say we head straight back to the ranch. I'll send a few cowboys to round up the rest once this breaks."

As the men nodded and grunted their agreement, John's

thoughts turned anxiously toward Whitehorn. How had Jane weathered the storm? Would this show of the Big Sky's ugly temper have sent her scurrying back East in spite of her promise to wait for him?

They were a good day's ride from the ranch, with a branch of the Yellowstone River in the way. Not to mention how this enormous herd of cattle would slow their progress. He could only try to keep his mind focused on the job at hand and hope Jane would honor her word.

Through the morning and early afternoon, Caleb's crew drove the cattle, which only wanted to sink down onto the mud and wait out the storm. Rain collected on the wide brims of the cowboys' hats and sluiced off the back. Tired, hungry, cold and wet, they pressed on, hoping to glimpse the lights of home before day's end.

Riding ahead of the herd to scout terrain, John and Caleb crested a rise, then reined in their horses abruptly. Caleb loosed a stream of the foulest curses John had ever heard pass his lips. John was tempted to add a few Cheyenne profanities of his own.

They stared down at the swollen, turbulent waters before them.

''This storm must've dumped a pile of rain up in the mountains.'' Caleb slumped in his saddle. ''It's going to be a miserable job fording these cows across that mess.''

John swiped the back of his hand across his mouth. ''Have we got any choice?''

After gazing upstream, then down, Caleb shook his head. ''One way it gets wider and the other way it gets deeper. Trying to go around it will take us days out of our way.''

''I'll go tell the men.'' John rode around, alerting everyone about what lay ahead.

By the time the first cow made her way across the raging

stream, half wading, half swimming, the crew all knew
their tasks. A couple of the best ropers positioned themselves on either side of the river, downstream from the
herd, to lasso any calves that might lose their footing. A
small number of men led the first of the herd across and
kept them moving once they reached the opposite bank.
Others drove the animals from behind and kept a lookout
for stock straying up or down the near bank.

The thin trickle of cows making their way across gradually swelled as pressure from behind nudged the front
ones forward.

In the barely controlled confusion, Floyd Cobbs managed to come unsaddled, and for a while it looked like he
might be swept beneath a churning sea of bovine hooves.
Then Ravencrest wheeled his pinto and managed to catch
Floyd's arm. The young Cheyenne pulled the cowboy up
behind him, and the tough little range pony struggled
ashore, carrying them both.

Seeing Floyd's horse struggling in midstream, John
nudged Hawkwing into the water. "Might as well get our
baptism now as later, old friend. Let's go."

He shivered as the water crept up his legs, though it
wasn't as cold as he'd expected. Then again, perhaps he
was too thoroughly chilled from the rain to notice much
difference. Reaching out to grasp the reins of Floyd's
mare, he called soothing Cheyenne words to her. Whether
that helped, or whether she just needed the familiar assurance of a tug on her bridle, she settled down and headed
for shore.

John was concentrating so intensely on retrieving
Floyd's horse that at first he didn't notice the commotion
from both sides of the river. When he heard the men shout-
ing his name and pointing upstream, he glanced that way
just in time to see a large tree bearing down on him.

In the endless few seconds while he urged both horses forward, John found himself wondering how the tree had come to be sailing downriver. Perhaps the earth around its roots had dried and been blown away during the dry summer. Then wind and the force of the river must have uprooted it.

It went speeding past him with inches to spare.

John opened his mouth to say, "That was close."

At the last moment, the tree trunk fishtailed, and a thick length of root snagged him. For an instant his boots caught in the stirrups and he feared he would be yanked clean in two. Then one boot pulled loose and the other foot worked free.

A heartbeat of relief drowned when the river's powerful current hurtled the tree into the fording cattle. It smacked John into the hindquarters of one shorthorn, then dragged him on, momentarily stunned. Before he could recover his wits, the tree spun, hauling him underwater.

Vaguely aware that his belt had somehow caught on the tree root, he thought he should do something to free himself, or at least raise his head above the water. As a strangely seductive sense of warmth and peace began to steal over him, John tried to remember why he should struggle. A vision of Jane beckoned him and he longed to surrender to it.

Perhaps this was the only way he could be with her.

"Ruth! Caleb? Come in." Jane struggled to hide her surprise as she ushered them into William and Lizzie's front hall. "You must be here to meet your new nephew."

Peering over Caleb's shoulder, she hoped to see John striding up the porch stairs behind them. She fought down a pang of disappointment over his absence. If Caleb had returned from the roundup, John would likely be paying a call soon.

Perhaps he was in town at Harry Talbert's this very minute, having a bath and getting barbered after his weeks on the range. By the look and smell of Caleb, he'd dispensed with those niceties.

"Lizzie had her baby?" Ruth appeared dazed, as if she was walking in her sleep.

"A boy, you say?" Caleb tried to smile, but made a miserable job of it.

A queer flutter of panic down deep in her belly reminded Jane of the first time she'd stepped into the Kincaids' kitchen. Something was very wrong and everyone knew what.

Except her.

"Yes, and a big, strapping fellow, too." John. Something had happened to John.

If she kept on talking and didn't stop, no one would be able to tell her. And if she didn't hear, it wouldn't be true.

"A real Kincaid, William says. Arrived the other night in the middle of that dreadful storm. I had a devil of a time hunting down Dr. Gray. Finally found him in the saloon, mind you. Not drinking, of course. Just stitching up a couple of fellows who'd gotten in a fight. Thank goodness your cousin James was there to arrest them, for he had a horse and wagon ready. Otherwise—"

"We didn't come about the baby." Ruth cut Jane off when she paused to gulp a breath. "I reckon you've probably guessed that by now."

Jane clamped her lips shut and nodded. She looked from Caleb's blue-gray eyes to Ruth's dark brown ones, searching for some sign of hope in either pair. Instead she found only a reflection of her own anguish. She longed to turn and run until she was too far away to hear them. Or perhaps cover her ears and hum very loudly. Sooner or later, though, she'd have to stop and face the truth.

"Take me to him." Perhaps John was still clinging to life and her presence could make a difference.

Caleb scraped his hat off. "We can't, Jane. That's the trouble. All the Cheyenne and as many of my ranch hands as I can spare are out combing both sides of the river for him right now. I wish I could tell you and Ruth to keep hoping, but that wouldn't be right. I saw the whole thing...."

In broken words he told her how they'd had to drive the cattle across a swollen river. How one of the cowboys had come unseated, and John had plunged into the water to lead the riderless horse to safety. About the uprooted tree that had dragged him downstream, through the fording herd and away.

Jane listened. Unmoving. Unblinking. Unbelieving.

Of all the dangers this land could throw at her and those she loved, she'd believed they were safe from her worst fear. They'd never found the body of her shipwrecked father, and now Jane wondered what had killed her mother in the end. Despair or hope?

"Come back to the ranch with us, Jane." Ruth took her hand. "I'll send Mrs. Muldoon to help Lizzie. Your place is with us."

Somehow Jane found her voice. "Maybe later, Ruth. For now, I have to stay here. Lizzie and William need me."

If she let Ruth and Caleb take her back to the ranch, comfort her, cosset her, she would shatter as easily and irrevocably as an eggshell. But if she kept moving and working, if there was someone depending on her, she might just hold herself together. The way John would have wanted her to.

"We need you, too, Jane. Besides…" When Ruth tried to persuade her, Caleb shook his head at his wife.

"Go up and visit with Lizzie." Jane almost didn't recognize her own voice, it sounded so hollow. "I have to fix dinner, and you must stay to eat."

She needed to keep her hands busy. Do the chores she was accustomed to doing at the time she was accustomed to doing them. Cling to some tattered shred of routine and normalcy in a world suddenly turned upside down. Without another word to Ruth and Caleb, Jane took herself away to the kitchen. There she stoked the fire in the stove and began peeling potatoes.

She didn't feel like crying. Her heart didn't even hurt. From old, bitter experience, Jane knew this blessed numbness would soon wear off. Then pain would land on her with the weight of a granite boulder. She would either become strong enough to carry it or it would crush her, the way it had crushed her mother.

No, Jane would not let that happen. If she did, it would make a mockery of all the qualities John had tried to foster in her.

Before Mama had run away to marry against her family's wishes, she'd been a child of privilege. Pampered and indulged until she'd come to feel entitled to pleasure and endless happiness. When life had turned and treated her harshly, she'd had no resources of character to draw on.

For the first time she could recall, Jane looked back on her own past struggles with gratitude. They had made her who she was. Appreciative of life's smallest pleasures. Sympathetic to others in trouble. And stronger than most people might realize.

Herself included.

Somehow she survived that day, her body going through the motions of her household duties, while her thoughts swirled in a thousand different directions at once. Her detachment was not so complete, however, that she failed to note a muted glow of admiration in Caleb's cool eyes and a tone of newfound respect in his voice.

Her composure began to chip away at bedtime when she peeked in on Lizzie to ask if there was anything she needed before Jane retired for the night.

"No, dear," Lizzie murmured, casting an anxious eye toward the cradle. "Even if there was, I wouldn't tell you. You've been amazing today, keeping the house running, when I can hardly guess how you must be feeling. Are you *sure* you wouldn't rather go spend a few days out at the ranch? Will and I would feel just awful if we thought you were pushing yourself to stay here on our account."

"It's kind of everyone to want to look after me." Jane shook her head. "But I need to learn how to look after myself. And I need to keep busy. Out on the ranch, there'd be so many...reminders."

Lizzie patted a spot on the edge of her bed, and almost against her will Jane accepted the unspoken invitation.

"He loved you, you know." Lizzie clasped Jane's hands. "More than you may realize. Probably more than he ever realized. For the first little while I knew John Whitefeather, I was scared to death of him. He had this anger in his eyes, and I felt like whatever was bothering him must be partly my fault. After you came to Whitehorn he was a different man."

The first true pain of grief pierced Jane's swaddling of disbelief. She would never see John again. Nothing in the world could be worse than that. As she struggled to hold her heart together, Lizzie's voice seemed to reach her from a long way off.

"Toward the end of my labor, when the baby was coming, I was sure I was going to die. I was scared and sad that I'd be leaving the folks I love. But I knew I wouldn't trade my short life for a longer one without Will. I'm sure John felt the same about you.''

Jane couldn't speak and she couldn't stay. Lizzie's sympathetic wisdom might thaw the cracking sheath of ice around her heart and trigger an avalanche of pain. Giving Lizzie's hands a squeeze, Jane fled to the privacy of her own room.

Drawing her knees up almost to her chin, she curled up on her bed, lost in a blackness deeper than night. One for which she could not imagine sunrise. With a dry ache gnawing at her heart.

She would have given anything to be able to soothe it with the tears that had once come so easily to her.

Would he ever be dry or warm again? John wondered as he pulled himself up the muddy riverbank. He vaguely recalled his struggle to free himself from the tree that had tried to drown him and carry him away. Instead of yielding to a rosy dream of Jane, he'd channeled all his fading will and strength into fighting his way back to the real woman.

Too many people she'd loved had slipped away from her. Damned if he'd be one more.

When he finally recovered consciousness, John found himself washed up on an outcropping of rock. His whole body felt like it had been pummeled almost to jelly, and he knew it would hurt even worse if the numbness ever wore off.

Shivering and gasping for breath, he gazed around, hoping to see some familiar landmark or a place of shelter. He didn't recognize anything on the rolling prairie, but the distance of the Crazy Mountains in the west told him the river's swift current had carried him far from the roundup.

A weak but insistent bawling drew John's gaze back to the river. "Maw! Maw!"

The white face of a shorthorn calf poked out of some bushes, now partially underwater. It must have been one of Caleb's herd, John decided, carried downstream by the same tree that had abducted him. The calf made a feeble attempt to scramble up the riverbank, but its hooves could find no purchase in the slick mud.

John knew if he tried to drag it up the bank, the calf might pull them both back into the river instead. But it was the only other warm-blooded creature around, and he couldn't leave it to die when it had fought to survive this long.

Unbuckling his belt, he slid as close as he dared. If the roots of those bushes gave way, both he and the calf would be in big trouble.

"Hush now, little white face," he murmured in Cheyenne. "Maybe you and me can help each other get home to our kin."

When the word *kin* passed his lips, John knew he didn't mean his Cheyenne band, or even Ruth and her family. He meant Jane.

Pulling the long strip of leather into a loose loop through the buckle, John managed to get one of the creature's hooves through it after several failed attempts. When the calf thrashed and rolled its eyes, John wondered if this foolishness was going to cost him his life. He knew he had to try, anyway.

He talked to the calf some more and stroked its nose. A rough tongue thrust out and swiped across his hand.

"All right, little one, it's time to get you out of the water before you pull this bush out by the roots. Come on now."

John stretched out on his belly and began to tug on his belt. It was hard to get much force behind his grip in this position, but trying to anchor his feet in the sodden earth of the riverbank would be way too risky. Inch by inch, he dragged the heavy little animal up the unstable slope until it finally got something solid under one of its hooves. A final desperate lunge brought it sprawling onto solid ground.

"Good for you, little white face!" John rubbed its hide to warm it up. "You and me may make it back home in one piece, after all."

To his surprise and relief, John realized his heart was beating stronger and he felt warmer. When he tried to rise to his feet, though, the stabbing pain in his booted ankle made him cry out.

The calf bawled, too.

"Don't worry, it's just my leg. I must have twisted or busted something when it caught in my stirrup."

Surveying the landscape, John assessed his options. If he stuck to the river, moving along the bank, chances were good he'd meet up with somebody looking for him. But how long might that take on a busted ankle? Long enough for Jane to hear he'd been killed and leave town?

If he struck out south, away from the river, he'd eventually come to the tracks of the Northern Pacific Railroad. He wasn't going to make very good time crawling on his hands and knees, though.

As if it could read his thoughts, the calf shook itself and struggled to its feet.

"One good turn deserves another, little friend." John grabbed the end of his belt with one hand and pulled himself up on his sound leg until he was able to throw his arm around the calf's neck.

The creature bawled and bucked, but John hung on, murmuring a mixture of Cheyenne and English. He hadn't spent most of his life gentling animals for nothing. The calf soon calmed and began to walk in roughly the direction John wanted to go.

The clouds parted, and before they'd ventured too far, the sun appeared and began to beat down on them.

"You know, the thing I hate most about this country is that it never does anything by halves." Wiping the sweat from his hairline, John asked himself what kind of idiot made conversation with a calf.

A few more halting steps and they crested a gentle rise. Before them lay the tracks of the Northern Pacific.

John sighed. "Come to think, that's what I love most about it, too."

Chapter Nineteen

"Jane, the telegraph dispatcher brought this wire message over to the bank for me to give you." William Kincaid handed her a piece of paper. "He said it's from Boston. Not bad news, I hope."

Boston. The word still made the back of her throat tighten.

"I hope so, too, Will. Thank you for bringing it." Something to do with Emery, no doubt. Well, she was beyond his power to hurt, now.

Unfolding the paper, Jane read the dispatcher's meticulous print. Then she read it again. And a third time. Each word separately she understood, but taken together they made no sense.

"It *is* bad, isn't it?" Will's tone of solemn concern warmed a tiny spot in Jane's cold, aching heart. "Don't worry. Lizzie and I will help you out any way you need. So will Caleb and Ruth...all the Kincaids will stand behind you."

"I—it's not *bad*." She handed the paper over to see if he could make anything of it. "Just puzzling. Can you tell me what it says?"

As he read the telegram, the banker's tensely furrowed

brow relaxed. The corners of his mouth began to curl upward. "What is it about the message you don't understand? This appears to be from the lawyer you sent that money to. He says your Mrs. Endicott has been looking high and low for you ever since you disappeared from the hospital in Boston. After reading the letter you sent, she's disowned her scoundrel of a nephew and thrown him out. It says you are...and have always been...heiress to her fortune, and she's frantic to have you back home as soon as possible."

That's what she'd thought it said, but it couldn't be true. Could it? Understanding those clicks from the telegraph must be a tricky business. Perhaps the dispatcher had just taken it down wrong.

"Well, well, well." William shook his head, beaming. Then he called out to his wife who was rocking the baby in the sitting room. "Lizzie, wait till you hear! We've got a Boston heiress working for us."

"What are you going on about, Will? You didn't stop in at the Centennial Saloon on the way home, did you?"

Back in the kitchen, Jane swayed on her feet, then sank onto the nearest chair. She felt as though she had just downed several strong drinks in quick succession.

Heiress to Mrs. Endicott's fortune? The very idea was preposterous. Why had Mrs. Endicott never hinted at such a thing? Why had Jane and Emery needed to keep their engagement secret because his aunt wanted him to marry a girl with better prospects?

"Oh, my stars!" Jane whispered to herself. "*That's* why Emery wanted to marry me. I always assumed he'd get Mrs. Endicott's money, but he must have known it was coming to me."

In the light of that insight, so many confusing aspects of her life in Boston and her relationship with Emery suddenly made perfect sense. His need to isolate and control her. His violent flashes of temper. The unexplained sense that he'd resented her presence in the house, even though he'd claimed to care about her.

Lizzie tiptoed into the kitchen. "I got Will to put the baby up in his cradle. Now I'm going to make you some tea, Jane Harris. What a shock this must be to you—a pleasant one, but a shock just the same. And after what you've already been through." She shook her head.

"Sit down, Lizzie. You really shouldn't be out of bed yet, much less working in the kitchen." Jane pulled Lizzie down onto a chair beside her.

The two women sat in silence for a moment, each mulling over what this telegram from Boston would mean for them.

"I suppose you'll want to head back East right away." Lizzie fumbled in her pocket and produced a handkerchief. "Don't mind me blubbering a little. Haley says it happens to most women a day or so after they've had a baby. We'll cry at the drop of a hat."

She dabbed her eyes. "I'm really happy as can be for you. If anyone ever deserved to come into a nice fortune it's you, Jane. But I get lonesome just thinking of you going so far away."

"It still hasn't quite sunk in." Jane shook her head slowly, as if trying to adjust her mind to the news. "I suppose going back to Boston is the only sensible thing to do."

If such a telegram had been waiting for her when she'd arrived in Whitehorn three months ago, Jane would have hopped the next train East so fast it would have caused a minor tornado. Mrs. Endicott was offering her the one thing in life she'd always craved.

Security.

With Emery gone she'd never again need to fear for her safety. Mrs. Endicott's fortune would protect her from the specter of poverty. Even the emotional sterility of the house in Beacon Hill would numb her shattered heart.

Not so long ago, she'd been ready to barter her soul to find such a safe, tranquil haven. Now it loomed before her like a prison.

"Of course, you're welcome to stay with us for as long as you care to," Lizzie offered.

Stay in Whitehorn to be constantly reminded of John? To witness the wedded bliss of Will and Lizzie and the other Kincaids, until her bitterness and envy poisoned her affection for them, warping her as Emery's covetous resentment had warped him?

"I appreciate that, and I'll certainly stay until you can find somebody else to help you out." Jane sighed, conceding defeat. "Boston is where I belong, though."

Lizzie nodded. "I understand. Everyone will. A woman can't turn her back on an opportunity like this. Don't you worry about us, though. I'm sure Ruth wouldn't mind letting that Mrs. Muldoon come here for a while."

Maybe if she could get out of town fast enough, Jane reasoned, the past three months might feel like a dream or a particularly vivid story she'd read in one of Beadle's dime novels.

"Do you suppose Will would mind driving me in to Big Timber to purchase my train ticket?"

An hour later, with no more worldly goods than she'd brought to Montana, Jane drove down the main street of Whitehorn. The passage of traffic on the muddy roads had turned them into rutted pig wallows. The false fronts of the town's businesses looked rather shabby, and the whole place smelled of horse manure, damp sawdust and raw spirits.

Jane wasn't sure she could bear to leave it.

She tugged on Will's sleeve. "Would you mind if we stop here for just a minute?"

The banker cast a glance at the Double Deuce Saloon, then cocked an eyebrow at Jane.

"I saw some of Caleb's ranch hands go in," she explained, "and I'd like to say goodbye to them."

Jane couldn't bring herself to part from Ruth and Barton face-to-face, fearful she might change her mind about leaving. But something compelled her to pass a final word with the men who'd last seen John alive.

"If that's what you want." Will pulled up to the boardwalk and helped Jane down from the buggy. "I'll just be over at the bar if you need me."

She found Caleb's men at the corner table where John Whitefeather had been sitting the first time she'd laid eyes on him. They were all drinking sarsaparillas.

When he glanced over his shoulder and recognized her, Floyd Cobbs jumped to his feet and pulled out a chair. "Miss Harris, ma'am. Good to see you again. Will you join us?"

"Thank you, Mr. Cobbs, I will."

For a long awkward minute, they all sat. Clearing throats, but not speaking. Desperately avoiding eye contact. All their thoughts clearly turned in the same direction.

"They'll find him alive yet, don't you worry," said Clel Harding in a voice so hollow it was obvious he did not believe his own words.

"Them Cheyenne're great trackers," Floyd chimed in. "Real smart fellers."

The other men spoke admiringly of the Cheyenne and how John had recruited them to help with the roundup.

More and more John's name crept into the conversation as the men recounted his actions on the range in hushed, respectful voices.

Jane listened in silence, wounded, yet strangely comforted at the same time.

"Something was weighing on his mind, I reckon." Clel took a swig of his drink. "I seen him and Mr. Kincaid talking by the fire."

Something weighing on his mind? Jane stifled a whimper that rose in her throat. Had John's preoccupation with her and their impossible relationship cost him his concentration just when he'd needed it most?

"It's all my fault!" The thought had flared in Jane's mind, but the words had come out in a man's deep baritone.

Floyd Cobbs raised a trembling hand to shield his eyes. "I—if I hadn't fallen off my horse like some dang tenderfoot, he'd have never been in the middle of the creek when that old tree came a-sailing down."

"Don't blame yourself." Jane patted the cowboy's arm. "I know he wouldn't blame you."

John wouldn't blame her, either, she realized. And he wouldn't want her punishing herself. Was that part of the reason she'd decided to return to Boston?

Around Jane, the Double Deuce fell ominously silent, except for the sound of a single set of footsteps behind her. The fine hairs on the back of her neck bristled. Had Emery come to get her, at last, now that his aunt had thrown him out and he had nothing more to lose?

A tight, cold ball of fear vaporized in her chest, like snow in a furnace. Jane rose and turned to face him.

So certain she'd see Emery, at first her mind refused to recognize the tall, battered man limping toward her. Their eyes met and his smile lit up the dim interior of the Double Deuce Saloon.

In a voice raspy as tar paper he asked, "What does a fellow have to do to get a sarsaparilla around this place?"

Feeling like she'd died painfully and been just as painfully reborn in a matter of seconds, Jane ran into his open arms as the Double Deuce exploded with joy.

Will let him have his drink of sarsaparilla, which John drained with scarcely a pause for breath. Then he had to answer enough of the cowboys' questions to satisfy them that he'd really survived. Once they were convinced, they poured out of the Double Deuce, threw themselves into their saddles and galloped off to bring the good news to the Kincaid ranch, Sweetgrass and the remaining Cheyenne who were combing the banks of the Yellowstone for his body.

Through the haze of celebration, John clung to Jane's hand as though she might slip away from him at any minute.

"Enough of this," said Will at last. "You need to be seen by a doctor, John. Dr. Gray is supposed to be coming out to our place to check on Lizzie a little later. Why don't you come back there and wait for him?"

"Whatever you say, Will." Now that he'd reached his destination, John could hardly keep his eyes open.

He wanted to talk to Jane. To sort out everything between them and tell her what a cowardly fool he'd been to doubt her. Even if she doubted herself.

Then there was the question he wanted to ask her. By now she must have a pretty good idea whether or not his child was beginning to grow inside her. The fact that she'd lingered in Whitehorn made him hopeful.

Such talk and questions needed more privacy and more

energy than John could muster just then. So he settled for clinging to Jane's hand and nourishing his soul with the sight of her beautiful face.

Lizzie Kincaid almost fainted dead away when they walked through the door, John supported by Will on one side and Jane on the other.

"Sorry to turn your house into an infirmary, ma'am," he croaked. "I hear congratulations are in order."

"Good heavenly days! John Whitefeather." Lizzie collapsed onto the rocking chair and pulled out a handkerchief to catch the tears that abruptly poured down her cheeks.

"If you're sorry to see me, I can go away again," John joshed her. Had the bartender at the Double Deuce spiked his sarsaparilla? He felt giddy and light-headed.

"Go away? I should say not!" Lizzie blew her nose. "Will, you just take him into the little back bedroom beyond the parlor. I don't want to see him have to climb stairs. I declare, you look like you lost a fight with a grizzly bear, John!"

"Not a bear, ma'am," he chuckled. "Just a river. I wonder who's got that calf of mine. No slaughterhouse in Chicago for her, no sir. That little heifer can graze and calve until she falls over dead of old age."

He barely heard Will mutter to Jane, "Any notion what he's going on about? I hope the poor fellow didn't hit his head too hard."

The next thing John knew, he was lying in bed, flinching from the gentle swipe of a washcloth over his scrapes and bruises. He managed to winch his eyes open a sliver.

"I'm sorry if I hurt you," said Jane, "but Dr. Gray told me it's important to keep your wounds clean. He'll be right back to look at your leg and at the bump on your head."

She smiled, an expression that held more worry and

wistfulness than joy. He wanted to gather her close and see what remedy they could find for *her* wounds.

"I've got a powerful thirst."

"Shall I fetch you some water?" Jane rose so quickly, it was all he could do to reach out and catch her sleeve.

"Not *that* kind of thirst." He pulled her back toward him.

"Have you been thinking about me as much as I've been thinking about you since we parted?"

His eyelids ached to slide shut, but he forced them open.

"Of course I thought about you." Her voice sounded choked with emotion, and the forest hazel of her eyes glittered, as if with dew. "I thought I'd never see—"

While she was speaking, he drew Jane close enough to kiss. Before she could finish, he kissed her.

Had she thought she would never see him again? Then perhaps she could understand his fear that one day she might walk out of his life. She might see how it had held him back from committing his whole heart to her, as he longed to.

For now, he settled for committing his lips to hers. Becoming reacquainted with their ripe sweetness. Awakening potent memories of the night they'd first discovered each other as man and woman.

He sensed a struggle within her. One part eager to respond to his kiss and all that it implied. Another part still hesitant, still wary. Had she remained angry with him because his very real attraction for her had begun as a pretense?

Then maybe he would have to gentle his Jane all over again. Slowly, tenderly winning her trust anew. As he watched her ripen with his child.

Nothing less could have induced him to break from that kiss of reunion. But he had to know.

He withdrew just far enough to let the words out. With his hand tangled in Jane's silky hair, he pressed her forehead to his and searched her eyes. "Do you know yet? Whether we have a baby on the way?"

The subtlest rub of her brow against his told him she was shaking her head.

Before he could ask if it only meant she still wasn't sure, Jane whispered, "For a few days I'd thought it might be, but it isn't. You won't be obliged to make an honest woman of me."

"How's our patient doing?" Dr. Gray gave a warning rap on the doorsill, then strode in.

Pulling away from John's feeble grip, Jane fled the room.

If he'd had strength to match his annoyance, John might have strangled the good doctor with his own stethoscope!

Instead, he yelped as Dr. Gray probed his swollen lower leg.

"No bones broken, as far as I can tell," said the doctor, "but you'll have to stay off it, soak it and keep it elevated until those muscles heal. Let's have a look at that gash on your forehead."

John submitted to the examination in stony silence.

"Well, considering your ordeal, you're not in bad shape." Dr. Gray poured some medicine into a spoon and shoved the cloying liquid into John's mouth before he could protest. "Nothing modern medicine can do for you that rest and nourishment won't accomplish." He flashed a wry grin. "A pretty nurse won't hurt, either."

"What was that stuff you gave me?" John wiped his mouth with the back of his hand.

"Just a touch of laudanum to help you sleep soundly. Wouldn't want you thrashing that leg around." The doctor chuckled. "I must say, I've never seen a woman so improved as your Miss Harris. Traipsed all over town the night of the storm to track me down. Through three different saloons, no less. I never guessed she had that kind of pluck."

John's eyes narrowed. "Haven't you got other patients to see?"

Ignoring John's black stare, Dr. Gray tucked his stethoscope and the laudanum bottle back in his satchel. "As a matter of fact, the sheriff wants me to check out that pair of fools he has cooling their heels in the jail. Come see me at my office if you aren't feeling back to your old self in a week or so."

"Say, Doc..."

John didn't want to beg a favor of a man who clearly admired Jane more than he had any business doing. How soon might it be before anyone else came to check on him? He didn't trust either his strength or his balance to go hunting for Jane on his own.

"Would you ask...Miss Harris to come back in? I reckon I could use a drink of water to get the taste of that medicine out of my mouth."

Before the doctor could say yes or no, a commotion of voices and footsteps approached, and Ruth burst into the room with Caleb hot on her heels.

"*Ah hestatanemo!*" His sister hurled herself on John, speaking rapidly in Cheyenne. "I never thought I'd be so happy to see anyone! It was bad of you to give us such a fright. What did the doctor say? You need a good poultice on that cut. Bless all the spirits of the Big Sky for keeping you alive! Stay out of flooded rivers after this, you hear me? What are you laughing about? Did that doctor give you whiskey?"

"Just sleep medicine, little sister." Strong sleep medicine. He felt like his bones were starting to melt.

John glanced past Ruth to Caleb. His brother-in-law looked as though a crushing burden had just been lifted from his back. Yet Caleb's overwhelming relief still held a faint, bitter aftertaste of worry and grief.

"You look damned ugly, old friend." Caleb shook his shaggy blond head. "But it's sure good to see you this side of heaven. We got the herd in. I struck a sweet deal with the railroad to ship 'em back East early."

"That's good. My friends from Sweetgrass?"

"We sent the word out to them that you're alive. They did a fine job on the roundup. Put a couple of them in a proper saddle and teach them to throw a lasso, they'd make top-notch cowboys. I think I've got that young Ravencrest fellow about ready to come apprentice at the ranch next winter."

"Hush, Caleb," said Ruth. "Can't you see he's sleeping?"

He wasn't, quite. John just couldn't hold his eyelids open one more second, nor could he make his mouth move.

Another set of footsteps entered the room, and he listened hard, hoping to catch the sound of Jane's voice before sleep overcame him in earnest.

"Seems like good fortune's smiling on everybody," said William Kincaid. "Our baby arriving nice and healthy. Caleb getting the herd in. Jane coming into all that money. Now John practically rising from the dead. We'll all have plenty to be thankful for in our prayers. Why don't you folks come have a cup of tea and something to eat? I imagine John'll sleep for quite a spell."

"What's this about Jane getting money?" Ruth's voice moved away from the bed.

John struggled to stay conscious, hoping Will, Caleb and

his sister wouldn't get out of earshot before he found out what Will was talking about.

"That's right, you won't have heard yet. That woman Jane used to work for in Boston plans to leave the girl her fortune. Always did, as near as I can make out. Jane sent all the pay Caleb gave her back East so the old lady could buy back the brooch Jane pawned."

"Well, I'll be," murmured Caleb.

The voices were retreating.

"I think she wrote a letter, too," said Will. "Telling the old lady what was what with her scoundrel of a nephew. This morning a wire arrived from Boston asking Jane to come home."

Though he could still hear the drone of voices in the distance, John could no longer make out the words. He'd overheard all he needed to, though.

Jane had a chance at the kind of affluent life she deserved. The kind of undemanding life she needed. And there was no baby to bind her to him.

As the laudanum dragged him into the murky depths of sleep, John almost wished he'd let the river have him.

Chapter Twenty

Jane kept a vigil by John's bed that night, watching him sleep. Her gaze lingered over the finely chiseled contours of his sun-bronzed face. Dwelled longingly on the firm, narrow lips that had coaxed such pleasure from her body. Passed like a visual caress over the mane of dark hair splayed across his pillow.

So recently her heart had ached with emptiness, like a starving belly. Now it swelled so full of love and wistful desire that it hurt all over again.

For a mad instant, after he'd kissed her out of her right mind, she had almost answered his question about the baby with a lie she wished was true. Would it have been so very wrong to say she was pregnant, or even that she was still uncertain, buying her time to conceive?

Yes. It would have been wrong. As wrong as stealing Mrs. Endicott's brooch. As wrong as seducing John to gain his protection. Doing wrong sometimes proved an overwhelming temptation when right wasn't just a straight and narrow path, but also a rocky one on the edge of a steep precipice.

Somehow she'd found the courage to tell him the truth. Then she'd felt his disappointment—a pang so intense it had pierced her heart, too. Immediately she'd regretted her foolish honesty. Had John wanted her only because he thought she might bear his child?

Why did it matter, anyway? she asked herself. John had escaped death…this time. She'd experienced a grim foretaste of the pain she might have to live with one day. And she'd seen for herself how cruel and capricious the Big Sky could turn, without warning. Even if John wanted her to stay, for all the right reasons, how could she, knowing at what perilous risk she placed her heart?

John stirred and his eyelids fluttered. "Damn, I hurt!"

So do I.

"Almost makes me want to swallow another dose of that medicine."

Jane remembered the laudanum she'd been given in the Boston infirmary. Going back to Mrs. Endicott's would blunt all the pain and unpleasantness of life in much the same way, making everything as placid and effortless as a drugged doze.

"Is that you, Jane?" John squinted at her in the flickering candlelight.

"Yes."

"I didn't expect to find you here when I woke up."

She shrugged. "Someone had to keep watch in case you needed anything in the night. William and Lizzie have to see to…their baby."

She'd hesitated over the word, half-afraid, half-hopeful it would give them an excuse to talk about their hopes…or fears.

Instead John said, "I'll be fine until morning if you want to go get some sleep."

"Is that your polite way of asking me to leave?"

"You know I don't set a whole lot of store by fancy manners. Do you want to stay?"

How could she leave?

Jane nodded.

Without any introduction, he asked, "Were you sorry or relieved when you found out...you know...that you weren't..."

It had been only last week. With all that had happened since, it seemed like a hundred years. Yet the pain was still fresh in her heart.

So quietly she could barely hear herself, she whispered, "I wanted to die."

Had he not heard her? Or had he turned a deaf ear because it wasn't what he wanted to hear? Perhaps he just sensed she had more to say.

She did. "I thought you were gone. Lost like my papa. And I couldn't bear not having anything left of you."

The tears she'd longed for last night fell now, though Jane wished she could hold them back. She hated the thought of John marrying her out of pity. Especially when she wasn't certain she wanted to marry him at all.

If he asked, would she have the strength to refuse him? Or the strength to accept?

John moved around in the bed, as though trying in vain to get comfortable. "Sounds like there's been a lot going on around here since I went out on the range."

Jane rummaged in her apron pocket for a handkerchief. He was probably just making small talk to give her time to compose herself.

When she didn't answer, John spoke again. "Dr. Gray told me how you hunted him through nearly every saloon in town to come tend Lizzie when she had her baby. Weren't you scared?"

"Terrified." That probably wasn't what he wanted to hear. He needed a strong, courageous wife. "But Lizzie had to have the doctor, and there was nobody else to go for him.''

John nodded as though he understood. ''You're so scared to stick up for yourself, Jane, but you'd brave a trip to hell for the folks you care about.'' His voice held equal measures of admiration and regret.

She had never thought of it that way before. Until she'd come to Whitehorn, it had been so long since she'd had anyone to care for and protect.

Heaving a deep sigh, John winced. ''Will you pull your chair a little closer and hold my hand?''

I shouldn't. I shouldn't. I shouldn't.

''I suppose so.''

Her hand felt too good, too right in his. She wanted to strip down to her shimmy or further, and lie on that bed beside him. Guide his hand to her breast or between her thighs.

''I reckon you must have been scared to write to Mrs. Endicott, too.''

John's words quenched her passionate impulse...for the most part. ''Of course I was scared. For all I knew she might find a way to have me arrested. When I heard you walking into the Double Deuce yesterday, I figured Emery had come to finish me off. Who told you about all that, anyway?''

''Will mentioned it to Caleb and Ruth when they thought I was asleep. I hear you're an heiress now.'' The muscles in his hand tightened, though not his grip on her. ''Congratulations. I reckon it pays off sometimes to do whatever scares us most.''

''Lots of things in life are a gamble.'' Jane wanted to let go of his hand, but she couldn't. ''Sometimes they pay off big and other times you lose...everything.''

John Whitefeather and the Big Sky represented a gamble

for breathtakingly high stakes. Beacon Hill and Mrs. Endicott were a sure thing.

What was it about this man that made her such a reckless daredevil with her heart?

"I won't pretend I'm not tempted to run off back to Boston." Jane shrank from looking into those relentless blue eyes, but she made herself do it. "I was pretty certain I loved you, but until I thought I'd lost you, I didn't know how much."

John hissed with pain as he wrenched himself up from the pillows and pulled her into his arms. "Those are just about the sweetest words I've ever heard."

He pressed his lips to her brow and kissed his way down the side of her face to her lips. The heat of his firm, muscled chest penetrated her calico shirtwaist.

She wanted him so much it frightened her. "Please don't make me lose my head and throw away my choice about this."

John froze, more truly frightened than when he'd faced death on the river. Would Jane still consider hightailing back East, in spite of how she felt about him?

"Is that what you think I'm trying to do?"

"No. Maybe. When you hold me and kiss me, I like it so much, I *can't* think."

"All right, then." Like a warrior casting aside his most potent weapons, he let go of her and collapsed back onto the bed. "Do you want to go to Boston?"

She threw the challenge right back at him. "Do *you* want me to? Do you want me to stay, even if there's no baby? If I go back, I'll have enough money that I can afford never to marry. Nobody in Beacon Hill will ever know about you and me, so you won't need to marry me just to salvage my reputation."

What could he say? John wondered. What did she want

to hear? His reasons for wanting her in his life had nothing to do with fatherhood or honor, as important as those were to him. Did he dare tell her so?

All his life he'd sought acceptance. Rejecting the white world, before it could reject him. Prepared to sacrifice everything for the Cheyenne, just so he could belong *somewhere*.

He could reject Jane first, foolishly hoping it would hurt less than if she turned her back on him. Or he could pour everything into winning her. Even if it wasn't what she truly wanted.

Was there no other way?

Tell her the truth, perhaps, then let her choose. Leave himself wide-open to hurt. Having thrown down his weapons, must he surrender his shield, too? Did even a Cheyenne warrior have that kind of courage?

"I want what's best for you, Jane. Babies and Cheyenne honor were just excuses to do what I was too scared to do for the real reason. I can't give you the kind of life you could have in Boston with Mrs. Endicott's money."

She jumped from the bed. Wrapping her arms protectively across her chest, she faced him. "It isn't the money I want or the things it can buy. Don't you see that? It's the safety. You can give me so much. Everything I want but that. The more I love you, the worse it'll hurt if I lose you."

"I know. I'm scared of losing you, too. Scared that one day you'll find life in Montana too hard and you'll go away. But I think winning you is worth the risk, Jane Harris. Nobody can keep trouble at bay forever, if it wants to find them. No matter where they live or how much money they've got. All we can do is treasure the time we have together and try to grow the courage we need to take whatever comes."

"You make it sound so easy."

"It's not. We've both lost too many loved ones to be fooled into believing that. But there's no better teacher of courage than the Big Sky. I reckon you've already begun to find that out, Snowbird."

She stared into his eyes, and he saw all his own doubts and fears mirrored in her. He saw something else, too. Her newfound courage, like a wobbly legged filly. Would she be willing to nurture it into a full-fledged Montana maverick?

As Jane turned and walked away from the bed, he closed his eyes and held his breath. A warrior must never cry out his deepest pain. If she'd made her decision, he must honor it.

John heard the door close and the bolt slide home.

A single hot, stinging tear escaped from beneath his closed eyelid and rolled down his cheek.

Then he heard the softest and most beautiful sound in the world. The rustle of clothes parting from a woman's sweet body.

When his eyes flew open, Jane flashed him a self-conscious glance. "I locked the door so nobody'd walk in on us tomorrow morning."

The tempo of her undressing slowed and a teasing smile hovered on her lips. "You *were* watching me that night I took off my clothes in front of the window, weren't you?"

Desire, gratitude and love swamped his heart. Unable to speak, he nodded.

With her eyes locked on his, Jane removed each garment with lingering sensuality. Until John's longing reached a pitch that made him forget all his hurts.

"This bed's a good size and I don't take up too much room." Jane snuffed the candle and slid under the covers beside him. "I know you must be sore and exhausted. All

I want is to lie beside you, feel the warmth of your body and the beat of your heart to reassure myself this isn't a dream.''

John pulled her into his arms. ''Is that *all* you want? Or can I prove to you just how alive I am?''

In the darkness her flesh melted into his. ''I'd like that.''

Twining her arms around his neck, Jane pressed her lips to his with a provocative force that made his head spin.

''I'm still sort of dizzy, though.'' He collapsed back onto his pillow. ''Do you remember that morning in my cabin, when *you* made love to *me?*''

''I seem to have a vague recollection.'' She slid one leg over him, straddling his belly. ''It started something like this, didn't it?''

The moist heat of her breath whispered over his lips. John lifted his face to engage her. They shared a deep, blissful kiss of devotion and contentment. Of promise and hope.

Before the sweet torment of her soft breasts against his chest and the tempting wriggle of her hips turned his blood to liquid fire and his mind to mush, John spoke the words he needed to say.

''Now, before there's any chance of a baby coming, I'll ask you again, Jane. Will you agree to marry me? Give up a rich, safe life in Boston to be a ranch foreman's wife? I'll hold you to your promise this time, mind.''

She brushed her ivory-smooth cheek against his stubbled one, and John nearly lost his resolve to wait for her answer. ''Life with you may not be safe, *Taa'evâhe'hame,* but it will always be rich. I'd rather have one happy week with you to cherish for the rest of my life than fifty placid, barren years.''

Her voice sounded a little uncertain, even a little frightened. But completely resolute. Unlike the first time she'd accepted him, it was clear Jane knew exactly what she was risking.

Then, as if the decision had somehow liberated her, she gave a husky, mischievous chuckle. ''I'll haul a preacher in here tomorrow to marry us, if that's what you want. Or we can hold off until you're back on your feet. But from this night on, I plan to share your bed, mister, so you'd better not wait too long to make an honest woman of me.''

''Bearspeaker would never let me hear the end of it.'' John Whitefeather's chuckle subsided into a husky growl of desire as he gave himself to his woman.

Tonight and forever.

Epilogue

1902, Sweetgrass, Montana

The little newcomer stared warily at the large house of undressed timber as she clung to the hand of her younger sister.

Jane Whitefeather eased herself down to perch on the lowest step. It wouldn't be easy for her to get up again, with her belly swollen like a ripe melon. But experience and intuition had taught her that frightened children relaxed more quickly when adults didn't tower over them.

"Welcome to Sweetgrass, little daughters," she said in awkwardly accented Cheyenne as she held out her hands to them. "My parents died when I was only a little bit older than you. I was very sad and frightened. But this is a good place. Here, you don't need to be frightened, and you may be sad until happy feelings sing in your heart again."

Two dark heads turned toward one another. The little orphans exchanged a look, then gravely sat on either side of Jane. In front of the Olivia Endicott Memorial Home.

Jane still shook her head in disbelief, remembering how Mrs. Endicott had blown into Whitehorn five years ago, like a one-woman Yankee tornado. All her ailments forgotten, the formidable old lady had rapidly become as ardent a champion of Indian rights as she'd once been of the temperance movement. Though Jane hadn't welcomed her coming, they'd grown closer as the months passed. So close that John and Jane had named their first child after her.

As the two little orphan girls stared in fascination at the Sweetgrass settlement, a mixture of timber houses and traditional tepees, Jane's gaze strayed to the small graveyard atop a nearby hill. Both Mrs. Endicott and her little namesake rested there now, and not a day passed but Jane yearned for them with a sad sweet tug at her heart. Losing their baby had been at least as hard on John as it had on her, but their shared sorrow had drawn them closer than ever.

"Do I smell bread frying?" As if summoned by her thoughts, a familiar deep voice sounded behind her.

Jane turned to see her husband holding their son, Nathaniel. His nephew strode along at John's side.

"Barton." Jane beckoned him. "I'd like you to meet Annie and Rose Bushyhead. They've come to join our family. Can you show them the way to Auntie's fire?"

"Sure!" Barton lavished a gap-toothed grin on the little girls, who looked at each other and giggled. "Come on. Walks on Ice makes the best berry pudding."

As the children scampered off toward the village, John settled himself beside Jane.

Nathaniel squirmed in his father's arms. "Mama, Mama!"

John tried to hold him back. "Be careful now. With a baby brother or sister growing inside Mama, you're getting to be a heavy load for her to carry."

"Oh, I don't mind." Jane pulled the little fellow into an awkward but warm embrace, and rested her head against John's arm.

He bent over and planted a kiss on her hair. "I reckon those two little ones are going to be happy here."

Jane nodded. She knew it healed his heart a little more each time they welcomed another child of Cheyenne or mixed parentage to Sweetgrass.

"I thought I saw Will Kincaid ride off awhile ago. Everything's all right with Lizzie and the children, I hope."

"Couldn't be better, according to Will. I asked him to stay for a cup of tea, but he'd come on business. He tells me Mrs. Endicott's trust fund for the home is in good shape and the mortgage on Sweetgrass is almost paid off."

"Oh, John, that's wonderful! Everyone has worked so hard for this. Let's have a feast to celebrate." She glanced up into those extraordinary eyes, bluer than the sky above them. Eyes whose gaze never failed to set her heart soaring like the red-tailed hawk.

His long brown fingers closed over her delicate but capable hand, which bore a slender band of gold. "We've got something to celebrate that's even more important than burning the Sweetgrass mortgage. Or have you forgotten it's been five years since you made me the luckiest fellow under the Big Sky?"

The sun could have vanished from the heavens just then and John Whitefeather's smile would still have lit the valley.

"Only five years?" With a chuckle, Jane lifted her face for his kiss. "Sometimes it seems like you and I have been together as long as Bearspeaker and Walks on Ice."

His lips closed over hers as eagerly as on their wedding night, but with a hundredfold the tenderness and devotion.

"We will, Snowbird. We will."

* * * * *